Praise for
THE STOWAWAY

"*The Stowaway* moves forward from the very first page and never leaves the reader behind. Its subject matter, the lives of the poor under their masters, gives it a moral force akin to Zola. The firmness of the narrative structure . . . gives the novel an intense focus, as in Camus or Calvino. . . . Both a social document and an absorbing read." —*The Globe and Mail*

"*The Stowaway* is a terrific contemporary sea story. It resonates with the great themes of maritime literature and reminds us that the sea is, even now, an arena of suffering and high courage and a crucible of moral choice. The story of murder, fear and redemption aboard the *Maersk Dubai* comes vividly alive in this fine, compelling novel." —Derek Lundy, author of *The Godforsaken Sea*

"Engrossing. . . . Robert Hough, who demonstrated his considerable abilities with historical fiction in his award-winning first novel, *The Final Confession of Mabel Stark*, brings the story to life with meticulous, first-hand research and extensive interviews. This is a powerful novel that artfully combines the vivid, breathless pacing of the best adventure stories with the moral and metaphysical depth of the best literary fiction." —*Quill & Quire*

"Robert Hough's latest book mixes fiction and non-fiction to get at the truth . . . *The Stowaway* deals with a real-life adventure involving an epic journey and some well-considered heroics . . . similar to some of Norman Mailer's work . . . It's a story with real weight."
—*Eye*

"He weaves fact with fiction t[...]
—*The Chronicle Herald* (Halifax[...]

"It's a gripping yarn, a different kind of tale of good versus evil . . . Hough said he wanted to write an 'adventure story.' That's an understatement. It is really a thriller." —*Ottawa Citizen*

"The story is compelling, but it is in the version of the story that Hough has chosen to emphasize—the fleshing out of character relationships, and the manner in which he structures the novel—that moves it beyond a simple retelling of events to a work filled with suspense, excruciating choices and tragic ends. . . . Hough's choices create a gripping and empathetic tale." —*Calgary Herald*

THE STOWAWAY
ROBERT HOUGH

VINTAGE CANADA

Published in Canada by Vintage Canada, a division of Random House of Canada Limited, Toronto. Originally published in hardcover in Canada by Random House Canada, a division of Random House of Canada Limited, Toronto, in 2004. Distributed by Random House of Canada Limited, Toronto.

Vintage Canada and colophon are registered trademarks of Random House of Canada Limited.

www.randomhouse.ca

Library and Archives Canada Cataloguing in Publication

Hough, Robert, 1963–
        The stowaway : a novel / by Robert Hough.

ISBN 0-679-31300-1

        I. Title.

PS8565.O7683S86 2004a   C813.'6   C2004-905212-8

Text design: Daniel Cullen

Printed and bound in Canada

2 4 6 8 9 7 5 3 1

For Rudy, Jay, Ariel

A knocking comes at the door of the bosun's cabin, followed by a hoarse whisper, seeping through metal.

"Hey, Bose, time to get up."

Rodolfo Miguel stirs. His nickname is called again, and this time he mutters, "All right, Manuel, I'm awake." Beneath him, the big ship undulates, and produces the hollow groan of a hull on water.

The grey shrouding his quarters could be the light of early day, or the shadow of late afternoon, or the portent of a storm, and for a moment the bosun feels confused. Yet as his dreams dissipate, his situation crystallizes—morning shift, containers on board, early March, the weather brisk and overcast. He rises, rubs his eyes, and lowers himself to his knees, his forearms resting on crumpled bedding. For the next minute he is still, and alone, with God.

When he's finished his prayers, he changes into dark blue coveralls, straightens his bunk, and puts on the deck shoes he always leaves on a mat outside his cabin door. After crossing the corridor to the WC, he washes his round face and brushes his teeth and combs his thick, dark hair. Back in his cabin, he checks himself in the small plastic-framed mirror tacked over his dresser; in the weak light of the room, his skin looks coppery and dull, like a bell that's been exposed to weather.

He locks his cabin door and moves quickly through the halls of the seamen's level before reaching the stairs leading to the crew mess. When he enters, only two of his able-bodies, Manuel and Angel, are still there, lingering over coffee, smiling at their bosun's predeliction for sleeping until the last possible moment. Manuel rises, and sits when Rodolfo motions with his hand.

Rodolfo helps himself to food turned lukewarm in the service line—eggs, toast, strips of bacon shrivelled into corkscrews—and he pours himself coffee, flavouring it with cream and spoonfuls of sugar. When he sits, Manuel and Angel are taking deep, final pulls off their cigarettes, the air between them a wispy, corroded blue.

"So," Angel says, "what's it going to be like today?"

"Can't say."

"Maybe a storm?"

"Maybe."

"It could clear, too."

Rodolfo shrugs, and chews his breakfast. After a minute, Angel stands and heads toward the deck. Manuel says, "More coffee, Bose?" and when Rodolfo shakes his head, the AB rises as well, Rodolfo noticing the fine tremour in Manuel's fingers as he pushes his chair back into place. Often, Rodolfo worries about Manuel's health, for he knows he eats poorly, and smokes too much, and takes thing too seriously. As he walks away—"See you on deck, Bose"—Rodolfo asks himself how many voyages he's been on with Manuel. Has it been a half-dozen? More? At times he feels as though he knows Manuel's face better than the faces of his own children. *At least with Manuel, he's more or less the same every time we land on a boat together. But with my babies? Each time I come home, they're different. Each time I come home, they've changed.*

He swallows a mouthful of egg, and calls out, "Okay, okay. Tell the others I'll be there in a minute."

Rodolfo drains his coffee, and takes a last bit of bacon before scraping the remnants of his breakfast into a metal can lined with a green garbage bag. He heads to the deck. There, he spots his Taiwanese chief officer, who is slowly practising karate moves as he waits. When the officer hears footsteps, he stops, his hands momentarily suspended in the air.

"Chief," Rodolfo says, "sorry to be late."

"Don't worry. Is happen, Bosun. Is happen sometime."

"Yes, yes, with some more than other, no, Chief?"

The chief officer smiles, a lattice of creases extending from the corner of each eye. "The weather, maybe is bad today."

"Yes. Maybe. But could clear, also."

"You are know what to do today?"

Rodolfo nods.

"Good."

The two men chat in poor English for a minute more. When they part, the chief officer returns to the door of the accommodation, and takes the stairs back up to the bridge. From where he stands, Rodolfo can hear the man's footfalls resonating from within the stairwell.

Rodolfo's ABs have gathered next to the storeroom, where they are smoking cigarettes and huddling against the brisk, salty wind; when Rodolfo arrives, they are discussing whether the clouds will fade into streaks, or darken further and produce a chilled, spitting rain.

"Well, Bose?" one of them asks. "What are we doing?"

Rodolfo smiles, as though the question were a joke—they've been doing the same job since the voyage began in Bombay, and they all know they'll be grinding, stripping, and sanding the deck. All five of the ABs groan, throw up their hands, and jokingly complain. Then they dig out their sanders and head to the starboard aft, where they'd left off the day before.

Rodolfo begins his tour of the deck. As always, he starts with the starboard side, his eyes sweeping the metal surfaces of the *Maersk Dubai*. He checks that the container lassos are tightly winched, and as he passes the various hydraulic systems—hatch covers, windlass, mooring—he looks for rivulets of leaking motor oil. At the bow of the ship, he considers checking the void tank levels via the sounding tubes that reach to the depths of the hull, but decides not to—despite the choppiness of the ocean, and the intermittent listing of the past few days, there's no reason to suspect any of the holds have taken on water.

Instead, he moves to the port side and leans against the gunwale. The air is heavy with ozone. There are whitecaps and swells. The clouds are low-lying, full, and the grey-blue of a rifle. Rodolfo blinks away the salted mist, and peers far into the distance, to the place where the eye plays tricks on a sailor far from home—though there is nothing but ocean for thousands of kilometres, he imagines he can see an ochre sweep of hill and valley, and a yawning of off-white beach. He begins his tour back down the port side. The boat shifts and heaves beneath his feet, his sea legs responding in a way that is automatic, and not noticed by the sailor. Behind him, over the stern, comes a momentary break in the clouds. A shaft of sunlight, bleary and cream coloured, casts shadows for the first time since the big ship left Spain, momentarily warming the bosun's shoulders.

Then, just as quickly, the clouds reassemble, and the greyness of the day returns.

The bosun looks upward, his eyes narrowing. The weather, he thinks, could very well be like this for the rest of the journey: roiling and unpredictable, refusing to commit to storm or sunshine, threatening to keep them guessing all the way to North America. He checks more lassos, and he eyes the hydraulics on the forward port windlass. Everything is fine, or at least as fine as things can be on an aging boat like the *Maersk Dubai*. This gives Rodolfo a measure of satisfaction—a good bosun, he knows, is as valuable as the cargo stored in the ship's belly—and he promises himself that at the next port of call he'll splurge and call Maripaz, his wife since he was all of fifteen, and he'll tell her that he misses her, and that he loves her, and that all is well on board. Then he'll talk to each of his five children, and he'll tell them that one day, before they know it, Daddy will be home once more.

He hears a noise. Rodolfo stops, and listens; there is nothing but the rush of air over sea, and the sloshing of waves against metal. After a second, he shakes his head and moves on, thinking it was just one of the sounds that a sailor can sometimes hear in the breezes swirling around a big ship's prow: strains of a favourite song, or noises from a boyhood street, or the seaman's name, whispered in the voice of a loved one.

It comes again.

He stops once more, his thoughts so loud they are all he can hear. *A bird? A cough? Distant thunder?* He remains still for a full minute, and as he does he considers that perhaps the sound was supernatural, made by the same phantoms who steal wrenches, and overturn coffee cups, and hide packs of cigarettes every time a seaman turns his back. Rodolfo takes a few more tentative steps.

When he hears it again—clearly, this time, in a language that may or may not be familiar—he realizes that the noise is the sound of two people talking.

His hand goes to his bosun knife.

"*Amigos . . .*" he calls out.

Wind. Waves. The thrumming of rough water against the hull.

"*Amigos . . .*" he calls again, and this time he hears a muted answer.

"*Sí . . . sí.*"

Rodolfo moves toward the source of the voices, until he finds himself standing on a catwalk that crosses back to the starboard side. After another second, two men emerge from a compartment beneath the elevated crosswalk. The first is maybe twenty-five years old, a tall man with curly brown hair and a long forehead. The second is skinny and lank haired and young. They are trembling slightly.

"*Señor,*" the skinny one says, "*por favor, por favor,*" and they both make eating gestures with their hands.

Rodolfo asks where they are from, hoping they might understand English or Spanish. They peer at him, confused. Rodolfo repeats the question, slower this time, "*De donde son, amigos,* where do you come from?" which causes the two men to look at each other and speak in a language that, while containing Spanish words, emits from the back of the throat, the consonants sounding like a brush rubbing leather.

The older one's face lightens. "Algeciras!" he blurts.

Rodolfo Miguel pictures the Spanish port the boat had left a day ago, and as he does he feels his own face broaden into a grin. Though he's a big man for a Filipino, thick in the chest and arms, the smile causes his face to turn into something boyish, for he's also a man with freckles and teak-coloured eyes and a small, delicate nose. The stowaways relax slightly, the older one attempting a slender, uncertain smile.

"*Sus nombres?*" Rodolfo asks, pointing at their chests. "Your names? *Sus nombres?*"

They understand, and the older one says, "Petre."

"And you? *Y usted?*"

"Radu."

"All right, *amigos*. Come, *venga*."

Rodolfo leads the two men down the port side of the ship. It takes them fifteen minutes to reach the stern, for the boat is the length of a football field, and their progress is slow in the pitching, unruly water. At one point Rodolfo turns and, yelling into the wind, advises the stowaways to be careful, that a single moment of sea on deck could sweep them both into the water. The two men nod and smile and yell *OK* despite not having understood. When they reach the phone attached to the wall of the accommodation, Rodolfo holds up a finger—one moment, *un momentito*—and he dials upstairs to the bridge. He is told to report immediately. The stowaways follow Rodolfo up the six flights of stairs within the accommodation; throughout, Rodolfo chatters away in Tagalog, intending to calm the stowaways with the tone of his voice and the cheerful flow of his words. In truth, he doesn't know what will happen. Though he's never before encountered a stowaway—not in twenty years of sailing—he knows that the number of young men stealing away from desperate countries has been increasing of late. He also knows that port authorities have been raising fines for accepting stowaways, and on occasion refusing to take them altogether. And so, he's heard rumours, passed from port to port. Of a Greek ship forced to carry two Senagalese men for ten months.

Of a Dutch ship that had to house three Nigerians for the better part of a year. Of hollow-eyed Albanians, of nail-thin Chinese, of war-weary Croatians, caught in the limbo of ship life. By the same token, he knows he's probably worrying for no reason—these stories are passed around for the sole reason that they are so uncommon. In all likelihood, his stowaways will be turned over once they reach Halifax, giving Rodolfo an extra pair of rust scrapers during the crossing. Still, he feels concern. He is the bosun, and conditioned to spot problems before they come into being.

They reach the landing outside the bridge.

"Okay, *amigos*," Rodolfo says, "*no problema*, we have little chat with captain, *no hay problema*." Rodolfo then offers the humblest of smiles before pushing open the door, stepping over the flood barrier, and entering the bridge.

He stops. His lips part.

It is the look on their faces.

~

There are four of them—the captain, the chief officer, the second mate and the radio officer. Seconds pass. The wheelroom feels chilled. As Rodolfo waits for some sort of instruction, he's aware of the noises made by the bridge machinery—clinking, mostly, the notched progression of old mechanical dials.

Finally, the captain takes a few steps forward, and stops in front of Rodolfo. "Bosun," he asks in English. "These . . . these you stowaway?"

"Yes, Captain." Rodolfo is about to provide the details of his discovery when the captain lowers his gaze and begins to speak again.

"These men, they get on ship in Spain?"

"Yes," Rodolfo answers. "In Algeciras."

The chief officer moves toward the captain and, in a lowered voice, says something in Mandarin. The second mate and radio officer approach as well, the three officers now gathered around the captain, whose eyes keep flitting from side to side. The volume of their voices grows. The chief officer breaks away and approaches the stowaways. He stands, arms folded across his chest, appraising them. He asks a question, or at least Rodolfo guesses it's a question, for the chief officer has chosen to pose it in his own language.

The stowaways shuffle their feet and stare at the floor. The chief officer asks the question again, in the same indecipherable language, though this time his tone has sharpened, and the skin around his eyes has tightened, accentuating the wrinkles caused by decades spent in harsh sun. The captain approaches, as do the second mate and radio officer, and there's a tense quiet. Rodolfo focuses on a vein, blue and knotted, that has formed on the captain's forehead.

Suddenly, there is a squall of questions, some in Mandarin, some in English, the stowaways taking a half-step back, the chief officer barking something that echoes with anger and frustration. Slowly, the officers encircle the stowaways, the questions all in Mandarin now, the stowaways shaking their heads while saying, *"Por favor, por favor, por favor."* In Rodolfo's mind he pictures waves, for the voices keep building in pitch, and ferocity, before breaking into a lull and then, after a second's grace, mounting again. They keep coming, these waves of anger, until the captain, just thirty-four years of age and on his first voyage as master, snaps his head in Rodolfo's direction and says, "Bosun!"

The others fall quiet.

"Bosun!" he says again. "These men, they are speak Spanish?"

"No, no," Rodolfo says. "Maybe a few words."

"You know where they from?"

"I don't know. Romania, maybe, but I don't know."

"Then you ask where they from."

"But, Captain . . ."

"You ask, Bosun."

Rodolfo turns to the stowaways.

"*Amigos*, what is your country? *Su país?*"

The stowaways look at each other, mouths gaping.

"Your home? *Su hogar?* Brothers, where are you come from?" and even if the stowaways could have understood him in normal circumstances, they cannot now, for it is dawning on them that all the stories they'd heard back home—stories about what can happen if you pick the wrong boat with the wrong captain—were true. Rodolfo can see this understanding disfigure their faces and turn their skin the colour of ash. In a second, their hands are in the air, posed in a symbol of prayer, and they are pleading again, "*Por favor, por favor, por favor,*" Rodolfo barely having time to poorly translate one question before the officers bark five more—"They have passport? Gun? Criminal record? They have kill somebody? How they get on boat?"—until finally the captain turns and strides to the telephone connecting the bridge to the engine room.

The three other officers continue badgering the stowaways with a stew of Mandarin and English, the voices of the men in the room sufficiently loud that Rodolfo cannot hear what orders the captain is issuing to the engine room. He does, however, hear the noise made by the ship's engine change from a high-velocity thrumming to a steadfast chug. Rodolfo waits, and sees it. The big ship's prow begins to come about in a smooth, slow arc.

The other officers cross the bridge and gather near the captain. Their shoulders are hunched, and there's the low, staccatto hubbub of Mandarin. The stowaways look shaky and weak.

"Please, *amigos*," Rodolfo says to them, "do not have fear . . . *no preocupa . . . por favor, amigos*," and the stowaways start asking him whispered questions, either in their native tongue or their butchered rendition of Spanish. Rodolfo listens through one ear only. The other he uses to monitor his officers, who are still huddled in conference, the chief officer doing most of the speaking. Two words jump out at Rodolfo . . . *accommodation ladder . . .* and suddenly he's not listening to the stowaways at all, his concentration fully with the officers—on the way that they've ceased arguing, on the way their demeanours have grown solemn, on the way the chief officer is running a hand through hair dotted with grey. When the captain resumes speaking, his tone is low, and solemn, and firm.

Accommodation ladder.

Again, Rodolfo hears those two words, though he's not sure whether they were issued in English or in the little bit of Mandarin he has picked up as a sailor. He closes his eyes, and rubs them with his fingertips. His hand alights on the crook of the older stowaway's arm.

"Come," he says, "*venga,* I get you food, I get you *comida.*"

At this touch, the older stowaway grimaces, his eyes locking fearfully onto Rodolfo's.

"Come, *venga*," Rodolfo says again, and as he speaks he makes an eating motion with the curved fingers of his right hand. "Please, *por favor,* we get some food, some *comida.*"

The three men take the stairs leading from the bridge to the crew mess. There they find the second cook, a Filipino, who is smoking and pacing and wondering why on earth the boat is churning back toward Europe. When he sees the stowaways with the bosun, he understands that the rumour is true, that the bosun has indeed found some visitors. He fetches apples, bread, cheese and coffee. Despite their hunger, the two men cannot eat, their throats permitting only the passage of liquids. They sit, snuffling, taking loud sips of coffee, willing themselves to imagine that these minutes in a see-sawing mess hall are something they'll soon wake from, sweating and gripping at bedsheets.

Rodolfo walks into the galley.

"Bose," the second cook whispers, "what is happening?"

When Rodolfo tells him what he thinks the officers are planning, the cook can only shake his head and say, "This is bad, Bose."

The two stowaways finish their coffee. The cook pours them some more and, again, implores them to eat. They try, painfully, and when they're done Rodolfo takes them back on deck, where his ABs are waiting and wondering why they've been ordered to lower the accommodation ladder in the middle of the ocean. "What is it, Bose?" they keep asking, though before Rodolfo has time to formulate an answer the officers emerge and bark orders in English. Rodolfo and his ABs lash together empty barrels with rope. The stowaways watch as two of the men carry the raft down the ladder and lower it into the cold, wavy sea. It sinks instantly. The younger stowaway fights tears, and the older one stares into grey, simmering water. Seeing this, Rodolfo calls out, "No worry, is okay, *está bien,* no worry. . . ."

There is noise now, and confusion, the officers having ceded their authority to whatever experience is taking shape on the deck of the *Maersk Dubai.* Rodolfo yells to be heard. He orders his men to make a second raft, this one from barrels lashed to a palette. They put it into the water, and though it looks flimsy against the tossing sea it holds together, one of the ABs tying it off to the accommodation ladder. The Taiwanese officers crowd around the stowaways and order that the remaining deckhands do so as well. Seeing this, the stowaways drop to their knees and begin pleading in loud, panicked voices, the younger one bending over and kissing the feet of Rodolfo's old friend, Manuel Pacificador, who calls out, "What can I do? Please, *amigos, por favor,* what can I do?"

Rodolfo tries to look away, and cannot. The stowaways are given canteens of water before being herded onto the top rung of the ladder. The older one goes first, the younger one second, the captain calling that Morocco is very close and they have a raft and all they have to do is hold on and the tides will carry them in. The stowaways reach the end of the accommodation ladder, where they nervously feel for the first rung of the Jacob's ladder, which hangs like a rope to the surface of the ocean. When he is close enough to the water, the older stowaway takes a deep breath, crosses himself, and steps onto the bobbing, makeshift raft, which tips and takes on water but then gains an uneasy steadiness as he lowers himself to his knees. He spreads his legs wide for balance, and puts his face in his hands, and throughout the captain keeps yelling that they'll be fine, that Morocco is very close, that they'll be there in no time.

The younger stowaway refuses to move. His knees have fused, his hands have clamped to the knotted rope banister, his words have become a torrent. Though his language is understood only by the other stowaway, each and every person on deck knows that he is begging for mercy and God's forgiveness and the chance to see his mother just one more time. His nose is running, he has dampened his trousers, his lips are quivering and blue, and every time he calls out the older stowaway shudders, either in shame or pity or both, a salty moisture now seeping from the place where the base of his hands make contact with his eyes.

Otherwise, no one moves. No one. There's the sound of water sloshing against the hull, and there's the sound of the younger man weeping. The ABs start calling to him, telling him to leap from the Jacob's ladder to the raft, for the officers are planning to cut the rope and if he doesn't make a move now he'll hit the icy waters and drown immediately. So they yell, and shriek, and still they get no response. Finally, Rodolfo joins in, and when the frozen stowaway hears the bosun's voice, urging him onto the raft, he tearfully moves the rest of the way down the rope ladder. He steps onto the wet, bobbing raft. Next to the hull, he and his older companion look tiny, no larger than small dogs. Rodolfo watches intently, unable to avert his eyes, a senseless optimism having somehow convinced him that maybe the stowaways really can ride a frigid ocean current all the way to Tenerife, or Rabat, or Cádiz.

But no. Of course not. It's not possible. To Rodolfo, it seems there is no passage of time—not even the tiniest fraction of a second—between the existence of the stowaways and the non-existence of the stowaways. They are there, and then, simply, they are not. Rodolfo stands perfectly still, gaping not so much at the alacrity with which two men ceased to be, but at the impeccable ease with which evil appeared out of salty vapour, and claimed for itself the *Maersk Dubai*.

TWO

After spitting on the graves of the Ceaușescus, Daniel Pacepa leaves Ghencea cemetery and finds his way to the Piață Revoluției. He plants his feet at its centre, puts down his rucksack and closes his eyes. He imagines how it must have been on that frigid December afternoon: three hundred thousand poorly dressed countrymen, at first standing still and listening obediently and applauding at the prescribed moments. But then, shortly into his address, Ceaușescu looks out from the balcony of the Communist Party building and denounces the protestors of Timișoara, massacred just a few days earlier. Murmurs come from the rear of the crowd, interspered with a few hesitant boos. Ceaușescu can barely believe his ears, for these are his people, the people he and his wife have worked so hard for, and as he gestures for the crowd to stop they defy him, their jeers growing louder, and angrier, and soon there's an ocean of people, each and every one thrusting a fist into the air while chanting, "*Tim* . . . *ee* . . . *shwar* . . . *ah! Tim* . . . *ee* . . . *shwar* . . . *ah!*"

Which is followed by the order to fire. The bullets come from snipers' nests, installed in attics and dormers throughout Bucharest. As the tanks roll there is pandemonium, for even the

Securitate cannot control three hundred thousand people, who start chanting once again as Ceauşescu is seen fleeing the building-top by helicopter. This further emboldens the mob, and soon it invades the Parliament and the television station and the home of the dictator himself, so that by Christmas Day the tyrant and his homely wife appear on Romanian national television, lying side by side in a shallow grave, their faces twisted, their mouths parted, a bullet in the side of each head.

And for what? Daniel thinks. *So that seven years later Ceauşescu's cronies could still be running the country? So that nothing, not a thing, would change?* The thunder of revolution turns to the coo of pigeons. He finds himself alone, in the *piaţă,* feeling lonely and depressed—there are those, he knows, who believe the revolution wasn't even a revolution, that it was orchestrated by Moscow to get rid of a man they no longer had control over. He walks along the Strada Balescu, toward the centre of the city. He cannot stand what he sees. Everything looks grey and dirty, the people hungry. Every few metres he's approached by beggars, many of them children with filthy, outstretched hands. "When you get to Bucharest," his mother had said, "try to imagine how it once looked, without the grime and the beggars and the damn Gypsies everywhere. Try to imagine it before Ceauşescu knocked half of it down, before the buildings were covered with bullet holes. Try to imagine it when it was still the Paris of the East." Looking around, Daniel finds that his imagination is not nearly that vivid—he cannot believe that people bothered dying for this place, or that this was a place where his parents once found love.

He steps into a grocery. It is almost empty, save for an old ker-chiefed woman behind the glass counter and an older man look-ing over sticks of bread piled atop the case. Daniel crosses the shop, sawdust clinging to his shoes, and points to an end of blood sausage that is sitting, by itself, among jars of strawberry jam and plastic vats filled with watery cheese curds. As the woman reaches for his order, he pulls a roll of *lei* from his pocket. Seeing Daniel's money, her eyes widen and she puts the sausage down before grimly saying, "Wait, wait here one second."

She turns, and hustles through a doorway behind her. Daniel waits for a few seconds, beset with nervousness, an ache spreading through the tops of his shoulders. When the pain makes it all the way to the base of his head he exits the store just as three large men enter—they pass so closely Daniel can smell tobacco, and armpit sweat, and the dust on their clothing. Outside, on the sidewalk, he slips into the crowd, feeling stupid for having displayed his money so openly. At the end of the block, he stops and takes a steely glance backward—though the three toughs called by the old women are watching him, they've chosen not to pursue him in plain view of the other pedestrians. Looking straight at them, Daniel stands on his tiptoes, cups his hands around his mouth and yells "Fuck you!" The men sneer, and make obscene gestures, and motion that they want to fight.

Daniel makes his way to the Piaţă Universităţii, where he finds a bench. The warmth of the day seems to mock him, as does the city's immensity. Though he'd promised himself he would tour the place where his parents had gone to university, he now considers walking straight to the Gare du Nord, and getting on with his long journey west. As he stands, he decides to look for a place to have a quick drink before finding his way to the train station; a single morning in Bucharest has both jangled his nerves and left a parched, uncomfortable craving in his mouth. There don't seem to be any *hanuls* nearby, so after wandering south he ducks into a warren of narrow lanes lined with old stone buildings. Every minute or so, someone in an old, clanking Dacia honks, the pedestrians barely having time to flatten themselves against the building facades. As Daniel walks, he concentrates on looking like a person who needs to be somewhere.

At last he turns a corner and hears a violin, an accordion, and the harplike resonances of a *țambal*. Following the sound, he finds a door that opens onto a stairway leading down to a huge room filled with people seated at long, wooden tables. The room is so thick with cigarette smoke that everything—the band playing at the front, the loudly talking people, the framed pictures of royalty tacked to the walls—looks hazy and indistinct, as though in a steam bath. A barmaid notices him and takes him to one of the tables, where she seats him with a clutch of parents and grandparents and even a few children. He nods his hellos, and puts his pack between his feet. A minute later, his first beer and *țuică* are placed in front of him, the barmaid waiting as he discreetly digs just enough *lei* from his pocket. Before she walks off, he asks her for supper. She nods, and a few minutes later brings him a plate of boiled tripe and potatoes. Taking his first bite, Daniel thinks that maybe this is the reason people can stand living in the city: you can go out anytime you want and find a dinner like this.

He tucks in, the hot food filling his stomach and making him feel okay for the first time since leaving his town in Maramureș. He drinks more *țuică*, its fire soothed by glasses of beer poured from brown quart bottles, and pretty soon he's visited by an aching melancholy—he wishes that Elena, his girlfriend from up north, were with him, for he feels lonely and awkward sitting with this family of strangers. Yet by the time it's dark outside, he has started dancing, his arms linked around the shoulders of somebody's grandmother and somebody's bristly-faced husband and, at one point, someone's shy teenage daughter. The barmaids walk among the dancers selling little glasses of *țuică,* which the men down in one gulp and then toss into the air, the music punctuated again and again by bursts of shattering glass. Soon, Daniel is buying little glasses for the family he was so reticent to join early in the evening, as well as for their friends and the friends of their friends, and if he was careful about hiding his *lei* at the beginning of the evening he is not now, for he feels safe and drunk and surrounded by people who understand that sorrow is nothing if not a prerequisite for joy. As he dances he sings along, the words all having to do with love and pain and the exquisite brevity of life.

In the middle of one song he starts to feel a little woozy—all that smoke, he thinks—so he steps aside and rests, his hands on his knees, and it is at this moment that he sees her come toward him. She is older than he is, but only by a few years, and when she smiles he can see that one of her teeth is capped with tin. In that moment, Elena ceases to exist—though this woman is wearing a long skirt and a loose blouse, he can tell by the way her clothing hangs that she has a lithe, cool body, made taut by a life of movement. And her *eyes.* Never has he seen eyes that colour—two jade circles gleaming against skin as brown as a horse's flank.

She takes Daniel's hand, and in a moment he is whirling with this creature. She whoops and hollers as she dances, and when she raises her hands into the air, she looks nimble enough to take flight. The dance ends, and she bends over, laughing. The band starts a ballad, the melody carried slowly and sadly by the violin. She straightens and looks at him, a lock of dark hair hanging over her small, smooth forehead. When she smiles, Daniel marvels at the way that even something as homely as a tin-capped tooth can be a receptacle for all that is mysterious, and beautiful, about women.

"Who are you?" Her voice is raspy, and she speaks with a hint of an accent.

"Daniel."

"Well, Daniel. I am Bianca."

She is in his arms now, smelling of jasmine and burnt wood and plum brandy. She sways against him, her hips moving in a way that does not exist in the countryside but that clearly does exist here, in the Paris of the East, in the place where his mother fell for an aspiring writer named Ilya Pacepa. The ballad ends and Bianca kisses him, quickly, on the cheek. Daniel is about to ask her to dance again when he realizes that he needs to visit the lavatory. He pledges Bianca to wait, and as he urinates into a long ceramic trough one of the men from his table stands beside him and says, "Hey, better be careful."

"What?"

"The girl. Be careful . . ."

"Oh, I know . . ." and the fact of the matter is that he *does* know, for they have Gypsies in Maramureș too, living in camps on the outskirts of towns, crossing the countryside in carts or wagons or barely running Dacias. They have them, and he knows he should stay away, and for that reason the mere mention of what she is—*Roma, the girl's a Roma*—causes a staticky warmth to snake down his spine.

He goes back out and Bianca is waiting, arms crossed and looking down. They dance some more, and he buys her glasses of *țuică,* which she downs like a man. After a time, he leads her outside, to the end of an alleyway, where he pushes her into darkness. With her back pressed against pebbly stone, he kisses her while guiding his hands over the firm, clothed curves of her body. Then he is running after her, Bianca stopping abruptly at the curb on the main road and laughing when Daniel almost loses his balance and falls into traffic. Grabbing his hand, she holds it up in the air and tells him to keep it that way. She ducks into the shadows of a doorway, and waits until a cab pulls over, at which point she runs and piles in behind Daniel. When the driver orders her out, she unleashes a torrent of what Daniel suspects are curses, in a language as old and as strange as the devil.

"No," Daniel says. "We have money, we have *lei.*" The cab driver shakes his head and pulls into traffic, which causes Bianca to laugh triumphantly and sink into the back of the seat. Daniel looks through the taxi window at the city—at its fountains, its churches, its apartment blocks—until he feels almost pleased that he has come here. When her fingers touch his chin he turns; she smiles and looks into round, dark eyes.

"Oh my," she says. "You country boys—how can we girls stay away?"

With an exaggerated sigh, she rests the side of her head on his shoulder, as if wishing to take a small nap. A second later, her head springs up and she yells, "Stop!" The driver pulls over and she jumps out of the car. Daniel pays and steps onto the curb and notices, across the street, a sign for a Metro station called Crângași. The cab pulls away. Despite Bianca's urging, he doesn't move, for this place, this Crângași, is quiet and dark, and as he stands there it suddenly seems incomprehensible that one minute he was drinking *țuică* in the old city and the next minute he was here, with a woman like her, in this bleak paper-strewn neighbourhood. Her hand is on his elbow, and she's saying, "Come, Daniel, I have a place to show you . . ."

He follows her into a twisting of lanes and alleys, the streets now asphalt instead of cobblestone. Though the streetlights are protected by wire cages, half the bulbs have been stolen or smashed—as they move down the sidestreet, they keep entering pockets of shadow. Each time they do, Bianca squeezes Daniel's hand all the harder and says, "Careful, Daniel, don't be falling down."

She stops and pushes her shoulder against a metal door and they enter another crowded basement *hanul,* this one smaller and smokier than the other. Here, everyone seems to know her—men in patched, frayed jackets and women in long mended skirts keep coming up and greeting her and asking her how she is. When she introduces Daniel, she takes care to switch back to Romanian.

"Look at what I found, wandering the streets, a stranger needing company. Please, be nice, be nice, he is with me this evening . . ." and then they are all slapping him on the back and asking him questions about Maramureş and inquiring if, by any chance, he knows so-and-so in Satu Mare or so-and-so's cousin in Baia Sprie. They also bring him a cloudy, bitter-tasting *ţuică* that burns all the way down and keeps burning once it hits his stomach. When he pulls out some *lei* to pay they say, "No, no, put that away boy—is homemade, is free, is the way we do things here." Soon he is dancing again, and when he realizes he's left his knapsack at the first *hanul* he doesn't worry, for he figures he'll go back and get it later. At the back of the hall, the band starts playing a sad, slow song. Bianca takes his hand and they dance again, her head resting on his shoulder. As they sway, he seriously thinks that maybe, in another life, he was like her—he's never heard music that so accurately captures how it is to watch the sun dip glowing behind mountains, or how it is to realize that life is fleeting, and gorgeous, and cruel. When she realizes the music is making him maudlin, she lifts her head off his shoulder and says, "Hey now, boy, don't be that way. We are suppose to be happy tonight!" With that she motions at someone, and soon Daniel is given another glass of the foul-smelling *ţuică,* which he swallows in a single, incinerating gulp.

A numbness has seized his arms and much of his lower body. He finds it hard to speak, which is frustrating for he wants to profess his desire not only for her but for her eyes, and her smile, and her litheness, and above all else the sweet Gypsy sadness broadcast by the nuances of her beauty. His head spins, his vision blurs, the room takes on the same thick, yellowish hue as the *ţuică.* He loses his balance and falls against her, and for a crazy second he wishes he were the only man in a world of women who looked like her, and smelled like her, and moved like her.

"Oh boy," she says, "a little too much *ţuică,* no?"

"Yes," he says, suddenly hating himself. "I think so . . ."

"Sometime I forget that the Roma brandy it take a little time get use to, no? Is a little bit strong, no?" Daniel nods, and she adds, "Okay, so maybe you need air. Is not a large problem."

She puts his arm over her shoulder and walks him out of the *hanul.* Outside, she leans him against a wall and encourages him to take deep breaths.

"There," she says, "feeling a little better?"

"Yes," he lies.

"You want to come back inside?"

"No, I think another minute . . ."

"Okay, no problem. When you are maybe feeling a bit better, come on back, okay? And no more *ţuică.* I think maybe you have a little headache tomorrow, no?"

Daniel nods. As soon as Bianca goes back inside the *hanul*, he realizes he's going to be sick, his only hope being that he can stall it long enough that she doesn't see. He stumbles along cement alleys, making turn after turn, until he comes to a *piață* that is small and grimy and ripe with the odour of garbage. His vision has turned wavy, and across the *piață* he sees a car stripped of its tires and mirrors, and then the stripped car turns into two stripped cars, and then the two stripped cars turn into four stripped cars. Soon, an entire flotilla of stripped cars hovers over the *piață*. He lowers himself and lies on his side, resting on ground spinning as madly as a dervish.

~

He regains consciousness in a place neither light nor dark. He sits up, his back sore from sleeping on concrete. In the half-light, the walls look like thick black clouds. *Okay, don't panic, you can get up and walk right through them,* though as his head begins to clear he realizes that what he is leaning against is hard, and cold, and as real as life in Romania. His stomach drops, and he feels sick. He *has* been sick; the front of his shirt is messed with tripe and potatoes. His thirst is an agony, the pain in his head worse.

He hears snores. The bodies producing them are spread across the floor, their knees pulled upward, their bent arms serving as fleshy, numbed pillows. The noise in the cell begins to gnaw at him, growing louder and louder, and then it's reverberating through Daniel's throbbing head until he clamps his hands over his ears and thinks, *I deserve this, I do.* The air smells of urine and sweat, and though Daniel cannot see any rats, he can hear their nails, scurrying against stone. He rubs the cold out of his hands. On the far side of the cell is a small window, placed high. After a while, it begins to turn a muted orange. A swath of light cuts across the room, revealing Daniel's cellmates: rubbies, by the looks of them, stinking and bearded and accustomed to spending their nights in places such as this. Through the window, Daniel can see shoes and the bottoms of trousers, and he realizes the cell is in a basement.

His cellmates are coming awake now, their snores replaced by breathy yawns and cursing. Beside him, a big man stirs and groans. He sits. Though dishevelled and smelling as though he's bathed in *ţuică,* he's nonetheless in better shape than the other men, if only because his clothes aren't torn and he has both his shoes. He shakes his head, and as he does the few hairs left on the top of his head waver like antennae.

"Oh boy," he says to no one in particular. "Oh boy, oh boy. What in God's name have I done?"

He meets Daniel's gaze.

"Hey," the man whispers loudly, "you got a cigarette?"

Daniel shakes his head and looks away.

"Not one?" the man repeats.

"No."

The man coughs, and sniffles. "Your clothes," he says. "You're not from here, are you?"

Daniel's first instinct is to tell the man to mind his own business. Brusquely, he shakes his head.

"So where *are* you from then?"

"Maramureş."

The man laughs heartily, and slaps one of his knees. "Maramureş?" he says. "Really? Maramureş? From where in Maramureş?"

"A small place. Called Camarzana."

"Camarzana! Really! Well then, boy, you're looking at a guy from Baia Sprie!"

Daniel raises his eyebrows and eyes the man suspiciously. He doesn't even need to ask: the big shoulders, the bull's neck, the flattened nose. "You're from the mines."

"Yes! And you?"

"The strawberry fields."

The man thrusts his hand toward Daniel.

"What else is there, eh? My name is Gheorghe Mihoc."

Daniel takes the man's plump, coarsened hand. "Daniel Pacepa."

Gheorghe leans forward, his breath sour and hot.

"Well then, Daniel Pacepa. What brings you to beautiful, beautiful Bucharest?"

"I'm on the way to Spain."

"To Spain?"

"Yes."

"Algeciras, maybe?"

Daniel nods.

"What *is* it about that place? Sometimes I think that half the people in this cursed country are walking around with Algeciras on the brain. I take it you're going to get on a big ship?"

Daniel nods, and is annoyed when Gheorghe laughs.

"You know they say that in America you'll never find a square, ugly, Communist building." He laughs, harder now. "They say that every house is made from wood, and that they they pay you not to work!"

Though Daniel tries to smile, his face looks more tense than pleased. "Gheorghe," he says. "Is this your first time in jail?"

"Are you kidding? I know the Baia Sprie drunk tank better than I know the back of my hand."

"Then how," Daniel asks, "do we get out of here?"

~

When a meal of thin, greasy soup and stale bread arrives, Gheorghe and Daniel eat it with relish, licking their lips and rubbing their stomachs, as though it's the best meal they've had in weeks. Later in the day, a rhythmic tapping comes at the tiny window. When a guard passes in front of the cell, Gheorghe says loudly, "It's so nice and dry in here, eh, Dani? So nice to be out of the rain, am I right, Dani?"

At night, when the jail fills, Daniel and Gheorghe have to sleep sitting up, leaning against the cold wall, their shoulders touching. As Daniel drifts off, his dreams fill with barking dogs, and swirling red lights, and the revving of black vans, so that throughout the night he keeps waking up, feeling haunted and weak and alone. In the morning, the vagrants who came in the night before—the ones covered with scabies and sores and patches of dead skin—are turned loose, the men remaining being the ones who look as if they might be able to scrounge up a dollar or two for their freedom. After the drunks have been cleared out, and the two men have again smacked their lips over a breakfast of cold salty gruel, Gheorghe ambles up to the bars. A guard lazily approaches. There are words. Gheorghe backs away, shrugging his shoulders, feigning a lack of concern. A few hours later, he tries again, this time passing the guard a few bills. He returns to sit beside Daniel.

"Okay, it's done."

A different guard approaches with a ring of keys. He nods at Gheorghe, who stands and motions for Daniel to do the same. They walk to the bars and wait while the guard fiddles with the key ring. He curses under his breath, for both the latch key and the metal lock box are old and rusting and have chosen that moment to misbehave. Finally, the door swings open with a muted screech. The guard ushers Daniel and Gheorghe along a hallway and up some stairs. At the landing, he opens a side door, letting Daniel and Gheorghe into an alley. The door clangs shut behind them.

As Gheorghe stretches, Daniel feels a relief so profound he grows dizzy with it. *Never again,* he thinks. *Being locked up doesn't agree with me.*

"Ah," says Gheorghe. "Things are looking up. Can you believe, all that fuss for six American dollars? This world—it's a crazy place, don't you think?"

"Yes, it is that."

"Listen. A friend of a friend of my uncle has a construction company in France. I've got a job to go to there. It's where I'm going."

Daniel says nothing.

"I'm thinking," Gheorghe continues, "we could travel together for a bit. I could use the company. That is, if you want."

Daniel peers at him, appraising the offer.

"All right," he says. "If you want."

THREE

All twenty-two men are on deck, posted in a half-moon forma-
tion, staring at the spot near the port-side gunwale where the
stowaways had climbed, trembling, onto the ladder. The waters
are rough, the boat rising quickly and then, at the break of each
swell, dropping in a shower of froth. Despite the roughness of
the sea, there isn't a man on board who has to extend his arms to
maintain his balance or take a sudden sidestep when the ship rolls
in a trough.

The captain turns and, head down, marches toward the
accommodation. The chief officer shouts "Bosun!" and, a second
later, Rodolfo starts the gangway hydraulics, two of his ABs guiding the ladder as it folds, like an accordion, into its docket. The
rest of the men disperse—the bridge officers head upstairs, the
mess crew goes back to the kitchen, the engine crew goes below.
The remaining ABs drift toward the starboard aft. Each of them
looks dazed—that easily, all evidence has been erased, the event
now existing only in their memories. Up ahead, their tools lean
against the gunwale.

At lunchtime, Rodolfo accepts a tray of spicy fried chicken
and noodles from the Filipino second cook before moving to sit

with his ABs and two men from the engine room—the ship's oiler, Juanito Ilagan, and the pipefitter, Alfredo Panelo. As Rodolfo pulls his chair they glance upward, the oiler murmuring, "Hey, Bose." Other than that, nobody speaks. Occasionally, one of them takes a bite and chews, though mostly they push the food around their plates, creating stringy mounds that, a second later, they flatten with the backs of their forks. Rodolfo can hear the second cook working in the kitchen, and he can hear the sound of cutlery pivoting against hard plastic plates. Otherwise, there's a dull, thickened quiet, and it seems to Rodolfo that this absence of conversation has a weight, and that this weight is bowing the sides of the mess room, causing the walls to creak and complain. He sips his coffee and stares at his food. Though the dinner is one of his favourites, today it looks almost larval, as though it might start to writhe in front of him. He pushes away his plate, and takes another sip of coffee, and stares at the fake wood grain of the tabletop.

One by one, the men leave the table, scraping uneaten food into the trash cans located near the mess exit. Rodolfo goes to his cabin and tries to sleep. When he finds that this is impossible, he sits on his bunk with a pen and a piece of paper. He starts the same sentence four times—"Maripaz, my love, something happened on board today"—though each time he scratches out his words, crumples the paper, and tries again. He closes his eyes. The problem is that he can still see it all so clearly: the younger one clinging to the Jacob's ladder, refusing to let go, the stain on his blue jeans growing, the older one grimly clinging to the raft, his expression a grimace. The image throbs with colour, pushing at the boundaries of Rodolfo's mind, until it escapes and is in his cabin, a spectre projected on walls and on the ceiling.

He winces, and holds his head. He can feel his heart thudding in his chest, and he can feel his lungs cramping with each shallow breath. When he runs a hand over the blanket on which he is sitting, the fibres in the wool make his fingertips burn. He leans over and grabs the logbook from the drawer of his bedside table, a book kept for the captain or the shipping company should details of the voyage be needed. Out of habit he writes in English, refusing to let himself stop and think about the words he is putting down in the little lined notebook. When he finishes describing what he's seen that day, he returns the logbook to his bedside table.

Air, he thinks, *fresh air.*

He opens his cabin door, and finds the corridor empty. He takes the stairs to the mess level and hears voices in the recreation room. He follows them, but finds only a television set with a Jet Li video blaring—otherwise the room is empty. After turning off the video, he emerges on deck and takes a series of deep breaths. He walks along the starboard side. A third of the way along deck, he comes across Manuel, who is smoking a cigarette next to a firehose station.

Rodolfo stops, and the two men fidget, ashamed to meet each other's gaze. One is broad-shouldered and thickly built, the other small and pudgy with clear, orange-toned skin. Both were born in the northern province of Ilocos, and when they say hello with the same, choppy accent they are reminded that a world exists beyond the *Maersk Dubai*.

"Bose, would you like a cigarette?"

"No, Manuel, no . . ."

"I have plenty—it's not a problem . . ."

Rodolfo shakes his head while mustering a weak smile. "You know I don't smoke, brother."

Manuel nods. "Yes, I know, I just thought . . ." For a few seconds both men are quiet again. "Bose," Manuel finally says, "he kissed my feet."

"I know."

"My feet," Manuel says again, "he kissed my feet. He was begging for his life."

"I know."

"He was begging . . ."

Rodolfo nods yet again—*yes, my friend, I know.*

"Can you imagine, Bose, if that'd happened to us? Can you imagine our families? How they would feel?"

For a moment, Rodolfo thinks he might faint. Manuel snuffles and lights a second cigarette, Rodolfo catching a whiff of sulphur from the matchhead. Seconds pass. Then, because Rodolfo is the bosun and this bestows on him a measure of responsibility that, at that moment, he in no way wants, he decides he has to voice what every Filipino on board has been thinking since that morning.

"Manuel," he says. "We saw what they did."

The AB looks at his feet. His expression seems to fold in on itself: his eyes squeeze shut, his mouth quivers, his nose runs. He takes four or five jittery puffs on his cigarette.

When Rodolfo speaks again, his voice is little more than a whisper.

"Manuel," he says. "They could do that to us."

~

That night, Manuel sleeps in the spare bunk in Rodolfo's cabin. As an added measure of security, they prop a metal chair beneath the lever-style door handle. They sleep fitfully, and dreamlessly. Though they don't realize it, in other cabins similiar safety measures are being taken: knives placed under pillows, lug-nut wrenches waiting on bedside shelves, bad dreams endured with one eye open. Around two or three in the morning, the weather calms. A dark mash of clouds parts to reveal a crescent moon, its rays casting indigo spears over black, shifting waters. The sailors awake to a cool, sunny day. As the morning progresses, a breeze kicks up, as do small foaming whitecaps. The boat churns forward, making decent time, Rodolfo and his deck crew continuing to purge the foreward aft of grime and rust. While the work is tedious, each man is glad to have something repetitive and demanding to occupy his thoughts.

It is hard, putting the incident out of their minds, for the chief officer and second officer are roaming the boat, talking under their breath, at times gesturing. Even the captain, who had always stayed hidden in his office, can now be seen on deck, trying to engage a nervous and mumbling seaman in conversation, as if he'd always been the kind of master the sailors get to know. The morning shift ends. Rodolfo's crew locks the equipment in the bosun store and heads to the mess.

There, waiting for them on the tables, are cartons of milk and bars of chocolate. The seamen sit, each man staring at what has been left in front of him. Suddenly, one of the ABs chortles, and it is only a matter of seconds before they're all laughing and ripping open milk cartons and slurping down the contents. Someone says, "I guess they're a little worried," which sparks a peal of bitter laughter. When the milk has all been drunk, they tear open the chocolate bars and eat them, too, Angel throwing a chunk in the air and catching it in his mouth.

The laughter stops as quickly as it started. There are a few more brief attempts at conversation, but they fizzle, the Filipinos suddenly realizing they're acting like the children the officers consider them to be. With this comes a return of the gloom that has been weighting the big ship, bowing the gunwales and thickening the air. Rodolfo looks down at his food: steamed green vegetables, fried pork, *halo halo*. He takes a dry, choking bite. Then he rises and goes to his cabin. He lies on his bunk and stares at the ceiling, exhaustion propelling him toward a brief nap; when he awakes, his shoulders ache, and his head feels dull with fatigue. That evening, he's on watch duty along with Carmelito and Joe—he has them check hoses and container lassos while he roams the deck. After a bit, he leans on the gunwale and looks out over churning white water. In the mist, he can see the shimmering faces of his children, and he smiles—he was barely more than a child himself when his first, a girl named Jinky, was born in a Manila hospital. He can recall it as though it were yesterday—the way her tiny pink face burrowed into the crook of her mother's arm, the way she latched on to her mother's breast with a silent, confident ease. He remembers it all so well, his contented little angel in a ward filled with screamers.

If only, he thinks, he was from a country that hadn't been ruined by a man and his shoe-loving wife. If only he hadn't been forced to go to sea.

He hears footsteps. Turning, he commands his face to lighten as the chief officer extends a hand toward him. Though the thought of touching it repulses him, he does so anyway; thick, leathery fingers fold around his, and a throbbing spreads through his knuckles. The chief officer releases Rodolfo's hand, and both men lean their forearms on the gunwale.

"You men do good work," he says in English. "They work very good."

"Yes, Chief."

"*You* do good job, Bosun."

Rodolfo nods. His heart is racing, and he can feel sweat form on his brow and under his arms.

"I have know many bosun. When the bosun is good, the men look at him to make example. The men look at him for what to do. You understand, Bosun?"

Rodolfo says nothing. The officer clears his throat. "Bosun, I was talk with the company today. They say they want to promote a few good men. They say they need, uh, recommendation." A wave breaks beside the boat, producing a sudden, spitting froth. "Is okay," the chief officer says, "I put in good word for you?"

Rodolfo blinks, slowly, and says, "Yes."

"Because you must know, Bosun, that you are the sort of man who can go far. Maybe become an officer, who know?"

"Thank you, Chief."

For the next few minutes, they have a halting conversation about the ballast holds, and the tendency for the *Maersk Dubai* to list in high water, and how if they had any sense they would have the containers reconfigured once they reached Halifax. The chief officer clears his throat.

"Bosun," he says. "Yesterday, the stowaways, is unfortunate."

Rodolfo nods weakly while continuing to look into darkness.

"It is unfortunate business."

Rodolfo parts his lips and quietly says, "Yes, Chief."

"But you know these stowaway, they come on board and they hide weapon and in the middle of the night they get them and use them. Maybe knives, guns, who know? This happen to me once, near South Africa. Is very difficult, with stowaway. They are more like, uh, pirate, you know? I have been to sea for many year, Bosun, and I know. I know."

No, Rodolfo thinks, *they were frightened. They were hungry.*

"Yes, I tell you, Bosun, the captain he is a smart man, making that decision. He was very smart. Is sometime happen you have to make the *tough* decision. Plus the condition of the sea much worse than we think, but who is to know? The ocean is always a mystery, so yes, is bad, but sometime bad thing happen on a ship, is that not right, Bosun? Do you not think, Bosun?"

I will not look at you, Rodolfo thinks. *I will not turn my head.*

"Bosun?"

"Yes," Rodolfo mumbles. "It was a mistake."

"Yes! A mistake. Is what you say. I am happy you think so. A mistake. I am happy we agree on this."

There is a pause.

"Bosun?"

"Yes?"

"Good evening."

~

He wants to tell the other Filipinos about his conversation with the chief officer. Yet he dares not, for the silence on board the *Maersk Dubai* is like some new regulation, one that upsets stomachs and frazzles nerves and sparks headaches. He tells only Manuel, never guessing that in other parts of the ship, other crew members are confiding that they, too, were promised promotions by the officers.

He struggles through his day. On deck, working alone, he hears the way that noises are amplified by worried ears. In the seamen's mess, the sound of the food being chewed drives him mad. Walking through the corridors of the accommodation, he hears whispers waft through deadened air, only to turn a corner and see a pair of cabin doors being gently pulled shut. The seamen's rec room stays empty, even though the officers have stocked it with beer and cigarettes; at most, someone might wander in for a few minutes and turn on a video before quickly losing interest. Often, the muffled sound of car crashes and gunshots and the screams of women echo through the big ship's hallways.

In place of the recreation normally practised by sailors—cards, videos, cups of coffee, gossip—Rodolfo watches. He keeps his eyes and ears open. He reads the information given by the state of a man's clothing, or by the flicker of a man's eye, or by minute changes in a man's scent. Small clues begin to form, so that slowly, Rodolfo begins to sense which of the seamen will remain scarred by what they saw on that March morning, and which of the seamen will grow to accept it.

A patient man, he hears things. A fight between the Chinese head cook and the Filipino second cook (and could this mean that the second cook is not totally loyal to his officer?). A rumour, passed around in Tagalog, that two Filipinos in the engine room, the oiler and the third engineer, had protested putting the stowaways overboard. Or the fitter, not quite disobeying an order from the chief engineer but, in response to instructions he thought were stupid, throwing up his hands and saying, "All right!" And, of course, there's Manuel—two days after the deaths of the stowaways, Rodolfo returns to his cabin and finds him sitting on the floor, back against the bunk, staring fixedly ahead. When he leaps to his feet, Rodolfo pretends not to notice that his eyes are reddened.

Indications. Suggestions. Perhaps meaningful, perhaps not, but in either case to be sifted through and picked over—at this point, it's impossible for Rodolfo to discern what may, or may not, be the information upon which his future may depend. If a tension has taken hold of the *Maersk Dubai*, it's the tension born of a place in which no feeling, thought or emotion is masked by the emollient known as conversation, the irony being that the seamen aboard the *Maersk Dubai* do not stop talking because they want to harbour their fears and suspicions. In fact, it's the opposite. They stop talking because they want to express them.

~

Dusk, and Rodolfo looks out over soupy, orange water. He spots a hazy shoreline, wavering like a desert mirage. Though he's too far away to make out individual features, like coves or rock faces or the tallest of trees, he has plied these waters many times, and he knows he's looking at a string of islands, their shorelines linked by the tricks played on the eye by distance.

Never have the Azores called to him with such insistency. He wants to go there. He wants to feel dizzy walking on ground that isn't pitching. He wants to eat fish soup, and sleep on a feather bed, and have a glass of tannic red wine. He wishes he could gaze on (though never touch) pretty, dark-haired Portugese girls. He wants palm trees, black olives, rocky coves. Most of all, he wishes he'd never seen murder—he wishes he had no idea, beyond the stylized choreography presented in Jet Li movies, what it looks like, or how it sounds, or the way it fouls the air.

He moves through corridors that, for some reason, feel fore-boding and unfamiliar, as though he hasn't walked down them a thousand times already. When he makes it to his cabin, he drops to his knees and puts his elbows on his bunk and links his fingers. He asks for strength, and for courage, and for the wisdom to put both to use. Before long, he has fallen into the comforting, wavelike motions of his favourite psalm, number ninety-one, the one that counsels believers that no harm shall befall them, and that no calamity shall come upon their home, *for he has charged his angels to guard you wherever you go.*

Slowly, the words of the psalm comfort him. He lies in his bunk and drifts off, only to awaken suddenly, jumping off his bed as though stirred by a loud noise. He rises and goes for a cup of coffee in the mess hall, thinking a hot drink might clear the cobwebs left by his nap. There, he finds the lone Filipino officer, the third engineer Ariel Broas. Since the incident, Broas has started taking some of his coffee breaks in the seamen's mess with the rest of the Filipinos, the overtness of this gesture indicating a steadiness of nerve that Rodolfo, in the adjudicating silence of the ship, has noticed.

Rodolfo sits. The two men nod at each other. Rodolfo takes a sip of coffee and puts down his mug. With each pitch of the sea, a small amount sloshes over the rim, runs down the side and adds to the pool forming at the base. They are alone, he is sure of it, and he decides he'll say something.

"Mr. Broas . . ." he starts, and with these words comes a sudden twitching in his stomach. "Excuse me," he says, his apology followed by a needling of pain. He looks down, tries to think of the words he was about to use, and finds that he cannot—it's as though they've been snatched away by an angry parent. The two men, bosun and third engineer, do not speak, though whenever Rodolfo looks up he can see that the Filipino officer's mind is working away—it's in the deliberate motionlessness of his eyes, and in the odd passivity of his expression.

Ariel Broas takes a sip of his coffee. He wears his hair slightly long, his ebony bangs framing a slim, boyish face. His hands are slight and unscarred, unlike Rodolfo's, whose hands are marked by twenty years' worth of nicks and cuts and the burns caused by rope. His pupils are steady, and black, and surfaced like mirrors.

"Bosun," Ariel Broas says. "There's a meeting."

Rodolfo blinks.

"Tonight, God willing, in Juanito's cabin. There's a meeting."

FOUR

In the glass-roofed Gare du Nord, Daniel watches as Gheorghe retrieves a duffel bag from one of the lockers.

"Come," he says, and Daniel follows him to a cavernous WC. It is cold and odoriferous, the walls lined with pale blue tile turned to rust at the edges. The room is also cloudy with smoke, the commuters puffing away even as they urinate, one eye squinting against smoke coiling off the tip of a hand-rolled cigarette.

Near the entrance, Gheorghe drops to one knee and rifles through the contents of his bag—shirts, socks, toiletries, cans of food and even the odd kitchen utensil, all jumbled and entwined, like clothes on a bazaar table. Finally, he extracts a shirt and hands it to Daniel. Daniel removes his own and throws it in the garbage before pulling on the oversized garment and looking at himself in the mirror. It hangs over his wrists and down to his mid-thigh, making him look thinner than he is. Purplish sacks cradle his eyes, and his hair, which normally hangs straight and black over his forehead, is poking upward, gelled with dirt. His face is puffy around the jawline, and there are pinkish, pebbly caverns etched into the cheek that had lain on cement the night before.

Beside him, Gheorghe hands a coin to the old woman attending the washroom. The big man then starts washing himself as best as he's able, removing his shirt and splashing himself on his chest and armpits before throwing handfuls of water over his bristly, pockmarked face. Daniel follows suit, and when the two men have cleaned themselves, Gheorghe rummages again through his duffel and produces a razor, which he uses with hot water and a bar of lye soap. When he finishes, he hands the shaving equipment to Daniel, who scrapes away the fuzzy beginnings of a beard. When he's finished, he puts his coat back on and inspects himself in the mirror.

Yes, he thinks, *better.*

Later, he buys two tickets to Pitești, an ugly town famous for its Dacia factory and Securitate torture camps. The train will not leave till mid-afternoon, and the two men spend hours waiting in the chilled train station; if one wants to wander off and stretch his legs, the other stays behind and guards Gheorghe's duffel bag. At lunch, they eat cheese and hard rings of *covrigi* speckled with salt. Soon after, they go to the station's brightly lit cafeteria, where they spend the next few hours sipping beer and making conversation. The train arrives more or less on time, and the two men board. After the conductor has taken their third-class tickets and posted their destination on the luggage railings above their seats, Daniel falls into a deep, grateful sleep. The plan is: when the conductor is at the far end of the train, Gheorghe will get up and, with the aid of a felt-tip marker, change the *P* on their destination chit to a heavy, black-stalked *T.* This works, the conductor letting them sleep through Pitești, thinking that they're bound for Timișoara.

It is late now, the train shuttling through dark fields. Daniel awakens and, peering through his window, sees the occasional light burning inside a farmhouse. Many of the other passengers have either settled down to read or begun trying to sleep; across from them, a woman gives her toddler his evening bottle, the child so tired he can barely keep awake to drink. Daniel gets up, telling Gheorghe he'll switch their already-doctored chit with the chit of a pair of blond-haired travellers sleeping toward the back of the next car, who are travelling all the way to Belgrade. When he's finished, he rejoins Gheorghe, who grins and says, "The conductors, you know, they don't even care. They don't get paid enough *to* care . . ."

Daniel again falls into a light asleep, only to be wakened when the conductor comes and asks to see their passports, explaining that the train is about to cross the border. Daniel hands his over, saying nothing, the conductor peering at the document through bifocal lenses. Nodding, he looks at Gheorghe's passport as well before brusquely selling them each a visa. As the train passes into Yugoslavia, Gheorghe smiles and says, "Welcome to the world, Daniel Pacepa . . ." Twenty minutes later, the conductor returns, this time with two porters and a bitter expression on his square, creased face. Daniel and Gheorghe are put off in the middle of nowhere, the sun breaking over a barren Yugoslav meadow.

It is a cold day, the chill more in the wind cascading over the field than in the actual temperature. The station—a single, wood-beamed shelter decorated with torn schedules—is empty, and clearly hasn't been used for some time. Daniel looks around and sees they are surrounded by fields of canola stalks crackling in the breeze. He buttons his jacket, holds the lapels close to his throat, and turns to Gheorghe, who is also looking in every direction while saying, "Shit, shit, shit. That conductor really fucked us, dropping us here."

His hand darts out, and he points with his forefinger. Daniel turns and spots it too—a truck, so far away it's the size of a child's toy, moving silently along the horizon. A few seconds later, it disappears, the two men again feeling the intensity of their solitude. For a moment they stand and listen to wind blowing over the field. Then they set off along the railway tracks, toward the edge of the canola field, where they find a farmer's path that heads in the direction of the road. They start along it, only to find that the hard, frozen path soon dwindles to a barely trampled impression, before ending altogether in a wall of brittle grey plant stalks. Daniel stays in the larger man's wake as he barrels through the field, overturning plants with his huge feet. After ten minutes or so they stop, the two men crouching down to take shelter in the middle of the field; out of the wind, they feel warm from exertion. They wipe their brows and watch their breath condense in the cold, dry air. After a rest, they press on, eventually emerging at the side of a two-lane highway, their shoes now wet with frost.

Daniel gazes in either direction, the road so long and straight it seems to curve slightly at the outskirts of his vision. Each time a car comes, Gheorghe hides, leaving Daniel to wave his arms and call for help and generally try to look as meek as his features will allow. After four or five cars pass them, Gheorghe emerges, saying, "You look too serious—that's your problem. You look too fucking *glum*." For the next hour or so Gheorghe tries his luck, the big man holding his thumb in the air while grinning. They are there for hours. Long after they have given up hope, and have started walking in the direction of what they think is the nearest town, a troop carrier filled with soldiers pulls over and lets the two men board. Since Gheorghe has playing cards and a bottle of *ţuică* bought from a Bucharest platform vendor, they are taken straight across another border, and all the way to the city of Zagreb, Croatia. That night, they find their way through a city of buildings marred with bullet holes and mortar rounds, at one point eating a bowl of cabbage flavoured with bacon in a chilly, bright, tile-lined cafeteria. Later, they find the square outside the train station, where Daniel buys two bottles of Croatian vodka with the last of the *lei* he has brought from home. When night falls, they skirt the train station and find the path leading to the switching yard, which they follow to a place where the fence has been loosened and an impression dug into the stone-flecked earth. Gheorghe sends Daniel through on his belly, before throwing his duffel over the fence and crawling under himself. They brush themselves off and look around for station guards.

It takes them an hour of stumbling around in the dark, of ducking every time they hear a noise, of giving a wide berth to the cones of yellow light that stand, like sentinels, every forty or fifty metres. Finally, they find an idling freight train pointed west. They wander up and down the track until they find a car with its siding left slightly ajar. Gheorghe places both hands on a metal door and pulls, causing the sudden, sharp screech of metal on metal.

They freeze, waiting to see if the noise will bring a guard. "All right," Gheorghe says, and he pulls himself up the siding rail and steps through the darkened aperture. Daniel hears the thump of a falling body, and he sees potatoes skitter out of the siding and land on the tops of his feet. He hoists himself up, and for the next little while the two men mould high-backed seats out of mounds of seed potatoes. When this is done, Gheorghe stretches out, his hands clasped behind his head.

"So now we enjoy the ride. At least we aren't going to go hungry, eh, Dani?"

Daniel chuckles weakly, trying desperately to hide the thick, dulling fatigue that has overtaken him. The train begins to vibrate, and loose potatoes, softened and covered with eyes, begin bouncing against the metal floor. Daniel crawls to the siding and peers out. The rail station is moving now. Soon, the city is sliding past, the tenements a dark brown blur, and Daniel is reminded of the battered apartment where he'd lived with his mother and the large family of his uncle Stefan. Farther into the city, they pass another perforated building, this one located right near the tracks. Pinprick lights beam from every other window, and the thought that every light may represent a story like his own makes him feel sad, and short of breath, and craving a glass of *țuică*.

Loose potatoes are thrumming against the floor of the freight car, producing a noise like the hammering of an old washing machine. Daniel crawls around the floor, throwing errant potatoes back onto the pile so as to reduce the noise, only to find that every time he adds a potato, three new ones loosen. He gives up and returns to his space near the doorway. It is impossible to get comfortable—the floor is covered in small ridges, and the car is fumy with the dull methane odour of potatoes unearthed too long ago. When he calls out something to Gheorghe, his voice is a comic warble. Gheorghe shrugs, indicating he can't understand him, so Daniel pulls out one of the vodka bottles and crawls across the car to hand it to Gheorghe.

Gheorghe beams, and yells, "This should keep us warm, eh, Dani?"

Daniel nods, and returns to his spot near the siding. There he spins open the top on the other bottle and takes his first appreciative glug; compared with *țuică* it tastes like tap water. He takes another, deeper drink from the bottle, and soon finds that the alcohol decreases the intensity of the vibrations travelling up through his spine and neck, and the sensation of cold transmitting through the cloth of his pants. After a time, his head begins to throb, though it does so pleasantly, the pressure behind his eyes blocking out the smell and the noise in the rail car. The pain in his joints recedes, and he feels warmer. He drinks more, and when the bottle is half gone he even starts to feel a little happy, for he is blearily imagining the life that he'll have in America—strolls taken in parks, glasses of perked coffee had in fancy cafés, Hollywood films watched in red-curtained cinemas. He imagines comfort, and autumn leaves, and zoos, yet as he drifts closer and closer to sleep, those images bend, and waver, and darken, such that by the time he's asleep his dreams have turned to dogs and black vans and shoutings in the night *and this time he sees it all over again, as though it happened yesterday, the black vans screeching into town and the red lights swirling crimson, and as they speed through narrow streets there comes the wail of sirens and the footfalls of villagers* and then, without realizing it, Daniel is yelling in his sleep, his feet kicking at the ribbed metal floor. Gheorghe is above him, calling for him to waken, and when this fails he grips Daniel by the forearms and says, "Hey, Dani. Hey, boy! Wake up! You're having some kind of nightmare!"

Daniel's eyes pop open. He suddenly feels cold all over.

"What were you yelling?" Gheorghe asks. "Something about black vans? About the Securitate?"

"Yes," Daniel says, though when he realizes he's been dreaming about the old Romania, he pushes the knowledge away.

"Well, don't," Gheorghe says. "You don't have to; those days are over."

Daniel sits up and looks around the rail car. It is still, a wedge of light coming through the opened siding. The potatoes have settled from their original mounds, more or less covering the floor in an even blanket. He is still breathing hard, and finding it diffi-cult to talk, for the thought that maybe this trip will be too much for him—that maybe he's not as tough as he needs to be—is crossing his mind for the first time. He finds the vodka bottle at his side, and takes two or three large swallows. The liquor hits his nervous stomach and burns, a sensation that immediately causes Daniel to relax and feel more hopeful.

"Where are we?" he asks.

"Italy, I think. We've been stopped here for an hour, more or less."

Daniel crawls to the side of the car and peers out. In the dis-tance are cows, lazily chewing in a pasture, and somewhere far beyond that are mountains, looking hazy and brown. Every few minutes one of the cows raspily moos, a sound that makes Daniel think of home. Suddenly, he realizes that the last thing he ate was a fish sandwich, bought in the Zagreb train station, and that he's ravenous. With his back against the rail-car siding, he bites into a potato, glumly choking down its cloying flesh.

The rail car shudders, and shunts backward—for a moment Daniel worries that the train has, for some reason, decided to head back from where it came from. He can see exhaust and dust rising outside the opened siding; the wedge of sun cast over the floor of the car looks speckled. The train lurches in the wrong direction, stops, and then shuttles forward again. For the next ten minutes or so, it jumps forward in hesitant, irregular sprints, like a child learning to broad jump. Finally, the train settles into a constant, slow, forward motion, its velocity no more than five or ten kilometres per hour. As Daniel bites into his second potato, Gheorghe leans out of the car, the remaining hairs on the top of his head streaming in the breeze.

"There it is," he says, "the big city—take a look . . ."

Daniel leans out as well, his hands holding tight on to siding rails. He can see squat buildings up ahead.

"Well, Dani. Who first?"

Daniel looks at the hard ground sliding purposefully beyond the bank of the rail bed, and he thinks that anything is better than being stuck in this rail car filled with rotting potatos. With a quick curse he throws himself into the air. For a second he hovers over moving ground, and then he is rolling, a thudding pain in his side and shoulder. He comes to a stop and looks up. A little ways behind him, Gheorghe is sitting in the pasture, reaching for his fallen duffel. He stands and brushes dust from his pants and coat.

They spend the rest of that day walking into a little town somewhere near Milan. Though the weather is warmer than it was in Yugoslavia, they find that a chill has seeped into their bones, causing their teeth to chatter and their bodies to shiver. Slowly, the walk warms them, and when Gheorghe comments that he's not so cold any longer Daniel thinks, *Yes, he's right, it's about time.* When their legs grow tired, they stop and eat the potatoes that Gheorghe was smart enough to stuff into his pockets. When they become thirsty, they drink from farm wells, taking turns pumping blue metal handles until water pours into the other man's mouth. At one house, Daniel takes a pair of apples from a bushel he spots resting on an outside picnic table, and they savour them while cutting through a field cleared for seeding. Finally, the field gives way to a narrow track, which they follow into the town.

The streets are filled with people eating in restaurants, a sight so wonderful that Daniel and Gheorghe keep their heads down, working hard to ignore all of the things they cannot have: fresh pastries, proscuitto the size of babies, balls of pecorino hanging from cheese-shop awnings, pretty brown-haired girls without a hint of the toughness, or the sadness, ingrained in the souls of Romanian women. (*Oh my,* Daniel thinks every time he sees a girl with dark eyes, or a button-shaped nose, or hair gathered upward, revealing the long, graceful line of her neck.) On the steps of an ancient stone church they smoke cigarettes and quietly sip the last of the vodka. A clanging comes from the belfry. As it echoes through the town, they get up and wander away, as though ordered off the premises.

Along a narrow cobblestoned lane they find a bakery. Here, Gheorghe uses an American dollar to buy a stick of bread that's hard on the outside and fluffy as a kitten on the inside; its flavour makes them both feel hungry, and tired, and wishing they weren't so dirty. They walk on, coming to a small, one-room bus station. Inside, they study a bus schedule while counting out the last of their money. Soon, they are smiling, for they realize they have just enough for some cafeteria sandwiches and two seats on the gruelling twenty-hour ride to the city of Marseilles, a place so far from the chilly, bat-infested villages of Maramureș it might as well be on the moon.

FIVE

He sneaks through the ship's interior, turning right and then right again, following the U-shaped hallway to where the ship's oiler, Juanito Ilagan, has a larger cabin at the end of the corridor.

He can hear voices coming through the door; again, he looks from left to right. When he knocks, the door opens just enough to reveal the right half of the oiler's face. Juanito nods and indicates Rodolfo should enter.

"Come," he says, "please, have a seat . . ."

The fitter and the electrician are sitting on the bunk against the nearer wall, talking to the second cook, who's taken a space on the bed on the far side of the room. They pause to nod politely at Rodolfo before resuming their conversation, Rodolfo seating himself next to the cook. A moment later, the door latch turns, and Ariel Broas walks in and takes the chair beneath the porthole. He turns and nods to Rodolfo, and because he does not likewise greet the other three, Rodolfo understands that he, as the lone representative of the deck crew, is the new member of the group.

The conversation resumes, the sailors talking of baseball games listened to via scratchy shortwave radio transmissions, the enjoyment not so much the game but the connection with home;

of politics, both from Manila and the provinces, and how there's always trouble in the cities, rice fields and jungles of their country; of some Bollywood videos an Indian crew left behind, and how the actresses always break into dance the moment the skies darken with rain, their saris soon soaked through and clinging like Saran Wrap; of the condition of the food—which, in reality, is as good as can be expected, given that the ingredients are generally frozen or freeze-dried, but which gives them an opportunity to rib the second cook about the spiciness of his *gulaman,* the texture of his *halo halo,* the crispness of his deep fry. Rodolfo is happy to once again hear the banter of sailors, all quips and barbs and needlings, though it does feel as though they're doing something wrong by enjoying themselves.

He relaxes, slightly, and learns things about the engine crew: that the oiler, Ilagan, used to be a professional karaoke singer, and that he came from the same province as the officer, Broas. That the second cook, whose name is Ricardo, is intent on marrying a girl back in Manila, should her parents ever give their consent. That the electrician, an older man named Wilfredo, used to be in the Filipino navy. That the fitter, Alfredo, is also from Ilocos, the northern province where Rodolfo was born.

"You know," Rodolfo says, "my AB, Manuel, is from there as well."

"Which one is he?"

"Manuel?"

"Yes."

"A small man, a bit older than the other ABs. A little too much weight . . ."

At this, the other sailors nod, for they understand Rodolfo is talking about the nervous deckhand, the one rumoured to be having the most trouble dealing with what they all saw that morning.

"And what of you, Bosun?" the electrician asks. "Have you always been a sailor?"

"Oh no," Rodolfo says. "I used to work for the city—my wife's uncle got me the job. But working in politics, it wasn't for me. It wasn't for me at all."

"Why not?"

"All the wheelings and dealings, seeing how things get done, seeing how palms get greased. Oh no, it wasn't for me. So I talked it over with my wife, and I told her how I felt, and she said, 'Okay Rudy, if you're going to make a change you might as well do it now, when you're young.' A few months after that I shipped out."

"And with every shore leave," the second cook jokes, "another baby! How many is it, Bosun?"

"Five," Rodolfo answers, "and counting!"

At this, everyone laughs; even Ariel Broas chuckles for a moment. Slowly, their laughter is replaced with the awkward silence of five men who have decided it's time they started talking about what they've come to discuss. Rodolfo looks from face to face. The oiler lights a cigarette. Ariel Broas clears his throat, and asks simply, "Do we know where they were from?"

"Eastern Europe," says Juanito. "I think. You could tell by the way they spoke."

"Yes," says the fitter, "Serbia, maybe. There are lots of Serbs and Croats trying to get away from that place. Who can blame them?"

"Or Czech," says the electrician, "maybe Czech. Or Romanian."

"Yes," Rodolfo pipes up. "Romanian."

The others look at him.

"They knew Spanish words."

"So?" the fitter says.

"I knew a Romanian sailor once. He told me his language wasn't like the languages of the countries near his. He told me it had French words, and Italian words, and Spanish words. When I was talking to them, I heard words from those languages . . ."

"Didn't they get on in Spain? Maybe they learned those words there?"

"Maybe," Rodolfo says.

"Did you get their names?" the second cook asks.

"Yes . . . one was named Peter, I think, and the other was named something like Rada, or Radu, I'm not sure."

"It doesn't matter," Broas says.

The others look at him.

"What matters is whose fault it was. I blame the shipping company. The captain did it because he was following orders."

"I don't think so," Juanito says.

"Yes. I think so. He would have radioed the shipping company. They would have told him to do it. That's what would have happened."

At this, everyone but Rodolfo begins talking, in voices lowered to a hissing whisper, someone saying, "No, no, it was our weak and stupid captain," and someone else saying, "No, the chief officer was behind it all," while another man says, "Yes, I agree with Ariel—it was the shipping company." As he listens, Rodolfo realizes that the discussion is making him feel light-headed and weak.

"Bosun," Broas says. "What do you think?"

Five sets of eyes turn to Rodolfo. He shakes his head and says, "I don't know. It was all those things, maybe, or none of them." He pauses, and struggles to find a way to say what he really feels. "When I looked into the eyes of the officers," he says, "I saw a coldness there. I saw they were without God."

A few seconds pass.

"Yes," Broas says, "you're right. I saw that too . . ."

"So what do we do?" Juanito asks.

"We wait. There's nothing else we can do."

"Does this mean we'll do something later on? Does this mean we'll do something eventually?" the fitter asks.

Broas pauses for a moment, as if to think.

"Yes," he says. "We will."

~

The meeting breaks up around eleven, shortly before Broas starts his evening watch in the engine room. Rodolfo goes to his cabin. Though he's as quiet as possible, he cannot stop the door from creaking as he makes his way to his bunk. Manuel opens an eye against the light that widens, and then narrows, over the room.

"Bose," he says, "why are you late?"

"Shhh, my brother. Go to sleep."

"Where were you?"

"Shhh, Manuel. Sleep."

"Is something happening?"

"No, brother, nothing . . ."

Rodolfo pulls off his clothes and folds down the blanket in a crisp triangle. He crawls in, pulling the blanket to his chin. The two men lie in darkness, the moon casting a circle of dim, silvery light on the floor between them. Neither can sleep. Manuel asks if he can smoke, and when Rodolfo says, "Sure, it doesn't bother me," he lights a cigarette. Rodolfo listens to him rhythmically draw smoke into his lungs, the room filling with the barley scent of

American tobacco. As a sailor, he's grown accustomed to the smells encountered on a big ship—to diesel fuel and unwashed bedding, to cooking oil and burning tobacco, to the acrid smell of a city, carried by breezes, as they near the harbour of a poor country.

He soon finds himself thinking of home, as though he were looking at snapshots on a child's viewfinder. He thinks of his favourite noodle stand, of the places he'll take his little ones when he returns, and of the small gifts he'll buy for Maripaz when they're together again. He then thanks God for allowing him to have such comforting thoughts. There are men on board, he knows, who've not been so lucky—who have divorced, who have lost children to illness, who did not have enough to eat when they were growing up. After a time, his thoughts slow, and time begins to curl in on itself. He sleeps, soundly, for the first night since *the incident,* his dreams occuring in deserts, and forests, and other places without water.

The next day, around mid-afternoon, Rodolfo is on deck. The sea is strong, a steady rolling of waves pushing against the progress of the ship. The list lights mounted on the stack keep flickering from white to red to white to green, a constant visual reminder of the sea's unsteadiness. He can see the officers conferring on the bridge, so he steals along the starboard side, his path obscured by a bank of containers. He reaches the accommodation, and takes the stairs to the seamen's deck. Once there, he walks to the oiler's cabin. He knocks, and Juanito answers, looking surprised.

"Bosun . . ." he says.

A moment passes, both men fidgeting.

"Oiler . . . it's about Manuel."

"Yes?"

"I think he'd like to join us. I think it would help him. He has been . . . well, he's been as upset as any of us."

Juanito eyes him for a moment, and then shakes his head. "I don't know," he answers. "My room is crowded already. I should have a talk with Ariel. I don't know, Bosun."

Rodolfo's eyes flicker from left to right. He feels naked, being in the hallway, having this conversation. He lowers his voice. "One of the stowaways," he says, "kissed Manuel's feet."

Again, Juanito shakes his head. Rodolfo says nothing, for he knows full well what is running through the oiler's head—the young stowaway, tears streaming down his cheeks, on his knees and kissing Manuel's shoes.

Juanito nods, and steps back inside his cabin. "Okay, Bosun," he says before shutting the door. "Of course, of course, bring him. He is welcome."

~

That night there are seven of them, three on each bunk, with the officer Broas again claiming the chair beneath the porthole. Though the stowaways are not discussed this time, Rodolfo understands that by being there, the men have reached a tacit agreement—when the passage of the *Maersk Dubai* is over, they will somehow tell what they saw that morning. In the meantime, they'll offer each other company, humour and, should the need arise, protection. (Of course, they have decided one other thing. The other Filipinos on board—the ABs named Angel, Carmelito, Marlou and Joe—have not found themselves here, in the cabin of the oiler, and should therefore not be trusted.)

This solidarity, along with the passage of days, helps. Each time one of the Taiwanese officers asks Rodolfo for something, he feels a little less panicked, and a little less like this is the moment when the officers will decide to rid the ship of witnesses. Though he still has dreams of the stowaways being sucked under by the churning wake, they are not coloured so luridly. A measure of chatter, at times brightened with laughter, returns to the seamen's mess. At first, Rodolfo has trouble joining in, for it feels like a betrayal of the dead men, yet after time he starts to question how he could hurt them by, say, laughing at one of the second cook's awful jokes, or admiring a sunset off the bow, or savouring the way barbecued pork tastes after a morning of labour. His shoulders and neck do not ache with the same ferocity, and the dull ebb of his headaches abates. Prayer, too, helps, Rodolfo understanding that hardship exists for one reason and one reason only: to deliver him more eagerly, and more eternally, into the embrace of God.

Two days from Halifax, petrels appear, frolicking above the boat, occasionally swooping at fish thrown up by the wake. Ten kilometres from port the big ship stops, and the anchors are dropped. In the distance, Rodolfo can see the hazy outline of a bulk carrier, also stopped, awaiting a berth. They are in anchorage for a day and a half. The pilot boat arrives, and the pilot comes aboard to help navigate the *Maersk Dubai* to shore. As the big ship nears the berth, a mooring tug moves to its side and manoeuvres it into place. Throughout the docking, the smaller boat throws up mushrooms of white, foaming sea water.

They are in Halifax for ten hours, the stevedores and onshore crane operators responsible for loading and unloading the boat. Rodolfo and his ABs continue stripping, grinding and sanding the deck. In the engine room, filters are cleaned and injector valves replaced. In the mess, the second cook chops enough onions for a week, his kitchen filling with a vapour that would leave a lesser man gasping for breath. The boat leaves for Newark, where the sailors are again confined to the ship. Then, in Miami, they are allowed to leave the boat for an hour only, the Filipinos all rushing to the long-distance phone shops that line the port, only to find there's a problem that night with the trunk lines. They return feeling glum, and lonely, and remembering the terrible moments they've had during the voyage. The ship proceeds to Houston, or more precisely to the docking facility at the mouth of Trinity Bay called La Porte, Texas. Here, an official shore leave is finally granted, and Rodolfo heads to a shop called Best-Price Phone Calls. The place is loud with chatter and ringing telephones. After waiting in line for twenty minutes, he's handed a pass card for cabin number 4, which he finds in a line of wood-panelled booths along the left side of the shop. He nods his thanks, and enters the relative quiet of the cabin. He places a call to Manila.

When Maripaz answers the phone and hears her husband's voice, she squeals. "Oh, Rudy, it *is* you."

"Yes, yes, I miss you so much . . ."

He can hear the usual clamour in his small house, for even though it is early morning there, the television is playing loudly, and the younger of his children are calling for attention, and the city itself provides a constant backdrop of traffic sounds and raised voices. As sometimes happens when he goes a long time between phone calls home, Maripaz is sniffling and wiping her nose, and then laughing at the silliness of her reaction.

"Oh, Rudy, I had a feeling that something bad was happening."

"No, no, everything is fine."

"Really?"

"Yes, of course, it's just I've been working very hard—they haven't been giving us shore leave . . ."

The phone is snatched from his wife's hand by his eldest daughter. After a brief conversation—he can't believe how much like an adult she sounds—Jinky passes the phone to each of his children, right down to the toddler, Joshua. Upon hearing the sound of his baby's voice, Rodolfo grows suddenly weary. Maripaz comes back on the line, and when she asks the same question as before—"Is everything all right? Are you sure everything's all right?"—Rodolfo almost tells her about the stowaways.

Instead he says, "It's nothing, dear. I'm tired. Very tired. We're working very hard. The boat—there are some problems with it."

Just then, the attendant knocks on the glass door of the booth, holding up fingers to indicate that Rodolfo's call is getting expensive. Rodolfo nods and says his goodbyes more hastily than normal. He steps into the hallway that divides the shop in two. Outside, the night is hot and humid, and it reminds him of home. He stands still, hating the sensation of being in his own skin. Oddly, he feels as if he's in a movie—this moment linked to another moment, and that moment to the following moment, and if he could only press fast-forward he'd know why this entire experience requires him to be feeling the way he's feeling now.

He goes back to the boat and jots down the details of the last day or two in his logbook. He has dinner, he returns to his cabin, he reads from his Bible before falling asleep. The next morning, at breakfast, he sits with Juanito and Ariel Broas; in between swallows of egg, Juanito says how he'd gone to the Mission to Seafarers the night before, and that the priest there had turned out to be, of all things, a Filipino.

Later, the three men go to shore together, Juanito heading for the phone shop again, as he had trouble with a phone card the night before and still hasn't spoken to his wife and children. This leaves Rodolfo alone with the Filipino officer. There is a moment of discomfort, for despite the meetings in Juanito's cabin he still doesn't know Broas well, and like most people is a little intimidated by the third engineer. Broas nods toward the Mission to Seafarers, and it takes Rodolfo a second to realize that this is an invitation to go with him.

They walk side by side, not talking. The mission is within the confines of the port, housed in an aluminum-sided building set on blocks. Inside, other sailors are playing cards and drinking beer—Sri Lankans, by the look of them, skinny and dark skinned and wearing shorts. There is also a table full of Greek officers arguing loudly, and some Senegalese crewmen watching football on television. At a table near the corner, seated in front of a mound of paperwork, dressed in light pants and a checked short-sleeve shirt, is a man who could only be the priest that Juanito had mentioned earlier. Broas and Rodolfo approach. They all introduce themselves—the priest's name is Albano—and sit.

"Our friend, he told us you were Filipino," Broas says.

"Yes," Father Albano says, "I'm from Manila."

"Really?" Broas motions at his own face. "You look more . . ."

"Chinese? Yes, I know. Half the time, Filipino soldiers start conversations with me in English, or Cantonese if they know some. I like to answer in Tagalog, just to watch the expression on their faces!"

The three men chuckle. For Father Albano, this is nothing out of the ordinary, Filipino seamen appreciating the comfort, and the familiarity, of a priest from back home. For a pair of sailors two months into an eight-month passage, he's a comfort item, like the stained glass of a neighbourhood church or the smoking-oil scent of a favourite noodle stand. The words that come out of his mouth, he knows too well, are by and large inconsequential—much of his ministering is performed by the hue of his skin, and the shape of his face, and his familiarity with the clamorous side-streets of Manila.

Yet as he makes small talk with the two men, he senses that they are suffering from something beyond the garden-variety loneliness that builds during a voyage. The smaller one may hide it better than the stocky one, but it's still there, in the way the muscles in his forearms twitch, and in the way he clenches his jaw when thinking. The bigger one—the one who'd introduced himself as a bosun—keeps taking quick sidelong glances at the young officer, as though he expects the smaller man to do or say something. The conversation continues: gulf weather, Texan barbecue, news from home, movies. As they talk, the little voice upon which the priest relies, honed during thousands of conversations with upset sailors, grows in his head. Soon, he is listening to *it,* rather than to the words coming from the mouths of the two men.

Broas signals that the conversation is over by glancing at Rodolfo and nodding. The two stand, and it's all the priest can do to stop from saying, *No, wait, tell me what it is.*

Instead, he stands with them, pushing back his chair as he asks a question. "How are things on board?" and even before Ariel Broas manages to compose himself and say, "Fine, fine," the priest Albano can see it, seeping from each of them, an aura of dread.

SIX

My dearest, dearest Dani,

Oh my love, how I miss you and need you and wish we were together, at all times and forever. And, oh, the number of times a day I imagine us in New York City, being happy and working at good jobs and maybe, even, who knows, with little Danis running around and laughing and being bad boys like their father. At night, I push my face deep into my pillow and try to imagine what it would be like to be without problems. During the day, I'm moody and not myself, and people know to stay away and not bother me because I'm a girl whose sweetheart has left for America, and there is nothing I can do but wait.

I am knitting you a sweater. When I get stuck on tricky parts, like under the arms or around the neck, I'm encouraged by the thought that it will keep you warm in the Big Apple, but then I start to sniffle, for there is nothing more I want than to be there, with you, in the United States of America. Other times, when I'm tired of knitting, I try hard to think of all the things that bring me joy and I think, okay, any world that has these things must also be a world that can allow my sweetheart to be alive, and healthy, and happy. This helps.

Dani—there is something I must tell you. The other day I was at home and I heard a knocking at the door. When I opened it I saw a woman named Maria Săngeorzan, who is a friend of my friend Marta from Satu Mare. She had come because her husband, Petre, and her second cousin Radu had left for Algeciras about six weeks before you, and she wanted to come and meet me because she'd heard you had done the same thing. I looked at her and she smiled weakly so I asked her in and we had some coffee, and it was then then that she asked if I had heard from you recently. I told her I had, and was about to pull out the postcard you sent from France when I noticed that she was looking downward at her fidgeting hands. At this point, I realized something was wrong, and that this was the real reason she had come. I asked her what it could be.

Elena, she said, I am worried. I haven't heard from Petre since his last note from Spain and I'm sick with worry. So I told her that there must be some explanation, that he must be very busy getting settled in New York City or that perhaps the mail is slow, and she kept shaking her head and saying, No, no, no, Elena, something has happened with him. I have a feeling in my bones.

Of course I told her again that everything must be all right and that she would hear from him soon, but all the while I was really thinking that her husband had probably met up with some American girl and hadn't worked up the courage to tell poor Maria that he wouldn't be sending her money for a ticket to America after all. After a while, Maria left, and I was struck by an even worse thought, that maybe something had happened to Petre, though what that could be I refuse to even think. (Dani, if I asked you to come home, would it help? No, no, I promised myself I wouldn't . . .)

Well, I must go now. There are a million things to be done here and I tell you I can't wait till the day when I can say goodbye forever to the goats and sheep and doing laundry by hand. I see your mother most days and she misses you terribly but at the same time I can see she is happy for you.

One million kisses and hugs and other things besides,
Your love Elena

P.S. Maria told me one other thing you might find useful. In one of his letters from Algeciras, Petre said they were staying at a place called El Faro. He said it was free and clean and that they are known for helping out travellers in trouble and that many Romanians stay there. One thing, though—it is a religious place so you have to act that way too.

P.P.S. Oh my love. Come home.

Daniel is propped on his elbows, his fingers beginning to tingle, his toes pressed against a slender, creased mattress. When he goes to put the letter back in the envelope, he hears the sound of something shifting inside. He holds his penlight to the envelope, and sure enough he sees a thin, square impression. Inverting the envelope, he shakes it, and she lands on his pillow smiling. The photo must have been taken at last year's Easter celebration, for she is in traditional dress—white long-sleeved blouse, brocade vest, black ankle-length skirt. Her light brown hair is piled atop her head, accentuating both the roundness of her eyes and the way that her long, pale neck widens, ever so slightly, as it meets the underside of her jaw. Her eyes are a deep, luminous blue, and her teeth are as white as the snow-capped peaks in the back of the photo. Yet it is the self-conscious way her fingers hold the hem of her skirt, show-ing off its embroidery, that causes him to wish, above all else, he was in a place imbued with the scent, and the laughter, of women.

He slides the photo back in the envelope, places it under his pillow, and drifts back into a light slumber. When he comes to, the room is bathed in a creamy half-light. Some of the men are already awake and padding off to the toilets. Around him, he hears coughing, and whispers, and noses being blown.

He goes to the mess trailer, where he eats eggs and toast and sausage with the other construction workers, all of whom are ille-gals from Eastern Europe—Romanians mostly, along with a handful of Albanians, Bulgarians, Ukrainians, Moldovans, Belarussians, and a lonely Azerbaijani with a reddish tint to his skin. They are barely awake and unshaven, sitting in pockets of twos and threes at the long table, the men mostly keeping their heads down while they eat. When Daniel is partway through his breakfast, Gheorghe comes and sits beside him, nodding cheer-lessly before tucking into the food on his tray. By seven, all of the men have eaten and are tramping from the trailers to the giant house frame on the hill. The sun is a thick, white haze, and already there are insects, whirring over dandelion stalks.

Daniel retrieves his broom. He starts in what will be the ser-vants' quarters, at the southern end of the house, and begins sweeping up sawdust, packing materials, fallen insulation, wire cuttings, bits of PVC tubing, cigarette butts, bottle caps, and the other detritus of a construction site. As he works, the foreman, a Romanian named Goran Vereş, paces from room to room, barking orders in French and Romanian and a half-dozen other languages. He is far from happy. The house is behind schedule, and he continually warns that if it's not completed by autumn he'll fire them all and get some North Africans to finish the job—at least they don't complain about a little heat. Around him, men are hammering, running wire and installing plumbing, and because they're trying to do it all at the same time, they constantly get in each other's way, and arguments are constantly flaring up.

From the servants' quarters, Daniel moves to the kitchen and then the dining salon, the latter so big it could easily contain the trailer in which the construction workers sleep. From the dining salon, he moves to the great room, with its towering cathedral ceilings and worn stone fireplaces at either end. He sweeps what will be the entranceway, the library, the billiards room, the trophy room and then finally he reaches the master bedroom, a large pod perched on a ridge so that the owner will one day be able to draw back his curtains and gape at vineyards, olive groves and the distant sea. Daniel leans on his broom. It's mid-morning, and already he's sweating—by the time he walks back to the other end of the house, the floor will be covered again with cigarette butts and tubing ends and wire clippings, and his task will start anew. Glumly, he rests his hands on the end of his broom, something that causes his gaze to fall on his own, sweat-covered arms. They are long and sinewy, and he surprises himself by thinking that his arms are the arms of his father, an educated man who had written poems and plays during his university days in Bucharest. Looking closer, he's also amazed to find that his fingertips are still slightly darker than the rest of his hands, as though permanently stained by the strawberry farms of Maramureș.

With this thought he turns and looks through wall frame after wall frame, toward the far end of the house. He sees the foreman, Goran, stomping from room to room, calling angrily, and though Daniel cannot hear what he's yelling he assumes it must have something to do with their coffee break, for the men are putting down their hammers and stepping carefully around their work stations.

He finds Gheorghe in the middle of the Great Room, sawing two-by-six planks for special fits. One by one, he feeds pieces of wood into a rotary saw, a plume of sawdust emitting from the manifold; as it falls, it sticks to the sweat on Gheorghe's arms and face, creating a blond film. When he spots Daniel, he turns off the machine and removes his breather and pushes his hearing protector back off his head, so that it drapes around his neck. As they step outside of the house, Daniel says, "I'm leaving today."

Gheorghe puts his hands on his lower back and stretches. Sunshine glints off his face, catching the sawdust stuck to dark stubble. "I see," he says, and is about to walk toward the dining trailer, where they'll both get buns and cups of coffee, when he stops himself.

"Look at this house. *Look* at it. One day, Dani, one day . . ."

"Yes, I know. We'll be rich as kings."

"I have an idea," Gheorghe says. "Since you're leaving, let's have a little celebration tonight. We'll go into town with the other Romanians, have a drink or two, maybe dance with some French girls. What do you say?"

Daniel looks at Gheorghe and realizes, with a start, that he will miss the miner from Baia Sprie.

"Yes," Daniel says. "I think that would be a good idea."

~

That night, after showering, they shave and comb their hair; as they dress, they try not to look at one another, as they are all slightly self-conscious that they have nothing to wear but blue jeans, light brown work shoes, and shirts made from soft, heavy cotton.

There are four of them. As Daniel and Gheorghe are both from the region of Maramureș, they are the targets of good-natured jokes about being hicks from the country, about having sex with sheep, about marrying their sisters and producing dim, stunty-fingered babies. (Hearing these jibes, Gheorghe throws his head back and laughs loudly before bellowing, "Shhh . . . don't tell anyone!") Eugen Brădescu is from Transylvania, and because he is tall, and because his nose is beak shaped, and because his eyes look perpetually heavy, they tease him about being a relative of Count Vlad himself. Hearing these jokes, he chuckles, his Adam's apple bobbing, even though the jokes don't quite make sense, for as every Romanian knows Dracula was not from Transylvania at all, but from a region to the south of the Carpathians called Wallachia. The fourth, Nicolae Pană, is from Bucharest, and is jokingly accused of being arrogant and snobbish, all of which is funny, as he's a carpenter, and a father, and as humble as a man can be.

Both Eugen and Nicolae are married, though only Nicolae has children. Eugen has been to university, and in fact was in Timișoara the night the riots broke out. Daniel and Nicolae know some French, having studied the language in high school. Of the four, Gheorghe is the only orphan, and he is also the only one to have spent more than a few days in a Romanian prison, the result of an incident with a stolen car when he was young and foolish and so drunk he'd forgotten what had happened by the time he had his two-minute trial. Beyond that, their differences end, for they all know what it's like to visit the Black Sea, to almost die of *ţuică* poisoning, to feel the delicious ache of a broken heart, to cry aloud at a folk song, to serve in one of Ceauşescu's fanatical goose-stepping youth groups.

They walk to the village, oak branches melding and forming a rough arcade above them; the light trickling through casts a patchwork on the path. On either side are rustic little farmhouses, and stone walls trellised with climbing roses, and olive groves turned a sepia colour in the last of the daylight. The farms start appearing closer together, until they are farmhouses no longer but the homes found on the perimeter of a settlement.

It looks ancient, this little town outside of Marseilles. The winding streets are fashioned from cobblestone, and there are geranium boxes in the windows facing the lane. The doors on the houses are big, roughly hewn, and strapped with metal; attached to them are copper door knockers, some as large as kittens. For Daniel, the town feels familiar and, for this reason, inviting—he can't believe they've kept themselves hidden, in a camp smelling of soup and dirty shirts, for nine whole weeks.

The four men reach a square with an old stone church. They look around, taking in the view. After a bit, they wander down a side street extending from a corner of the square. They pass windows bearing the words *pâtisserie,* and *boulangerie,* and *banque,* all written in the same swooping gold script. They also find more than one restaurant, though these are formal places, with tablecloths and written menus, and the men are looking for the sort of place where people unwind and have a drink and mingle with their neighbours. A block away from the southwest corner of the square, they find such a place—it's big and whitewashed, with a long wooden bar and old farming implements tacked to the wall. The ceilings have heavy wooden timbers painted black.

They find chairs at one of the tables and sit. At first their chatter is animated and gleeful, though after some time passes and they haven't been served, their conversation becomes somewhat forced. Gheorghe finally cranes his neck in every direction and says loudly, "For the love of God, who's working here?"

Both Daniel and Eugen diffuse Gheorghe's comment— "Patience, miner, patience"—and Nicolae jokes that maybe the sun has made the people lazy.

Daniel looks toward the bar. There are a half-dozen people there, middle-aged men with large noses and drinks in their hands. The barmaid is an older woman with pale skin and long, thin forearms; when he catches her eye, she gives the faintest impression of a nod before calling out something that Daniel doesn't catch. They wait a minute longer, and then the saloon doors leading to the kitchen swing open. A young woman wearing an apron and a light grey T-shirt dampened in spots with dishwater walks out. Immediately, the four men feel better, for though the waitress is not quite pretty—she has the same features and gaunt complexion as the barmaid—it is nonetheless true that there is a loveliness residing in her youth and in the self-conscious way she pushes a lock of hair off her face.

"*Oui?*" she says.

Nicolae Pană tells her in passable French that they would like very much to have dinner. She motions over her shoulder to a blackboard tacked to the wall, near where her mother is wiping the surface of the bar. Upon it are written two selections: *entrecôte* and *couscous*.

The four men start conferring in Romanian, it being the opinion of Daniel and Nicolae that the first item might be some sort of meat, whereas the second item is anybody's guess.

"*L'entrecôte*," says Daniel, and when the other men nod in agreement, he holds up four fingers and says, "*Quatre, s'il vous plaît.*"

"*Et du vin?*"

Daniel misses the question, so he turns to Nicolae.

"*Oui*," says Nicolae, "*vin rouge, s'il vous plaît.*"

The food is wonderful. *Entrecôte* turns out to be a steak, cooked so rare that the gravy is heavy with the tang of blood. In the middle of the table, the girl puts a huge bowl of *frites*, which are fluffy and hot on the inside and crispy brown on the outside. On each of their plates, there's a heaping of green beans flavoured with a mixture of tomatoes and garlic and herbs.

The wine comes in low, brown earthenware jugs, and it tastes of plums and black earth. When the first two jugs are empty, the girl replaces them. As she leans over the table, Daniel catches a glimpse of bra through her sleeve, and it is this sight, along with the wine, that makes him feel as though things will be all right in their tiny portion of the world that night. He stumblingly asks her a question about the green beans.

"*Les haricots?*" she says. "*Aimez-vous?*"

Daniel responds with a casual *oui* and when she asks the question of the entire table, they all nod and call out, perhaps a little too loudly, "*Oui, oui, oui!*" She smiles broadly and leaves, returning later with two more jugs of wine. When she notices they've eaten all of their *frites*, she brings a second bowl, the men groaning and their eyes widening. This causes her to smile and say, "*On mange bien ici.*"

The four men are full, and glad they've come. They are also filled with wine, perhaps a bottle's worth each. Yet as they tuck into their dessert, some sort of pudding with a hardened sweet surface, it's not drunkenness they feel but a warm, connected joviality.

The bar is filling up. The patrons are mostly farmers, thick-armed men in overalls and rubber boots, their women tanned and dressed in blue jeans. The four Romanians pay their bill and move to the bar. When Daniel asks the barmaid what people like to drink here, she grins and pours them each a strong, local, dark-coloured liquor. The men clink their glasses and drink, and because the warmth spreading down their gullets and into their stomachs reminds them of the heat caused by *țuică,* they feel all the more pleased. They order another round, and another. Soon, they forget they are poor construction workers in the south of France, in the middle of an unseasonably hot spring. Even the restaurant seems to have turned into a Romanian drinking hall, for there's no denying that the place is rustic, and that the ceiling beams are roughly hewn, and that the area around the bar is now alive with voices. *All it needs,* Daniel thinks, *is sad music and dancing, and who knows? Maybe that will come later.*

As the four men drink and joke and feel good about having had the courage to come into town, they fail to notice that four young men have come into the bar and have picked a spot a few feet away from Daniel's back. Since the Romanians do not notice the men coming in, they also do not notice that their hair is so short that the pink skin of their scalps shows through. Nor do they notice that they are wearing heavy black boots and braces, or that their upper arms bear the tattooed insignia of the National Front.

The Romanians are drunk and laughing and forgetting what things are like—what things are *always* like—back home, so they also do not hear the four young men talking about them, and gesturing toward them, and saying in loud beer-soaked voices that *they* are the reason people cannot find work today in France. The four Romanians notice none of this, for they are noisy and garrulous themselves, and it is Gheorghe who loudly announces that he feels like smoking and is going to get a pack of those strong French Gypsy cigarettes. He wanders off and, in his drunkenness, has trouble operating the cigarette machine on the opposite side of the room. As he pounds the top of the machine and haplessly pulls at knobs and levers, he simultaneously laughs and swears and sings the sad folk songs that pop into a Romanian's head when he's drunk. This leaves Daniel with Eugen and Nicolae at the bar, talking and joking and failing to notice that the patrons who had stood near them a minute earlier have moved to other parts of the cavernous room. Meanwhile, the four young men with shaved heads have moved closer, their comments growing louder and uglier as they drink more beer. The young waitress comes by, ignoring the four young men with shaved heads and instead choosing to stop beside the Romanians. When the loudest of the young skinheads notices the way the waitress is smiling shyly at the tallest, and the youngest, and the best-looking of the foreigners, he cannot tolerate it, for he knows that this is exactly the kind of fraternization that is ruining the once-great nation of France.

So he takes a step toward Daniel and, when Daniel asks him what the hell he wants, grabs a handful of shirt, the muscles in his forearm writhing under faded kelp-coloured tattoos. As Daniel looks at the hatred beaming from the young man's eyes, he feels that he knows it, from another horrible place and time, and it is this recognition that causes him to seethe as well. The Le Pen supporter says something. He does not, however, say it in the French that Daniel learned at school. Instead, he says it in the French of poor schooling, of no jobs, of an alcoholic father and a depressed mother. He says it in the French of a poor man, and were Daniel to understand it, he would have heard the man say, "Why don't you fuck off back to wherever you came from, you fucking *bougnoule*."

What Daniel does understand is the intent in the young man's words, and in the murderous sheen of his eyes, and in the flexing of his farm-worked muscles. Daniel pushes him in the chest, the man shoving back with enough force that Daniel has to take a quick step backward to prevent himself from falling. Chairs topple, and heads turn, and the bar goes quiet, for the skinhead is now waving a knife, some sort of homemade contraption that is double-edged and glinting. He narrows the space between himself and Daniel, and lowers the knife to a point just inches from Daniel's nose. Nobody speaks, for all the men and women in the tavern are asking themselves what experience they are about to have on this night, in their local pub. There is movement from the other side of the tavern. Though Daniel can see Gheorghe coming up from behind, an empty wine bottle in his hand, he keeps his eyes trained on the young neo-Nazi—he doesn't want to give him or his friends any reason to turn and look. The young man smiles cruelly, his friends chuckling, his grin disappearing at the exact moment that Gheorghe Mihoc swings the wine bottle as though it were a blackjack.

The man yelps—*like a girl*, Daniel thinks—and doubles over, his hands darting to where the butt end of the bottle has shattered. In that same instant, Gheorghe whirls and slashes the bottle's jagged edge across the nearest of the young man's friends, leaving a sweep of pulp and ribboned T-shirt. Daniel then strikes the first skinhead so hard he feels the man's nose shatter against his knuckles. The skinhead falls, and Daniel and Gheorghe start kicking him in the ribs and face and pelvis. A second later, something snaps inside Eugen Brădescu and he, too, starts kicking the downed man, his unleashed fury coming with tears and whimpers and a torrent of curse words. Meanwhile, the other skinheads—one of whom is weeping and holding his mess of a stomach—stand and watch the beating, afraid to move or call out or so much as even blink.

When Daniel yells, "Let's go!" the Romanians race through the bar. Yet when they reach the exit, Daniel realizes that Gheorghe isn't with them. "Gheorghe!" he calls, though of course the miner pays no attention, for if Gheorghe is still stomping the downed man it's not because he's angry, and it's certainly not because he's worried the man will get up and cause further trouble. No. The reason he's ruining the man's face forever is that he wants to send a message to the three other skinheads, and to the rest of the people in the bar, and to whole of the world at large.

There is one thing, he wants to say, *you must understand. I am from Romania. I am from one of the terrible cold-water tenements that ring Baia Sprie like a shawl. I am Romanian, and I know that I am poor, and backward, and will always have to struggle in this world. I know this. But I have also seen things that you cannot imagine, and I have survived things you would not have survived. So please, make no mistake about it. I am Romanian, and so much harder than you.*

~

The four men run through silvery countryside, not guessing that back in the tavern they are being talked about in low, admiring tones, the truth being that the injured men had stolen from one too many shopkeepers, and had frightened one too many old people, and had put their hands on one too many teenage daughters. In a few minutes they reach the camp, where they wake up their foreman and tell him what has happened. He comes awake so furious that he wants to strike them, though he settles for calling them filthy sons-of-whores and telling them how much this is going to fuck up his schedule and did they have any idea how much pressure he's under from the owner, who is over eighty and nearing death and wants as much time as possible in his dream house?

"Goddamn sons of bitches," he keeps saying, "goddamn miserable *dogs*." Still, he pulls on a pair of pants and gives them each the wages he's held for them, telling them that if they weren't Romanians he'd be calling the cops himself. When this is done he grabs the keys to one of the trucks and tells them they have two minutes, and not a second more, goddammit, to grab their things. Twenty minutes later they're in Marseilles, where he drops them off in front of the train station and tells them that when the police come he's going to say that all four of them fucked off in the middle of the night, and that the only thing he knows is that he hopes they're gone for good. Then he speeds away, still cursing his own bad luck.

When the food stalls open they buy coffee and stale sandwiches. As they chew, they discuss their plans, each man hoping that the police are feeling lazy and won't come looking until after they've had their morning coffee. If all goes well, Eugen will take the early train to the outskirts of Paris, where he has a nephew who might be able to get him a job in the boot factory where he works. Nicolae has decided to take his money and start the long trek back to Romania, for he now thinks that nothing—money, freedom, the promise of a future—is worth what just happened here, in a place so far away from his children. Daniel and Gheorghe board a train heading west, but not before embracing the others and wishing them each good luck.

Shortly after the train leaves Marseilles, raindrops start splattering the window of their compartment in long, windblown streaks. Outside, the terrain is a deep forest green. On board it is warm and quiet. Daniel keeps flexing and straightening the fingers of the hand that had shattered the young man's nose. His knuckles are throbbing, and beginning to swell, and he worries that he may have broken them.

When a porter comes down the aisle with a trolley, Daniel asks for coffee. The man nods and gives Daniel a miniature pot of his own, along with two thin biscuits and a cup no bigger than a thimble. The coffee is hot and rich and delicious, and he wishes he could enjoy it without having to think about what might happen when the train reaches the border. He finishes the cup and pours himself another, savouring not only the beverage but whatever freedom he might have left. Closing his eyes, he leans his head back against the seat, and feels the motion of the train resonate through his body.

In the seat across from him, Gheorghe stares out the window and looks worried. His foot bounces against the floor of the rail car. His hair—five or six oily tendrils that reflect the light cast by the fixtures inside the compartment—has adhered to his scarred pate. There are puffy dark pouches under his eyes. The blood on his boots has started to dry, leaving crusty brown patches.

Just before the Spanish border, the train shudders to a halt, then lurches forward in a series of abrupt jolts. By the time it stops altogether, Daniel is so nervous he considers leaping from the train and making a run for the mountains. After an eternity, a border official opens the doors to their compartment and asks to see Gheorghe's passport. He looks at it for a minute through reading glasses, the flesh under his chin trembling slightly. Finally, he checks something on a clipboard he is carrying, and repeats the process with Daniel and the four other people in their compartment. With a cordial nod, he leaves, the door closing behind him with an airy sigh. Ten minutes later, the train begins to shudder and stumble forward before gaining speed.

When there's no doubt they have left France, Daniel and Gheorghe look at each other and grin. Gheorghe motions with his head and they stand, stepping over feet, and luggage, and a small white dog before making it to the aisle.

"Imagine," says Gheorghe, "all of this fuss, for a little fight between men. Back home, it would hardly be worth talking about, am I right, Dani? Oh, and by the way, did you notice that waitress? I think she wanted to have about a dozen of your children!"

Daniel shakes his head, though as he does he tries not to think of the waitress or the supremacist's bashed-in face or even the country of France.

They find their way to the hospitality car, where Gheorghe is all good cheer and magnanimity, slapping Daniel on the back and insisting on paying for snifters of nice French brandy. "Maybe it was fate," Gheorghe says, "that little run-in we had last night. Maybe it was a sign. You know, I had a little sign back in Romania, telling me it was time to leave the country, something that happened to me in the copper mine. It was a hell of a thing and maybe sometime I'll tell you about it. In the meantime let's have a toast, eh, Dani? A toast to America . . . to American automobiles and American hot dogs and the wonder of American dollars, no?"

Daniel downs his cognac. A gentle warmth spreads through his body.

". . . and American cars and American liberty and that boring, boring American game called baseball . . ." At this both men break out laughing, for it suddenly seems so ridiculous, the experiences they are choosing to endure just to get to a place where everyone lives like the better families back home, in houses built from wood. "Hey," Gheorghe exclaims, "I made him laugh! I can't believe it! I made him laugh! Oh my God, we need to get into fights more often!"

As they burrow deeper and deeper into Spain, the land levels out and the train gains speed. In the afternoon, the bar car fills with Spaniards coming to pass the time, and it isn't long before Daniel starts imagining he can understand the rudiments of what they are saying—really, the language is not that different from Romanian, as long as you can filter out the thick, lisping pronounciation. He and Gheorghe take seats near the rear corner of the car and make sure to keep to themselves. They are drinking seriously now, each man spending more of his construction money than he should, until it gets to the point where their good mood evaporates and is replaced by something murkier—something that deepens their breathing, and hazes their vision, and makes them teeter in their seats. They do not stop, and by the time they've changed trains and disembarked in the port town of Algeciras, they are exhausted, and sick, and so drunk it is all they can do to stand.

SEVEN

The accommodation ladder is lifted. The forward and aft mooring lines are winched into the hull, and a tug pulls the big ship toward the mouth of the harbour. Below deck, the main propulsion engine strains, and ink green water churns behind the stern. At first, nothing happens. Then, there is movement, as slow as an old man's speech.

Throughout the day other boats appear on the horizon, looking faded and still. Gazing north, the seamen aboard the *Maersk Dubai* can see the Florida Keys, curving away from them. After the boat has spent a day churning east, the islands are still visible from the stern, though from this distance they appear to form a single, hazy coastline. Ahead, there is ocean, and sky, and a wavering horizon. The big ship takes the rhumb line, straight across the Atlantic, avoiding the rough weather reported near the Gulf Stream. With time, the islands of the Caribbean disappear behind the curve of the earth, the *Maersk Dubai* now alone in a grey, infinite wash.

A measure of normality has returned to the ship. Talk of promotions has stopped, free beer and cigarettes have disappeared from the mess hall, and the gift of chocolate is not repeated. The officers no longer roam the decks, engaging the able-bodies in chit-chat, and the captain has retreated to his cabin, appearing only occasionally on the bridge. The only officer who maintains any kind of presence is the chief officer, who still practices karate and tai chi on the expanse of deck outside of the accommodation, oblivious to the glances of the seamen. The meetings in the cabin of the oiler, Juanito Ilagan, become less frequent, until they stop altogether—as far as Juanito and the others can tell, the immediate threat is over, their objective now simply to make it through the voyage, at which time they will decide what, if anything, they should do. In place of the meetings, the normal diversions of sailors return—cards, videos, gossip over cups of coffee—along with a blurring of the division that had existed between the sailors who met nightly in the oiler's cabin and the sailors who did not want to get involved. There are even brief moments of pleasure: a wild hand of poker, a rainbow stretched across the blue expanse of the sky, the second cook spilling a pot of hot coffee over his pants (and, even funnier, his bug-eyed retelling of the event later on). One afternoon, a school of dolphins frolics in the wake of the big ship. The news spreads, and the entire crew is soon at the stern, watching the animals arc, like shooting gallery targets, through the air.

Later that day, one of the engine's pistons stops pumping. Juanito and the second engineer investigate, and find that the piston case has cracked so badly they'll have to wait for dry dock to repair it. With only seven operating cyclinders, the engine now runs at higher revolutions, the noise in the engine room a high-pitched whine. The extra strain on the engine leads to other problems. A day or two later, Juanito is welding a damaged exhaust manifold when he feels a needling pain in his chest, directly behind the heart. He takes a deep breath, the pain neither diminishing nor worsening. He continues welding, though throughout his shift he occasionally massages the sore spot, at times wondering if he has eaten something that has disagreed with him, or if perhaps he has somehow pulled a muscle. Yet after his shift has finished, and he's had a supper of spicy Filipino stew, he notices his chest is no longer bothering him. For this reason, he doesn't mention it to the others.

The next day, shortly after descending into the chaotic rumbling of the engine room, he feels it again, a highly focused pressure a little to the left of the centre of his sternum. He stops, winces, and massages himself, wondering if the pain is really worse that day or whether he's just more impatient with it. Though he continues working, he finds he's having trouble concentrating—he keeps manipulating his posture and the way he holds his tools, so as to lessen the discomfort. Finally, he turns and spots the pipefitter working on one of the boilers that are lined, like sentries, along the back wall of the engine room. He walks along a grated catwalk, directly above the bilge pool, and reaches the opposite side of the room. Here, he taps the fitter's shoulder.

Alfredo turns, and the two men remove their hearing protectors. Over the noise of the engine block, Juanito asks, in a voice just below yelling, if the fitter's chest hurts. Alfredo's eyes widen, and when he yells, "Yes, Oiler, it does!" the two men understand they are not suffering from indigestion, or muscle strain, or heartburn, and that they are suffering from the pain caused by a gas leak. Together, they cross back over the platform and spot Ariel Broas heading toward them. He motions toward Juanito's chest, as though posing a question. Juanito answers with a bobbing of his head.

"Yes!" he shouts. "It hurts!"

The three take a set of stairs to the top level of the engine room, where Broas suggests the two crewmen get some fresh air while he talks with the second engineer in the control room. The fitter and oiler step outside the accommodation and onto the deck. To the north, the sky is beginning to darken and roil, and the wind swirling over the boat has turned cool. They shuffle their feet, and curse their luck, and wish they were home. Juanito lights a cigarette, turning his body to face the breeze, for as every sailor knows the worst way to light a match is with your back to the wind, the air having a tendency to whip around your body like a whirlpool.

There is the creaking of metal hinges. They turn to see Broas step on deck. He approaches them, rubs his eyes, and explains what they will do.

For the rest of that shift, and the shift after that, the three men search for splits in the exhaust systems servicing the main propulsion engine and the smaller auxiliary engines. They also comb the tubes servicing the compressors and condensers, thinking some errant CO might be seeping into the coolant systems, where it is then circulated throughout the engine room. It is long, tiring work: their chests ache, the heat radiating from the engine makes them perspire, and their detector is old, the needle fluttering like a loosened moth over the gauge. Still, they put their heads down and work, sealing every hairline crack, every fissure, every fitting that does not meet perfectly, until finally they concede that they have done everything they can out of dry dock. While their efforts have helped, at times a discomfort still burrows into the upper-left quadrant of their bodies, usually toward the end of a shift when they are tired and the joints in their shoulders and fingers are beginning to ache. Other times, they wear paper breathers, like those worn by plasterers, though these are hot and uncomfortable and tend to slip off. Mostly, they choose to take their breaks up on deck, where they gulp down lungfuls of sea air, the whole time thinking of soft bedding, and tropical nights, and the voices of children.

~

Land is spotted. For the next twenty-four hours it hovers in the distance, an indistinct blurring of green, and brown, and gold. Slowly, the deck crew begins to make out its features: the Atlas Mountains, the gap separating continents, Gibraltar. The boat passes into the Mediterranean Sea, the shores of Europe so tantalizingly close the sailors keep themselves busy so as not to die of longing. At the end of the week, the boat steams down the Red Sea and then tightly hugs the sand-white shores of Yemen and Oman. Here, Juanito hears the first joke made about the stowaways; one of Rodolfo Miguel's deckhands says, at a mess table, "I hope no Arabs find their way on board," to which another AB responds, "Yes, or the captain would throw him over!" There is brief, forced chuckling, though only among the deck crew.

The ship docks briefly in Dubai before crossing the Gulf of Oman. As it nears Bombay, the atmosphere turns cottony, and redolent with spice and brackish water. After taking on new containers, the ship leaves India by nightfall, crossing back over the Arabian Sea toward Djibouti. There the sailors spend a half day in steerage, waiting for permission to proceed back through the Strait of Djibouti.

Shortly after the ship has entered the Red Sea, travelling north this time, Juanito hears the oily water separator sputter and clank. A few minutes later, it starts producing thin coils of dark blue smoke, and a short time after that it issues a series of mechanical sighs. Broas inspects the situation, and then reports to the second engineer. From a catwalk above, Juanito watches the ensuing discussion—the second engineer gesticulating, Broas shaking his head in defiance, the more senior of the officers yelling something and turning away. For a few seconds, Broas stands by the bilge pool, staring at the murk, before he bounds up the ladder leading from the lower decks of the engine room. He jumps off and passes Juanito on the catwalk.

Juanito has never seen him this way—his features scarlet, the tendons in his neck distended—and it scares him, for he knows that the third engineer prizes control and reserve above all. Juanito goes back to work, half-heartedly draining one of the main engine's oil pans, though as he does he watches Broas jury-rig a sump pump that will expel the ship's waste directly into the ocean. By the time he's finished, his overalls are covered with handprints and muck. He also looks disgusted—bilge pumped straight into the ocean is a serious offence, one that could lose Broas his licence to operate a big ship's engine.

He is coming back now. As he passes Juanito, he stops suddenly and turns. His face is a tight sheet, his eyes slits. He yells something, a question or a command, Juanito isn't sure—Broas has a soft voice at the best of times, and here, in the engine room, amid the screeching of the engine, it is lost. Juanito removes his hearing protectors, and strains to hear the officer's words.

"Tonight," Broas yells, "I want to talk to you."

~

The rest of Juanito's day proceeds slowly. He welds, he showers, he tries to nap, though as he lies in his cabin he keeps slipping into a waking dream, the one in which he's still an entertainer in Manila, singing American pop songs at his uncle's nightclub on Roxas Boulevard. His head fills with stage lights, his ears with applause. If only he'd ignored his mother's wishes and turned down that first offer on a big ship—he could have become a politician, like so many of the film and music stars of the Philippines. He could have become the kind of man who can give his family everything.

At eight o'clock, there's a knocking at his door. He opens it and Broas enters, taking his customary seat beneath the porthole. Juanito lights a cigarette, exhaling smoke in a bluish plume through his nose. The two men sit without speaking. Broas sighs loudly, puts his face in his hands, and rubs his eyes. When he takes his hands away, blood has risen to the surface of his cheeks.

"Oiler," he finally says. "The incident today, with the separator, it made me . . ." He shakes his head from side to side. "It was a bad thing, Oiler, what they made me do. It made me want to . . . I don't know. It made me want to do something."

"Yes," Juanito says. "It's as if the officers think they can order us to do anything . . ."

"It was a mistake, doing nothing. It's *been* a mistake, all along. They think they own us now."

Juanito and Broas look at each other, their gazes then returning to the floor of the cabin. In a lowered voice, Juanito says it— "I'm feeling gutsy today"—and it's as if the air in the cabin thins, sharpening outlines and adding a resonance to colours. *So this is it,* he thinks, *this is the moment it starts.* Juanito continues looking at his feet. He can barely say it. "That priest," he mutters. "That priest in Houston. The one we all talked to . . ." He lifts his eyes, wanting to see how Broas will respond to his suggestion.

He nods, says, "Yes," and looks around. Juanito opens the drawer to his bedside table, where he keeps his Bible, some stationery, and a pair of reading glasses. The two men work steadily behind the locked cabin door, writing and rewriting, scratching out words and phrases and sentences, sometimes so fiercely the paper rips and they have to start over again. Balls of crumpled notepaper accumulate on the floor. They periodically gather them and burn them, Broas dropping them flaming into one of the seaman toilets while Juanito guards the door.

Beyond Juanito's porthole, the night is clear, the ocean as still as a shield of rock; this tranquility seems to mock the efforts of the two men inside. Each time they arrive at the point at which they are about to describe what happened to the stowaways, they are unable to write any further. Or they get testy with each other, and because they dislike confrontation, they tear the letter up rather than argue. Perhaps they feel they won't be believed, or perhaps they cannot find the words to accurately describe the captain's actions, or perhaps they are inhibited by the fear of how the officers will react if they find out what they've done. It doesn't matter—they only know they cannot put *it* into words, the experience they most want to reveal to the world beyond the big ship.

In the end, the two men write about the bilge water and the carbon monoxide leak (along with the the malfunctioning lifeboat mechanism, and the broken emergency fire pumps, and the faulty sterilizing lamps in the water fountains, so that when crew members need a drink they either have rusty water, or go all the way to the mess, where they pour themselves a cup from one of the jugs in the refrigerator). They leave out their most significant complaint, thinking that maybe, by the time they have the ear of the naval authorities, they'll have found the words to describe the experience they both had on a chilly March morning aboard the *Maersk Dubai*.

When they finally go to bed it is late. The next day, their movements are sluggish, and their responses slow, and it could be that their fatigue has something to do with what happens. Or it could be that they are on water, not land, a place where different rules apply, a place where ghosts exert the physical influence of mortals. Perhaps the phantoms of the engine room—the wrench stealers, the coffee spillers, the disappearers of a newly opened pack of Marlboros—are to blame. Or it might be that boats, like people, really can be cursed by experience, their souls rotted by the things that have occurred aboard them, the ghosts of the *Maersk Dubai* merely acting the way any guilty party would when under the threat of disclosure.

That morning, after breakfast, Juanito heads to the engine room, where he dons hearing protectors and watches Broas, who is talking with the first engineer behind the sheet of Plexiglas separating the control room from the rest of the engine room. After a few minutes, Broas comes across the platform to tell Juanito that one of the air compressors needs overhauling, as it is not functioning properly. The two men find the joint in the pipe where they suspect the blockage might be. They lean over it, examining it, the whole time swearing under their breath, for they are hot and sweaty and they both have dull headaches brought on by a lack of sleep. Broas asks Juanito to open the main air valve so he might listen for leaks. Juanito does this, and hears the gurgled rush of compressed air through the pre-start valves. He moves back over to Broas, barely a foot of sooty air between them. Broas bends over, moving his head close to the flange, turning his head to listen, not realizing that at that very moment the air being forced through the compressor is encountering not a leak but a dam of rust, and calcium, and dirt.

The pressure builds and builds, until it can no longer be contained by the rubber sheath of the compressor, the explosion occurring just one inch from the unprotected eyes of Ariel Broas.

EIGHT

Time passes slowly in Algeciras. Daniel and Gheorghe walk its streets, they smoke hashish in its parks, they make botched attempts at conversation with its tawdrily dressed women. At night, they sleep at the El Faro Guest House for Christians in the hillside slum known as La Bajadilla. Most afternoons, they buy a cheap bottle of whisky and head to the park, where they drink and talk and look up at clouds. On their sixth afternoon in Spain, they visit the neighbourhood brothel, the women pudgy and Arab and as sad as stray dogs; afterwards, Daniel feels the ache of misgiving, deep in the pit of his stomach. He tips the girl stupidly, and when Gheorghe sees this he follows suit, the visit all but depleting them of their construction money. In the middle of the night, with the moon lost behind a mattress of clouds, Gheorghe takes a brick he's found on the street and uses it to smash a hole in the door of a convenience store where they'd once been treated rudely. A half minute later, their footfalls echo through empty streets, their pockets bulging with pesetas and lottery tickets.

Mostly they pass their time at their favourite spot on the *paseo*, a place where there's a bench and a clear view of the harbour. Here, they watch for the arrival of a tanker, or a bulk carrier, or a container ship. Toward the end of one afternoon about two weeks after arriving in Spain, they leave their bench to buy pieces of chorizo on a bun, for the port is again crowded with nothing but the smaller tramp steamers and cargo boats, and the one thing the other Romanians staying at El Faro have told them is that the ship must be a big one, or you'll be found and put off before the boat even leaves the harbour.

"I swear to you," Gheorghe says as they chew their dinners. "This waiting around is going to kill me. It's going to fucking *kill* me."

Later that evening, when the daylight has all but dwindled, they return to their spot, and once again look out over the port and its oily, reflective waters. This time, they see something gigantic, stopped beyond the mouth of the bay, and for the first time they understand what the other Romanians meant when they talked about big ships. They decide to come back in the morning, and when they do the boat has drawn close enough that they can see it clearly through the misty, pollutant haze that shrouds the port. They both blink, as if to make sure their eyes aren't deceiving them. Then they watch, amazed by the tortuous process of docking a ship the length of a football field. Throughout the morning they leave their spot, and come back, and leave, and come back, and still the mooring tug is working away, its distant motor buzzing like a chainsaw.

That night, when the men assigned the other mattresses at El Faro have begun to rustle and snore, Gheorghe touches Daniel's shoulder. The two men dress, and tiptoe into the darkness of the living room. There are men sleeping there as well, so they have to be quiet as they slip out the door of the small kitchen.

They trudge along narrow, winding laneways, their leg muscles tensed against the decline into the city. Gheorghe retrieves the thick

L-shaped branch he found that afternoon and stashed in the window well of a nearby house; as they walk, he periodically taps it against the asphalt. Though it is well after midnight, there are still whole families outside on the fissured pavement, mostly Gypsy or Arab, though there are a few Nigerian clans as well. As Gheorghe and Daniel near the centre of town, the streets become empty. There is now cobblestone under their feet, the air thick with a fishy vapour carried in from the bay. They traverse Plaza Alta, the original centre of town, and in so doing pass a five-hundred-year-old fountain with tiles depicting life in the Middle Ages: book burnings and public floggings and the king's soldiers collecting tithes. A minute later, they reach the plaza where the market sets up every morning, the two men wrinkling their noses at the dull, settled-in smell of sewers and smoked ham. Soon they reach the *paseo* running along the city's shore. Even at this hour, it is crowded with vagrants and prostitutes and Arabs whispering, "Hey, *amigos*. Hashish, good hashish—why not buy from me some good hashish?"

They cross the *paseo*, reaching a traffic circle filled with hibiscus, acacia trees, and a statue of the guitarist Paco de Lucia. Upon reaching the far side, they start walking toward the ferry terminal that services tourists heading across the Strait of Gibraltar to Tangiers or Ceuta. The clamour of the *paseo* fades behind them. They can hear palm trees rustling, and they are conscious of the sound of their sneakers on the pavement. When they reach the huge, empty, illuminated terminal building they turn left, and find the spot where the fence has been knocked down. Here, they step into the shipyards.

Above them, a sliver of moon barely registers through dense low-lying clouds. A half kilometre ahead is the big ship, its hull marked with running lights. They head toward it, their view repeatedly blocked by the sides of transport trucks and trailers and container stacks and the massive fish-packing plant that runs along the shipyard's north side. At times they enter long stretches of shadow; when this happens, they have to walk with their arms stretched out in front of them, all the while listening for the hum of auxiliary motors, until they reach another clearing and can look up and see the boat docked in the bleary, bug-flecked night. Though they know there is a direct route through the shipyard to the berth (for they have seen it during the day, a snaking lane travelled by trucks and loading vehicles), they cannot for the life of them find it in this labyrinthian darkness. So they fumble along until they reach a pitch-black junction of crates and containers and parked forklifts. They stop, their skin growing clammy in the humid night air, trying to decide which gap to choose. Daniel picks one, and when they finally emerge they are met with squawking gulls, and salty sea air, and the side of the big ship.

They look up, mouths agape. Before them is five storeys of grey metal, arcing slightly over their heads, its summit marked by lights gone hazy and weak in the thickly polluted harbour air. Their brows dampen, and their pulses quicken, and for a moment Daniel wonders if he'll find the courage to do what he has come to Algeciras to do.

Gheorghe hands the grappling stick to Daniel and backs up about three metres. Then he runs, lobbing his body through foggy space before landing on the anchor chain. As his feet spin for a foothold in the huge rusting links, the force of his leap swings the chain into the hull. His body hits the side of the boat, the impact forcing air from his lungs. He makes a hissing groan, like a punctured tire.

Daniel calls in a loud whisper, "Gheorghe, are you all right?"

The big man nods without looking back. After a moment, he turns and reaches out; Daniel leans over the water to pass him the heavy end of the L-shaped stick.

Gheorghe begins to climb. It is difficult, for his right hand is holding the grappling branch, and the links of the chain are so thick he can barely grip them with his left hand. To overcome this problem he flexes his left wrist, forming a hook with hand and forearm; with this improvised tool he pulls his body up one link after another. Daniel watches from below, barely breathing, forgetting that his job is to keep watch for security guards. Gheorghe climbs higher and higher, his body falling away from the boat each time he replants his hooked left wrist, until finally he reaches the anchor portal. There, he pauses, his breath coming in quick, rasping pants.

It is this moment they are most unsure about, that has caused them the most concern during planning sessions in the parks and plazas of the city. Gheorghe arcs the branch over his head so that the crotch hooks the side of the gunwale, the heavy end reaching just above his head. For the longest time, he remains still, regaining his breath, one hand on the grappling branch and the other on the topmost link of the anchor chain. His sleeves are rolled up, and the muscles of his forearms pulse with effort. There is a moment when he looks down, and for Daniel this moment of hesitation seems like an admission of defeat. But then the big man kicks away from the anchor chain, reaches high with left hand, and pulls himself up and over the low metal gunwale.

It is magic, this moment, a miracle pure and unadulterated— Gheorghe, on board the big ship, looking over the gunwale, laughing and calling out, "Hey, Dani, what are you waiting for—the weather's nice up here!" and then holding his belly and laughing.

Below, Daniel backs up before flinging himself through moist air. The anchor chain swings him into the hull of the boat, smashing his side, and he makes the same wounded grunt Gheorghe made before him. He hangs on. His ribs ache. The chain feels warm, and scratchy with rust. He pulls himself up, hand over hooked hand, sweat rising against his shirt, before finally reaching the anchor portal, and in his mind he is already on board—the only thing left to do is grab the branch left hooked over the gunwale, pull himself up one arm-length, and let Gheorghe haul him on board. Yet what he does not know is that Gheorghe's weight caused a hairline fissure to open at the branch's apex, where it forms a ninety-degree angle.

Daniel takes the end of the branch. It holds for a second, and then splits with a loud crack. He plummets, silent, eyes wide with surprise, his body fixed in the shape of a cross.

~

When he hits the harbour there is no splash, for the water is too heavily weighted with gasoline, diesel fuel, fish oil, fertilizer, detergent, rust peelings, barnacle slime, algae and mud—he's less like a man falling into an ocean and more like a knife splitting jelly. The water folds around him, warmer than it should be, his eyes, nose, ears and lips burning. He kicks furiously, his shoes filling with murk, and for a moment he wonders whether buoyancy is possible in liquid this thick and reeking. A second or two passes. As he dares not open his eyes, he has little idea whether he is rising to the surface or sinking to the harbour floor. What he *does* know is that this is the loudest place he has ever been, for thoughts of death are screaming in his ears, and the pressure in his lungs is creating a low, bassoonlike moan. His head somehow breaks through the surface of the water. Gasping, he fills his lungs with cottony air. He points himself at one of the metal ladders affixed to the high concrete jetty and thrashes his way to safety. Hauling himself up, he sits on the edge of the slip and picks at the slime on his head, and arms, and shoulders.

"Hey!"

It is Gheorghe, several hundred metres above, leaning over the gunwale. Daniel looks up. As his eyes are filled with oily water he can see only running lights, looking smeary and mustard yellow. Gheorghe, meanwhile, peers from side to side, looking for guards.

"What happened?" Daniel calls.

"The branch broke. Listen to me, Dani. Find another one. Then come back, okay? I'll be here."

Daniel nods, though he knows that this is goodbye, that Gheorge's instructions are a way to avoid the awkwardness men feel at such times. Daniel gives him a wave and ducks into the maze of containers separating the boat from the shipyard entrance. His side aches with each breath, and he can still taste the harbour in his mouth. As he trudges along he cannot help thinking of Elena, and the way she'd cried when he'd told her he was leaving. He also thinks of his mother, who spent her life making traditional blouses to sell at the tourists markets of Cluj or Sighişoara, a job that turned her hands plump and muscular and sore—as he walks, it is those hands that keep popping up before him, like darting figments, their presence confusing him. He stops, and clenches his eyes, and forces them to go away. A modicum of strength returns to his legs, though the voices and images of his loved ones still struggle to get into his head and paralyze him. He keeps on, paying little attention to where he is going, until he realizes, with a start, that it's been ages since he has found a clearing, or spotted the looming walls of the fish plant, or seen the distant neon lights cast by the hotels lining the *paseo*. He listens, and hears only water, distantly shifting against mooring slabs. Reaching out, his hands come away sooty. Feeling panicked and stupid, he jumps, hoping to glimpse a reflection of light somewhere. Instead, he sees nothing beyond a muddy sky. His steps quicken. He scurries down alleyways, along paths, through gaps, for suddenly he cannot tolerate being trapped and wet and alone. After a bit he stops, panting, and curses a blue streak, for it suddenly seems so unfair that he is lost and alone and losing his mind in this darkened Spanish shipyard.

It takes a few moments before he pulls himself together and starts moving again. Turning a corner, he runs headlong into the shadow cast by a person much larger than himself. He leaps backward, hands up, ready to fight, before realizing the outline looks familiar.

"Gheorghe?" he whispers.

"Daniel?"

"Why are you here?"

"They found me. Threw me off."

"I can't believe it. It's really you?"

"Yes, goddammit, it's me."

They hunt for a way out, Daniel saying how he's been lost for who knows how long and Gheorghe saying, "I know, I know, it's a maze, this fucking place." Finally, they pass through a chasm sided by containers and there, in front of them, is the collapsed portion of fence. They step over and march past the darkened ferry terminal. Soon they are at the traffic circle, passing the statue of Paco de Lucia and the *paseo* running along the far side. When they reach the plaza where the day market sets up, they find that the bar anchoring the northwest corner of the market is, at four in the morning, still open, the owner and his friends having stayed up to drunkenly discuss the obsessions of all Algeciran males—fishing, lotteries, women, the bulls. Gheorghe and Daniel enter, one man dripping wet, one man dry as a bone, and while the owner's impulse is to throw them out it's clear that the man in wet clothes needs something to steady his nerves, and that the larger one is the type who might cause trouble if denied.

They sit, Daniel feeling embarrassed when his pants seep murky water. Slowly, the group at the bar—older men, with thick forearms and bulbous spider-veined noses—resume their conversation. When the bartender approaches, Daniel and Gheorghe order the favourite strong drink of Algeciras: a tall, thin glass filled with ice cubes and whisky.

"Well, Dani," Gheorghe says, "I suppose practice makes perfect, eh?"

Daniel grimaces and drinks, enjoying the warmth of the liquor as it spreads through his chilled body. They have one more, then deposit some pesetas on the table. Outside, the city is beginning to lighten with the first hazy rays of dawn, and the market vendors are starting to open their flimsy, tacked-together stalls. The day breaks hot and humid: just walking causes Daniel to perspire. They each buy a plum from a sun-baked old woman in a kerchief, who drops their money into a pocket sewn into the front of her dress.

The two trudge up the hill into the slums of Algeciras, Daniel bothered by the ringing noises a mind makes when exhausted. The cracked, concrete streets are filling with Arab and Gypsy children, along with their mothers, who are taking an early crack at laundry, their arms elbow-deep in blue plastic tubs filled with soapy water. Slowly, La Bajadilla turns into a checkerboard of orange and shadow. There are dogs barking, chickens squabbling, and the first callings of the lottery vendors. As always, Gheorghe and Daniel are greeted by the heroin sellers who loiter, night and day, in front of house number 33, on the corner of Calle San Luis and Calle Gerona. "Hola, Faro!" they call, their mouths nothing but black spaces and tin. Daniel detects the sarcasm in their voices, and he understands why it's there: they know he and Gheorghe are staying at the house for stranded Christian travellers, and the dealers believe that one day soon they too will be customers.

The two men knock on the door off the kitchen, at first sheepishly and then with force, hoping that one of the other Romanians will let them in. Instead, it is Lawrence himself, the director of El Faro, who opens the screen door. He looks at them wearily, his jaw clenched. His long hair is pulled back into a ponytail. He leads them into the kitchen, and motions at the table.

"Sit down," he says in Spanish.

Gheorghe, who cannot understand a word, looks at Daniel, who has already started to pick up basic phrases. Daniel nods toward a chair and they sit glumly at a chipped, stained table, obviously pulled from a dump somewhere.

Lawrence sits as well. He rubs his face and breathes deeply. There is a cup of herbal tea in front of him, and he reaches for it, taking a small sip. He puts the cup down, and again rubs his face. When he speaks, his voice is soft, his Spanish inflected with a Californian accent.

"It's just that it's so, so dangerous, what you tried to do tonight." He shakes his head. "Some of those captains, what they will do, what they have *done*. Do you understand?"

Daniel nods, for Lawrence is saying something about danger, about *peligro*. As if he didn't know that already.

"You have to understand that stowaways get thrown overboard. They just *do*. Believe me, their bodies wash up on the shores of Tenerife every single day. Am I getting through to you two?"

Daniel nods again—he's saying something about *cadáveres*, about bodies. "We're sorry," he says, "*lo siento*."

Lawrence sighs. "Look. This is happening too much . . . It's getting so we're going to have to tell Romanians they can't stay here any more. Do you want that to happen? Do you?"

Daniel says no, though he's just guessing that this is the answer Lawrence wants.

"Look. This is what I'm going to do. Tomorrow, I'm going to put you two to work. You've been here long enough, and the policy is you have to start helping us out. It might keep you out of trouble. Either that, or I'm afraid you'll have to move on. Is that all right?"

Daniel and Gheorghe look at each other, confused.

"*Work*," Lawrence says in a louder voice. "Tomorrow, you start to *work*."

Daniel understands, and he nods.

"Good," Lawrence says, at which point he lowers his head, clasps his fingers and, as the two Romanian men watch, begins to quietly pray.

NINE

Juanito stumbles backward, grabbing a guardrail for balance, his stomach and chest a hundred stinging pinpricks. For a few seconds he feels dizzy, and there is a sharp ringing in his ears. When he opens his eyes he sees that Broas is on his knees, bent over, hands pressed against his face, screaming. Juanito drops to the floor and tries to peer into his face.

"Ariel," he yells, "are you all right? My God, are you all right?"

The third engineer doesn't answer. Instead, he rocks on his knees, hands over his eyes. For a second, he goes quiet; then, through clamped fingers, Juanito can hear whimpering. He places a hand on Broas's back and leans toward him, again saying, "Are you all right? Ariel, please, are you all right?" Broas moans and takes a series of deep, shuddering breaths before beginning to swear, his curses coming through fingers turned crooked and white.

"Help me!" Juanito yells.

When he gets no response, he calls louder, and again hears only the syncopated thrumming of the engine. He looks up to the control room. When he sees that the second engineer is not there, he searches for glimpses of the fitter, or the electrician, or one of the other officers, until he understands that he and Broas are truly alone. He takes his officer's hands by the wrists and tries to pull them from his face, the whole time saying, "Let me see, Ariel, please let me see."

Broas fights him, pressing his palms even tighter against his face, again breaking into a rhythm of curse words and rocking and pleading, "Oh God oh God oh God." Finally, he stops moving. Again, Juanito pulls gently on his hands, attempting to lower them, and for a second it seems Broas will allow this, though when a space does form between his palms and his face he gasps, clamps his hands back against his eyes and tries to calm himself by taking deep breaths through his nose. This time, when Juanito pulls on Broas's wrist, he allows his hands to be shakily lowered.

"Oh, Ariel. No . . ."

Broas shoots his hand back to his eyes, and once again he groans. When Juanito asks if he can see, he whips his head from side to side, his upper body shaking with the motion, his lips quivering as he utters the words, "No, no, no." Juanito wraps an arm around Broas's shoulders, hooking a hand under his right arm. He stands slowly, Broas rising with him, both men extending an arm for balance.

There are two flights of stairs to the deck level, and another three flights to the level containing the ship's hospital. Their progress is slow, Broas having to feel for each metal step as Juanito guides him with his voice—"That's it, Ariel, a little to the left, a little bit more."

Every five or six steps he has to stop and let Broas rest, the wounded man calling, "No, please, Oiler, I can't . . ."

"Help me!" Juanito calls again when they reach the main deck, and this time the fitter, the second cook and some of the ABs come running, the second cook carrying the huge knife he uses to cut meat. They freeze when they see Broas, and the ghost-white expression on Juanito's face. Then they rush forward, even though there is little they can do, the width of the stairs barely permitting two men, side by side, to go up. Juanito and the wounded man pass. When the fitter notices that Juanito is trembling from fatigue, he offers to take his place; Juanito is about to say *Yes, thank you,* when Broas clutches tighter onto the side of the oiler's neck.

They reach the ship's hospital, midway along the lower of the two officer levels. The second mate, who is acting as doctor on board, arrives with the chief officer and the chief engineer in time to see Juanito lead Broas to the hospital bed. The second mate tries to pull away the patient's hands, and because Broas will not permit it the other officers hold him down while he thrashes and pleads and snaps his bleeding face from left to right. Juanito hovers in the doorway, shaking. Behind him, trying to peer in, are the fitter, the second cook, and Manuel. When the bosun arrives, Manuel steps aside and lets his boss see inside the room.

"What happened?" Rodolfo asks. "My God, Oiler, what's going on? What happened to Ariel?"

Juanito doesn't answer. He watches the second mate hunt through his medical kit. A small brown bottle is extracted, as well as mats of gauze, and tweezers, and rolls of white tape. The second mate applies a clear jelly to Ariel Broas's eyes. The patient howls and then calms, Juanito thinking there must have been some sort of freezing agent in the ointment. The chief officer then turns and notices that Juanito and the others are there, half in the stateroom and half out. He scowls and says something sharp in Mandarin before moving toward them. The tips of his fingers touch Juanito's chest to back him and the others out of the room.

The door shuts with a clang. The Filipinos stand staring at the door like passengers on an elevator, until slowly, one by one, they disperse.

~

For the first time since the voyage began, Juanito is welding on deck, repairing ballast pipes, working alongside the deck crew. It's a change of pace, working in the brightness of daylight, and it takes him time to adjust. Unlike in the engine room, where each piece of machinery represents something solid and real, you cannot work on deck without understanding that the ship is so alone it almost feels imaginary. The sun glinting off water, though beautiful, gives him a headache. The misty sea air, which hangs over the boat like a cloud, irritates his skin—Juanito begins to understand why the face of an able-body always looks pink and slightly raw, and why the creases emanating from a bosun's eyes grow deeper and darker than those around the eyes of an engine room boss. He even finds being on deck slightly claustrophobic—the hazy band of the sky and the solid blue of the sea feel like two planes that, at any time, could snap together like a film director's clapper.

In the hush of open air he finds that his mind begins to whir like the machines he's accustomed to tending. With this whirring comes a resurrection of memory, and suddenly he is there, again, on that awful morning, the two men clinging to the Jacob's ladder, one man wailing and one man struggling to contain his tears.

Throughout the morning, the able-bodies working on deck ask him, one by one, if he knows how Broas is doing. Each time, Juanito answers, "Better, I think," even though the last time he saw him he'd been sleeping. When his morning shift ends, he visits the Filipino officer. This time, he is lying awake on the ship's lone hospital cot, wearing sunglasses—he tells Juanito that his vision is blurry and shaded, as if he was looking at everything through a smear of dark blue petroleum jelly. Juanito helps him pass the time by chatting with him, and by reading him stories from the Bible.

In the middle of one passage, Broas interrupts him. His voice is low, and solemn: "They say my eyes will be okay."

"Thank God."

"They told me my eyes would be fine."

"That's good, Ariel."

"Oiler?"

"Yes?"

"I will see again, though it might take a while."

Juanito says *good* once more, though he's beginning to understand what it is that Broas really wants to discuss. He moves his chair a little bit closer to the bed. Whispering, he says, "Do you still have the letter?"

Broas nods, and turns his head in Juanito's direction. "They're sending me ashore in Malta," he whispers. "To see a real doctor. You'll come with me. I'll need help mailing it. Do you understand?"

"Yes," Juanito says. "I understand."

~

That afternoon, the second mate helps Ariel Broas move from the ship's hospital to his own cabin on the lower of the two officer decks—Juanito spots them moving slowly, Broas taking the timid, shuffling steps of the elderly. A routine develops. During the day,

the second cook brings Broas his meals, sitting him up and hand-
ing him his cutlery and directing him to his first mouthfuls.
Juanito visits at night, to keep him company and read to him. He
also helps Broas apply his medicine by squeezing a thin straight
line between his eyelids. He then asks him to blink several times
so that the balm mixes with tears and coats the marred surfaces of
the corneas. The letter is not mentioned again, and Juanito wonders if it is hidden somewhere in the room, tucked into a magazine perhaps, or stuffed among pairs of socks and underwear.

When the boat reaches the waters surrounding Malta, it goes
into anchorage while awaiting a free berth. They are there for two
full days. On the morning of the third day, Juanito notices a speck
on the water, at first blending with its Mediterranean backdrop,
then gaining the features of a pilot launch. An hour later, the big
ship is inching to shore, its progress guided by a mooring tug.
Juanito leaves the engine room and goes to Broas's cabin, where
he finds him sitting on the edge of his bed. He is dressed in an
officer's uniform and sunglasses, and his hands rest atop a cane.
Together, they listen to the whine of motors as the big ship is
manoeuvred into its berth.

They walk down to the deck, Ariel Broas holding the elbow
of the ship's oiler. They reach it just as the bosun and his ABs
begin lowering the accommodation ladder. The pilot and the captain emerge from the accommodation chattering in bad English,
Juanito realizing it's the first time in weeks he has seen the captain.
My God, he thinks, *he looks awful—his face is so pale; his uniform isn't
even pressed properly*. On deck, the pilot nods to the captain and
descends the accommodation ladder to the dock, where he looks
back up at the captain and gestures before stepping into a waiting
car. The captain waves back, smiling. Then, beneath the brim of

his hat, his eyes narrow, and the corners of his mouth turn down. Without saying a word to the assembled seamen, he heads back to the bridge.

Juanito holds Broas's arm as they take a step, and another, and then the chief officer joins them, his hand claiming Broas's other elbow. Time flits, creating a pastiche of images for the oiler: the bird-flecked jetty, the tightening of Ariel Broas's jaw muscles, the chief officer opening his lips and saying, in English, "Okay, Oiler, I take." When Juanito doesn't understand, the chief officer stops the three of them.

"Okay, Oiler," he says in a louder voice, "I take from here."

Juanito removes his hand from Broas's forearm. As the chief officer slowly guides Broas down the gangway, Juanito is relieved that he doesn't protest, or look over his shoulder. Instead, he keeps moving, tentatively finding each step with his right foot before letting his left foot catch up.

~

It is a day of pacing, of splashing cold water on his face, of jumping at every little sound, of wishing he knew a way to counteract the anxiety clouding his thoughts. At dinner, Juanito goes to the seamen's mess. There, he takes a seat by himself and picks at his food. A short time later, he's joined by Rodolfo, who says, "You look tired, Oiler. Not sleeping well?"

"No," he says. "Not really."

Juanito takes a bite of chicken and has trouble swallowing. An impulse passes through his head. *Tell him,* it says, and so he lifts his eyes and looks at Rodolfo, and he thinks how strange it is that at one time he did not know this man, that at one time they hadn't shared the same experiences. He's about to say something about the letter when Carmelito sets his tray on the table and sits with them. He takes a bite and, with his mouth full, says, "Ariel's back."

"He is?" Juanito asks.

"I just saw the chief officer bringing him on board."

Though Juanito wants to go immediately, he takes his time, for he doesn't trust the AB who has just conveyed this information, and he doesn't want to appear as though this news was meaningful in any way. He eats as much as he can, and has more coffee, the whole time acting as though the news of Broas's return is nothing beyond incidental. Finally, he stands and nods goodbye, dumping his tray on the way out. Once out of view, he moves smartly along the corridor to the heavy metal door marking the entrance to the stairs. He climbs the three flights and reaches the door to the first of the officer decks; for a second, he hesitates. Then he enters the corridor, looking up and down, before going to Broas's cabin. He knocks and enters, finding him sitting on his bunk, staring straight ahead. Broas immediately starts shaking his head back and forth.

"He watched me. Every second. Maybe he suspected, I'm not sure, Oiler. You must mail this in Algeciras."

Broas reaches into his breast pocket, pulls out the letter, and passes it to Juanito. It's folded into quarters, the creases so sharp and defined Juanito is afraid he'll tear it if he tries to unfold it. It is then that he realizes Broas has been carrying the letter in his breast pocket since it was first written.

"Ariel," he says. "Your eyes. Can you see any better?"

Broas shakes his head. "Yes, I can, a little."

Juanito leaves. He feels light-headed, and on the verge of dizziness. As he steals along the corridor of the officers' deck, he reaches out and trails his fingertips along the walls. He takes the stairs to the seamen level and reaches his cabin. There, he circles his oversized room, a hand to his forehead, his thoughts swirling. A second later, he is sitting on his bunk, slowly opening the creased letter. He reads it, and as he does he keenly remembers all the trouble they'd had the night they had written it.

He lights a cigarette and touches the flame of the dwindling match to the corner of the letter. When the flame creeps close to his fingers, he shakes the sheet of paper, scattering the floor of his cabin with ashes. After sweeping up the remnants, and carefully placing them in his metal wastepaper basket, he hunts for another sheet of paper. A moment later, he starts a new letter. This time, the words come easily, and true, as if they'd always existed. Reading it over, he wishes it looked more official, that it was free of errors and produced on a computer. For a moment, he considers burning it and starting over. Instead, he folds it into quarters, creasing the seams with his fingernails. Then he puts it in his own breast pocket and pats it for safekeeping.

A day later, the boat reaches Algeciras, the largest tanker port in Spain. They are in anchorage for a day and a half. During those thirty-six hours, Juanito finds he can neither sleep properly nor digest his food without a host of rumblings and needling pains. Finally, they are piloted to shore, and the big ship is docked against a concrete berth. He has been to Algeciras a dozen times, and though he cannot see the *paseo* from the deck of the *Maersk Dubai*, he can picture it—the swaying palm trees, the hashish dealers, the dingy hotels, the lottery vendors, the girls in tight Korean jeans, the newspaper kiosks selling dirty magazines and strong cigarettes.

Juanito coughs away an attack of nausea before going to find the chief officer. He finds him in the bridge, reading a Chinese newspaper; when Juanito enters he looks up, surprised. Juanito tells him he must go ashore, explaining in English that his wife's sister is having a baby and they've been having a hard time since her husband lost his job, so he has to wire some money and talk to his wife and see how everything is going. The chief officer remains mute as Juanito burrows deeper and deeper into the lie, telling him how close his wife is to her sister, and how they already have a child nearly blinded from diabetes, and how things are difficult—so very, very difficult—at this time in the city of Manila. Throughout, he hopes that the chief officer will mistake his nervousness for the sheepishness caused by having to ask a superior for a favour.

"All right," the chief officer finally says, "you have half-hour."

Juanito thanks him, and moves down the accommodation ladder. Upon reaching the dock, he walks quickly through the maze of buildings and stacked containers lining the harbour. He enters the first long-distance telephone shop he sees and takes a place in line, just in case he's been followed. As he waits, he keeps looking over his shoulder, so as to spot any Taiwanese faces, or the face of any of the four ABs who have shown nothing but loyalty to the officers. When he is three people away from the kiosk where he would normally ask for a phone booth, he slips out of line. He lets a few moments go by, loitering between the lineup of people and the wall of wooden phone booths. As he does, he monitors the faces of those in line—they are poor people, Arabs and Africans mostly, with the odd backpacker. Finally, when he's sure he hasn't been followed, he leaves the building, trying hard not to cast furtive glances in every direction. Outside, he stops at a magazine kiosk to buy stamps. Walking away, he plasters the letter with with far more postage than is required.

The letter box is black and wrought iron and mounted on a telephone pole—he can see it, a half block away, outside the Algeciras Hotel. He feels the perspiration from his hand dampen the letter, and for a moment he worries he may smear the address. The *paseo* sways and turns vaporous. The music coming through car windows and shop doors becomes something minor keyed and ominous, like the theme music played during foreshadowed moments. The colours of Spain intensify, Juanito suddenly conscious that he can see splashes of red, and orange, and black everywhere. The letter box approaches. Juanito no longer feels as though he is walking. He is an object, the letter box is an object, and the distance between them, through a contraction of space and time, dwindles, until they are side by side, an arm's length from one another, as close as two men waiting to board the same bus.

The ship's oiler reaches out and, with a prayer, pushes the letter through the slot.

TEN

Dear Elena,

As you can tell by the postmark, I've made it to Algeciras, and am staying at the place you told me about, slowly going out of my mind. It is hot here, and for a boy from the mountains it's hard to adapt to a place where the sun shines from dawn till dusk every day. The town is dirty and poor, the streets full of the most shifty of individuals. I have been put to work at El Faro's charity furniture shop, which is more boring than you can imagine—the store is an oven, and all I do is sit, watching the dust rise off furniture that no one would ever want. I can't even spend my days reading, for of course there are no places where I can buy Romanian books. In other words, I'm bored, and homesick, and suffering from the strangest of dreams.

But enough complaining. The good thing is that I am safe and healthy and learning Spanish very quickly, which should come as no surprise given that it contains so many Romanian words. I almost got on a big ship the other day, and as soon as another one pulls into port, I'll get on for sure. A week after that, I'll be in America.

There are other Romanians here—one from Moldova, another from the coast—and they've assured me that a port with laxer security doesn't exist in the whole world. Having been here for three weeks, I can understand why—the Spanish care about bulls, football, eating fish, playing lottery games and that's about it. All you have to do, I'm told, is wait until dark and then climb on board and hide. It's as simple as that. Then, when you give yourself up, they put you to work and give you food and sometimes they even pay you. So don't worry—what I'm about to do isn't dangerous in the least. In fact, after the difficulty of my trip to Algeciras, I'm looking forward to some fresh sea air, and I'm looking forward to being away from the problems of the world.

I must go now, Elena. I have to write my mother— I received a letter from her the other day—and I need to do my laundry, and I need to shop for some food, and of course I have to go to the harbour and look for a big ship.

With love,
Daniel

P.S. The last time you wrote you asked about those Romanian guys named Petre and Radu. I asked around, and some of the other Romanians who are living at El Faro told me that they *had* been here, but that they both got on board without any problems whatsoever. Please tell Maria that they've probably gotten jobs on the ship, and have decided to make a little money before starting new lives. As for not writing, one thing I've heard is that sailors can often go months without visiting shore, so I imagine they just haven't had a chance to post a letter.

Daniel leans back in his chair, puts down his pen, and rubs his eyes before folding the letter and sliding it into the back pocket of his jeans—later, he'll find an envelope somewhere. In the meantime, he wishes someone would come into the shop, which is at a dusty, round traffic circle called Plaza España, just down the hill from the El Faro house on Calle Lérida. Inside the traffic circle, there is nothing more than a mounding of tramped earth, without benches or fountain or tiles or even a circle of grass. From where he sits, at the front of the store, he can watch poor, dirty-faced children play—the Spanish call them *flaquitos*, or "little skinny ones." Sometimes they come into the store, and if no one else is looking he'll give them candies, or small glasses of Coca-Cola, or a peseta or two.

Squat, poorly maintained houses ring the plaza, and it is this sight—cracked walls, torn curtains, each door with two or three locks—that is slowly becoming Daniel's impression of Spain. And while it's possible to see small, heartwarming gestures—a flowerpot filled with begonias, a freshly painted door, a child doing homework on a stoop—this neighbourhood is nonetheless a shantytown, claimed by the illegal construction workers of Costa Del Sol.

The store, too, is a shambles. The idea is that people will drop off their used but still serviceable furniture, which El Faro will sell for next to nothing to the poor. In reality, the shop operates as a place for people to unload their junk without having to pay a dumping fee. Every square inch of the place is stacked with teetering backless chairs, with sofas losing their stuffing, with televisions that roll their images in a maddening blur, with easy chairs smelling of cat. Every day, pickup trucks pull up, and someone drops off a bureau with a missing drawer, or a washing machine that no longer agitates, or a cracked mirror streaked with quicksilver.

Jesus, Daniel thinks, *another truck is coming now*, driven by a Spaniard with tattoos on his forearm. The driver and another man hop out, lower the tailgate, and begin pulling at a sofa as ripped and torn as a magazine chewed by a house pet. Judging by the difficulty they are having, there's a mattress inside the sofa, its springs no doubt loosened and poking through. The sofa lands with a thud, raising a cloud of dust. The two men hop back in the cab and drive off.

Daniel goes out into the blistering sun; even this short walk makes him perspire. He looks under the sofa cushions and, sure enough, sees a metal mattress handle—in addition to being old and ruined, it's going to be as heavy as a stove. Daniel curses and heads back inside, taking the stairs to the second floor. Here, Gheorghe is working as an orderly at the El Faro drug rehabilitation centre—mostly he spends his time playing euchre and smoking hashish with middle-class German heroin addicts, a job he says he'd gladly do forever if only they paid him. Daniel pushes open the door and finds him in the middle of a hand of cards. He waits, looking around. The walls are decorated with posters of sad-looking teenagers in foreign jails, and there's a big metal coffee percolator on a counter. Despite the bank of open windows along the front of the building, the room is hot, and airless, and poorly lit.

Gheorghe stands and tells the other card players that he's needed downstairs. He follows Daniel, and for the first few minutes they rearrange the furniture in the store, disassembling a bottleneck that had formed at the entrance. They walk into the street. Only the occasional car passes, the quiet of siesta having descended. As they move, they're conscious of the sound of their feet striking the dusty roadway, and of the voices of the *flaquitos*, who stay outside even during the inactivity of midday. "*Hola, faro,*" they call, their voices almost ethereal in the hot stillness; while Gheorghe ignores them, Daniel looks toward them and nods, a gesture that makes the smaller ones giggle.

On three, they lift. The sofa bed is so heavy that Daniel thinks his grip might fail him and he'll have to set it back down. He breathes through gritted teeth, an ache invading his fingertips. Large damp spots form on the front of Gheorghe's shirt. They drop the sofa in the hot shade of the store and sit on it, breathing hard.

Gheorghe reaches into his pocket and pulls out a pipe and a brick of hashish. Seeing it, Daniel waves it away, saying, "No, not here—if Lawrence catches us again . . ."

"So what? So he throws us out? Listen, Dani, this morning I was down at the wharf. There's a boat there the size of the Black Sea."

Daniel fights the temptation to say, *No, Gheorghe, I can't spend days in a dark corner.* Instead he stiffens and says, "Good. Finally."

The hashish in Algeciras is so black and resinous that Gheorghe is beginning to acquire the smudged fingertips seen on the Moroccan dealers who, day and night, patrol the *paseo*. He flames a lighter under one corner of the brick, and for a few seconds black smoke spires toward the ceiling. He blows it out, and crumbles the drug into the bowl of the pipe.

He lights it and inhales greedily, the hashish turning the bright orange of a Chinese lantern. When he's filled his lungs, he passes the pipe to Daniel, who gives in and smokes as well. Usually, when he's under the influence of black Moroccan hashish, the hot hazy slowness of Algeciras feels more in line with his mental state, and therefore more tolerable. This time, as they pass the pipe back and forth, Daniel feels his thoughts curl, and turn fearful. Laying his head back on the edge of the sofa, he thinks, *Oh boy, maybe I smoked too much,* for his heart has slowed to a pounding lurch, and the air has turned into a patchwork of tawny red jigsaw pieces. He rubs his eyes and swallows away a rippling of nausea. Gheorghe stands and goes back up the stairs to his work, leaving Daniel alone and anxious and with a tightness gripping the back of his neck.

Five minutes later, one of the Albanians staying at El Faro comes and relieves him. Daniel walks into the stillness of Plaza España; he feels prickly, and so weird he shivers in the sweltering heat. He heads toward the centre of town, and as he does he pretends that he belongs there, that he understands the attraction of bulls and lottery games and the music of Paco de Lucia. He enters a shop and buys a can of beer, doling out the pesetas in silence so that the woman behind the counter won't hear his poor Spanish and give him the dour, patronizing glare that Algeciran shopkeepers reserve for Arabs, Africans, East Europeans and spoiled American backpackers.

He then walks into the main square and looks at the sixteenth-century stone church with the tiny wooden door. After finishing his beer, he goes inside. He sits toward the rear of the chapel, and puts his hands on the pew back in front of him. Resting his forehead on the back of his hands, he thinks of all the Sundays he spent in the Romanian Orthodox church back in his hometown, all of the men seated in the front of the church and all of the women in the back. Though he had always complained about

having to go, he understands now that he misses those mornings—
the hymns, the flickering glow of candles, the sliced-potato sandwiches he was given at his aunt's apartment afterwards. He stays
in the church for a long time. When he finally leaves, he heads to
the far side of the city, past the Colegio de García Lorca—it is said
that the great poet used to visit Algeciras often, back when the
city still had canals and a loveliness about it. After a bit, he comes
to a huge park crowded with orange trees. Every few metres there
is an office worker snoozing on the grass, or pairs of students
kissing. He roams the park for a few minutes. It is so hot and still
that even the birds in the trees appear to be resting. After a time,
he does something he's always wanted to do—he picks an orange
the size of a canteloupe from one of the trees and samples it.
Immediately, he understands why the Spanish never do this, for
the fruit is hard and sour and green.

He spits it out, and sits. The hashish has started to wear off,
leaving him feeling groggy and dry mouthed. He lies down.
Above him, sunlight fights through the leaves of the tree, speck-
ling his body. There is something relaxing about the sight of a big
white-hot sun, camouflaged by green and orange, and Daniel
gazes up at it for the longest time. *How strange*, he thinks, *that the
passage of my life has brought me here, to this moment in Spain, to a park
full of orange trees.*

After a time he closes his eyes. The slightest of breezes has
come up, cooling his damp skin. He can feel tree roots, grown
over and softened with grass, beneath him, and he decides that
what he needs, more than anything, is a rest. It doesn't take long
for his thoughts to turn soupy and coloured, and it doesn't take
long for him to hear it, coming closer, the oscillating wail of a
siren *for they always used sirens, better to put the scare into a whole village,*

Daniel throwing off rough woollen blankets and rushing to his bedroom window and there, right there, for the thousandth time, are black vans and German shepherds and swirling red lights, and then Daniel is sitting, gasping, commanding himself to forget it ever happened, an exercise that seems to be getting harder and harder with the stress of each passing day.

He looks around, hyperventilating so badly he thinks he might suffocate, here, alone and afraid in a park filled with secretaries. There is wind rustling the trees, and there are young couples peering at him, their mouths swollen from kissing. He puts his face in his hands and again struggles to silence the chaos in his head. When he fails he leaps to his feet, his throat a knot, and rushes through the park, not stopping until he reaches the first bar he can find. He goes inside, and when the bartender finally saunters over Daniel orders a whisky on the rocks, "*Un doble, por favor,*" and drains it on the spot so he can order another before the man leaves him. Minutes later he orders a third, spending the last of the pesetas in his pocket. He has been there no more than five minutes.

He stumbles out, the alcohol having exploded like a bomb in his veins—he walks a block, reeling from side to side, until he finds himself in front of the café run by El Faro. He pushes open a wooden gate, thinking he'll go inside and drink a free coffee and try to get his head together. Standing at the entrance, he looks around: there is a plastic fountain, and each of the tables has a Bible on it. Daniel sits at the nearest table, almost losing his balance as he lowers himself into the chair. After a time, Lawrence's Spanish wife, Rosa, comes and takes his order for coffee. She returns a few minutes later, though as she sets his coffee in front of him, she peers at him and asks if he's all right.

"*Sí*," Daniel says, "*sí, sí, sí.*"

"*Verdad?*"

"*Sí, sí . . .*"

The coffee is thick and strong, the grounds collected at the bottom of a tiny white cup. As Daniel sips it, he picks up the pocket Bible in front of him and starts flipping through the waxy pages, if only to see how many of the words he can understand. It is difficult, for the sentences are floating in front of his eyes, and his mind is as muddy as the coffee.

"Daniel?"

He looks up and sees that Lawrence and Rosa are standing above him. When Rosa moves away, Lawrence tilts his head in her direction and says in Spanish, "She told me you might need some . . ." He stops, and fumbles for words. "May I join you, Daniel?"

Daniel nods, and Lawrence sits, slowly pulling back a chair. For a moment, he says nothing. Speaking very deliberately, so that Daniel can understand every word, he says, "You know I was like you once."

I don't think so, Daniel says to himself.

"I was like you, reeking of liquor and hashish. Plus I took heroin. Did you know that, Daniel? That I was one of the heroin addicts helped by El Faro? Believe me, Daniel. Things could be a lot worse for you. Things *will* be a lot worse for you if you go on like this."

At this, Daniel wants to laugh. Did he really say he used to take heroin? The saintly director of El Faro? *Now,* Daniel thinks, *I've heard everything.*

He stares at the surface of the table, wishing only that Lawrence would go away and let him drink his coffee in peace.

Still speaking in the slowest and clearest of voices, Lawrence breaks the silence by saying, "You know what I do when I'm feeling the way you're feeling now? Look . . ."

He lifts the pocket Bible that is resting on the table, and places it on its spine. "I take the Bible, and I let it do this . . ." He releases the covers, allowing the book to fall open to a page toward the end of the New Testament.

"Now," he says. "I look for a passage that makes me feel better." He tilts the Bible toward him, and looks over the page.

"There," Lawrence says, "1 Timothy. *This is a true saying, and worthy of accepting, that Christ Jesus came into the world to save sinners.* Do you see, Daniel? *He* doesn't care what you've done. Believe me, He's seen it all. Whatever it is, He won't be shocked. He won't judge. Let's try again."

He closes the Spanish-language Bible and, again, places the spine on the table. He lets go, and this time it falls open near the beginning of the New Testament. Lawrence picks up the Bible, and lets his light blue eyes roam over the pages. "Here," he says, "Matthew 11:28. I like this one—*Come unto me, all ye that labour and are heavily burdened, for I will give you rest.* Do you hear that, Daniel? *I will give you rest.* He will, too. Now you try."

He hands the Bible to Daniel, who humours Lawrence by doing as he's shown, the Bible flopping open to the writings of the Apostles. Lawrence picks up the book, his beard parting to reveal a broad, warm smile.

"You've picked the Book of John, Daniel. I don't even have to read it, I know it so well. You've picked the part where Christ is in His garden, and He doesn't know whether He can do all that God has asked Him to do. He doesn't know whether He has the courage. Then, He hears a voice—a voice saying, *For God so loved the world, that He gave His only begotten Son, that whoever believeth in Him shall not perish.* That's the Book of John, that's what *that* is. That's John, chapter three, verse sixteen. You should think of that, every time you need courage."

He smiles.

"That," he says, "is probably the most important part of the Bible. And you picked it, Daniel. It was that experience that gave Jesus the courage to do everything he had to do. Do you understand, Daniel? Every experience we have is a gift from God, and because it's from Him it can and will change us, as long as we open our hearts and let it. Can you understand that, Daniel? It is the acceptance of experience that is His greatest gift."

He pushes the open Bible toward Daniel. Though Daniel did not understand all of what Lawrence has just said, he did understand much of it. He picks up the book and looks at the section, as if to prove to himself that the passage really exists. Lawrence leans toward him. His light, straight hair is untied that day, and it falls to the surface of the table.

"You can take this Bible if you want, Daniel. I know that when I'm feeling low, and tempted to return to my old ways, I just hold a Bible in my hand and rub the front cover with my thumb and immediately I feel better. Though if I do give it to you, you have to promise me something. You have to promise me you'll remember that He walks with you, at all times. *You* don't have to be strong, for He'll be strong *for* you. This is something I end up telling most of the Romanians who come to stay here, sooner or later: you don't have to be so tough, for He'll be tough *for* you. You can draw strength from that. He's there for you, always. *He* will make you strong."

Daniel lifts his head, and peers at Lawrence. He lifts an eyebrow.

"He will?"

"Yes," Lawrence answers. "He will."

~

That night, Daniel and Gheorghe lie on their mattresses, waiting, unable to close their eyes. When the bedroom fills with snores, Gheorghe whispers, "Okay." They both rise. Gheorge is already dressed in jeans, T-shirt and work shirt, Daniel in a pair of green cargo pants and a thin jacket. His photograph of Elena is tucked into his breast pocket. They each have a bottle of water and a pocket filled with peanut butter sandwiches, which they surreptitiously made after the others had gone to bed. As the two men are about to leave, Daniel touches Gheorge's arm and motions for him to wait for one moment. He steps over sleeping men, and reaches into his abandoned duffel, and retrieves the Bible that Lawrence let him have.

They tiptoe past the men sleeping in the living room, move through the kitchen, and slowly open the door leading to the darkened street. From the window well of an abandoned house they retrieve a strong nylon rope connected to a grappling hook, bought that afternoon in a hardware store and stashed by Gheorghe. They walk through La Bajadilla, a walk they've taken so many times the grade no longer registers in their calves. After passing through the Plaza Mayor, they cut through the traffic circle with the statue of Paco de Lucia, and walk the traffic lane to the ferry terminal. At the terminal they turn left, and find the knocked-down fence.

This time, the shipyard doesn't feel as dark or as puzzling, for the two men have spent so much time studying its paths and crannies from their perch on the *paseo*. It takes them less than ten minutes to emerge at the wharf. They sit, looking up at the grey, mountainous ship. When Gheorghe asks Daniel if he'd like to smoke the last of the hashish, Daniel says no, that from now on he's staying away from the stuff. Gheorghe shrugs his shoulders and prepares his pipe. Daniel can hear the sea sloshing against the wharf, and Gheorghe pulling smoke into his lungs with a hiss. Miles away, past where the harbour widens into the channel, a ship in anchorage issues the low moan of a foghorn.

It seems to Daniel that they sit there forever, studying the side of the ship, for Gheorghe seems to have fallen into a stupor—his mouth looks dry, his eyes puffy and red. This time, it is Daniel who takes the first leap off the wharf, and as he catches the anchor chain and swings into the big ship's hull he knows to cushion himself with the flesh padding his right shoulder. The swinging chain comes to a rest, and Daniel climbs noiselessly before hooking the rope over the gunwale and pulling himself on board.

This time there are no smiles, or laughter, or jubilant calls into the night. Instead, Gheorghe moves six metres backward, runs and then launches his big body through space. At the top of the anchor chain, he takes hold of the rope and pulls himself up one arm length before grabbing Daniel's extended left hand. At the same time that Daniel pulls, Gheorghe swings his right foot onto the gunwale and levers himself on board.

The two men look at each other.

"Okay, boy," Gheorghe finally says. "It's better if we split up, no? I'll see you later, after we show ourselves. Remember—two days, no more and no less."

Daniel nods. He moves along the port side, while Gheorghe takes a catwalk to the starboard side. The running lights illuminate the deck of the ship just well enough that Daniel can move safely, without tripping over container lassos or water pipes or flood barriers—everything has a dull, amber glow. About two-thirds of his way along the boat, he finds an open, recessed compartment beneath one of the catwalks. He enters it, and sits in shadows. Wrapping his arms around his knees, he decides that this compartment, tucked out of sight, is as good a place as any to wait for daybreak, and the morning departure of the *Maersk Dubai.*

ELEVEN

The crinkly pale blue envelope is placed on Father Albano's desk. Throughout the morning, it sits amid a scattering of letters, bills and cards, just one more thing demanding the priest's attention. Shortly after lunch, he finds himself with a few minutes to spare. He plucks the letter from the top of the pile and opens it with his thumb, taking no notice of whom it is from.

It reads:

Dear Rev. Albano,

Greetings in the name of the LORD JESUS. This letter intends to inform you about our situation on board M/V *MAERSK DUBAI*. It appears to us that our superior officers are creating violation regarding our contract intentionally . . .

. . . and then someone wanders into his office to ask for some advice regarding a Greek sailor who is complaining of depression. The person leaves, and the phone rings, and someone else comes into his office. Pretty soon, the priest has put aside the letter, for he is a busy man, and the truth is that it's not uncommon for sailors to send him letters of complaint, levelled against belligerent captains, unfeeling chief officers, and slave-driving chief engineers.

His day continues. The letter sits, open and facing straight up. An hour or two later, he picks it up, and begins to read it once again.

Dear Rev. Albano,

Greetings in the name of our LORD JESUS. This letter intends to inform you about our situation on board M/V *MAERSK DUBAI*. It appears to us that our superior officers are creating violation regarding our contract intentionally

. . . and this time, when the reverend stops reading, it's because something has tweaked his memory. Those two sailors who had come in the previous month, the two who had looked so bothered—weren't they from the *Maersk Dubai*?

He reads on, intrigued now, the letter saying,

Some violations they have been doing are as follows:
* Abuse of authority
* Non-payment of excess overtime
* The subsistence allowance
And our drinking water here is also of bad condition because all drinking fountains don't have sterilizing lamp. <u>The worst thing they did was the violation of human rights</u>, when they discharged two stowaways who came from Algeciras, Spain. In March 12, 1996 at about 10:00 a.m. to 1:00 p.m. <u>they forced the stowaways to go down from the ship in mid-sea</u> without informing proper authorities about the situation.

As far as we all know, human lives must be preserved and save at all cost. And we are also informing you that this ship is unsea-worthy since the lifeboat mechanism doesn't work well same with the emergency fire pump that doesn't start immediately when it's needed. And one worse thing they do during navigation is pumping out of bilge and sludge overboard. But during the ship's stay in U.S.A. they remove the pipe connection to avoid problem with the authorities. Our oily-bilge separator is in bad condition and they don't use incinerator, but they keep records in the engine room to be presented to any person of authority when required. We also suffer from chest pain due to carbon monoxide leaking from the Main Engine.

All of us here know very well that you in the Seafarers' Center are willing to extend help to anyone who needs it. That is why we are now begging you to please assist us with our problem.

Till here and hope to hear from you.

GOD BLESS YOU ALL.

Respectfully yours,
CREW OF
M/V *MAERSK DUBAI*

The priest's hands tremble as he reads the letter a second time, making sure he did not imagine the words. It's no use. They are still there on the page, staring up at him, refusing to dissipate, the plainness of the language indicating a bedrock of sincerity. He reads it a third time, and a fourth time, and then he reads the same underlined phrase—*they forced the stowaways to go down from the ship*—

over and over, finding that no matter how many times his eyes digest those words, he cannot fully comprehend the darkness hiding in their construction.

He then scribbles his own letter, to his colleagues in the Newark office, for he guesses that the boat's first stop in North America will be the port servicing the city of New York. As he writes, he keeps making mistakes, and starting over, and then returning to the letter written by the seamen so as to assure himself, yet again, that this is something that is really occurring.

In his note, he asks his colleagues in Newark to please take any and all measures—alerting authorities, Coast Guard, the harbour police—when the big ship docks. Then he feeds the note into the office fax machine, and he watches, pacing, as the machine consumes the letter to an accompaniment of scratching and clawing noises. When it has been transmitted, he finds he doesn't feel any better, for even though he's done the right thing, he has been pulled into an experience he did not, in any way, wish to have.

Minutes later, the priest in Newark responds.

"Father," his fax reads. "I've checked the shipping schedules. The *Maersk Dubai*'s first call is not Newark, but Halifax. The boat docks first in Halifax."

TWELVE

Gheorghe moves as quietly as he can, for this time he's determined to remain unnoticed. In semi-darkness he finds stairs up to a catwalk, suppressing a howl when his shin hits a perforated metal step. He creeps along the walk, careful to lift each foot. Halfway across, he realizes he's been holding his breath, and that his pulse is pounding in his chest and temples, making him feel slightly sick. He closes his eyes and breathes as slowly, and as noiselessly, as possible.

He resumes traversing the catwalk, his head pivoting from side to side, looking for the movement of shadows. Upon reaching the ship's port side, he turns and descends the metal steps, until his feet make contact with the deck. He stays still for only a second, though in that time he has the same thought he had when he was on board the other ship: the deck is so large, and solid, that it's hard to believe he isn't on land.

He looks toward the bow—the boat seems to stretch away from him forever, coming to an end not in a definite point but in a blur. He squints and moves forward, careful not to trip over any pipes, steps or flood barriers. To his right is a siding of containers, stacked like blocks, and to his left is the gunwale topped with an inky, thick night—though outdoors, he feels as though he's moving down a narrow, darkened hallway. As he nears the bow, the light cast from the tower at the rear of the boat is blocked by the containers; his way is now lit only by the murky glow of running lights. He slows and places each step more tentatively, for he's heard of stowaways who have broken their ankles while searching for a hiding spot on a big ship, only to be found writhing and holding themselves and pleading not to be taken off. Gheorghe reaches out and trails his right hand along the wall of containers, withdrawing it only when he hits a lasso reaching toward the deck.

He feels the gap before he sees it: a half-metre-wide fissure leading into the containers stacked on deck. Gheorghe looks at it, hesitating a second or two before entering. He's now entombed in darkness, guiding himself solely by touch, and it occurs to him that if the containers shift he might be crushed. Still, it's an outside chance, for the straps keeping them in place seem to be heavy and taut, and even if they did topple, they would lean onto one another rather than fall, a crevice still remaining below. After a few more steps, his left hand trails across another opening, this one leading to a channel that burrows into the centre of the containers; this space, Gheorghe realizes, would not be visible from either port or starboard. He steps into it, and finds that no more than a centimetre or two separate his shoulders from the walls formed by the containers. Here he lies on his back and crosses his hands over his chest. Above him is a strip of star-flecked night.

When he drifts off, his sleep is light and unsatisfying. Every twenty minutes or so he wakens with a new pain in his neck or lower back, and he has to adjust the way he curls his body on the hard metal deck. Mostly he sleeps on his side, his hands together and acting as a pillow, though in this position an ache comes to his hip and shoulder. He rolls over, only to awaken in a short while with the same pain pulsing through the other side of his body. The night is getting cool. He had perspired heavily when climbing aboard, and his sweat, which had refused to dry in the swampish air, is now causing him to shiver. Still, he is exhausted, and he keeps drifting to a place midway between sleep and consciousness.

Later, he stirs, and his eyes open for good. The banner of night visible in the gap above him has turned to a light, emerging violet. As dawn breaks, the violet slowly shifts to a coppery orange before becoming yellow and then, gradually, an intense, cloudless blue. Far off, he hears voices, spoken in an Asian language, and a minute after that he hears a power tool, revving and spitting fumes. *Sanders,* he thinks, and he smiles—tomorrow, when he's revealed himself, and is asked if he knows how to operate the kind of machinery used to take rust off an aging gunwale, he'll be able to say that he does.

He sits uncomfortably, legs drawn to his chest, and eats the sandwiches in his pockets. After a short while, his lower back begins to ache, his feet start to tingle, and he notices that a film of perspiration has formed on his upper lip. When his head begins to ache, he's beset with a nervous jumpiness—how stupid, he thinks, not to bring a bottle to get him through the first day of hiding. He stands. To keep himself occupied, he does vertical push-ups against the face of the containers and hums Romanian drinking songs to himself. At times, he catches whiffs of diesel fuel, carried over the deck. There are other noises now—it's clear that the big ship's engine is running, for he can hear a throaty rumble coming from the stern, and he can feel the slightest of vibrations transmitting through the soles of his sneakers. He can

also hear the whine of small motors, and he supposes this is coming from the tugboats that pull a big ship away from its berth. He
looks up at the sky, trying to gauge whether the boat is moving.
Though there are one or two thinly spun clouds, it's impossible to
tell whether their drifting is caused by wind or the relative movement of the boat. After a time, he resorts to dampening a finger
and holding it up, thinking that maybe the breeze will indicate
whether the boat is moving; this doesn't work either, for his hiding
space is airless, and quickly growing warm. His head pounds, his
hands tremble, and he's starting to feel the onset of chills.
Ruefully, he grins—with everything that has happened on this
trip, it'd be just his luck to detox on board a boat that has gone out
of service for repairs.

Still, there's nothing he can do but be patient, for he understands that the most important thing is to remain out of sight for
at least two days. That way, when he's caught, there won't be a
temptation to turn the boat around and deliver him back to
Algeciras (assuming the damn boat ever *does* leave shore). So he
waits. He daydreams. He wonders if Daniel Pacepa has found
himself a good hiding spot. He thinks of *ţuică,* of women he knew
in Baia Sprie, of all-night card games with fellow miners. It is all
of little help, for he's neither a patient man nor a man accustomed
to entertaining himself with thoughts. His thirst is a torment, no
matter how much of the water he drinks, though his desire to
leave his crevice and see what is happening is worse. After a time,
he begins to believe that the boat is, indeed, moving, for he
notices he can no longer hear the sounds made by seagulls, and
that he can no longer hear the sweeping noises made by traffic
along the *paseo.* As well, he notices that the engine now sounds
less concentrated, and he thinks that its throaty rumblings are no

longer ricocheting off the foothills ringing Algeciras. Taking a
chance, he sticks his head into the pathway that he took to reach
his hiding spot. He looks left, and he looks right. Beyond either
gunwale, he sees only light turned bleary with refracted sun and
seawater. He looks harder now, his eyes narrowing as he peers
beyond the starboard side. By the time he withdraws his head into
the chasm, he feels confident that if the boat were still docked, he
would at least see the outline of shore.

No, he thinks, *we're definitely at sea.*

Within the hour, he is proven correct, for when the boat
reaches open water it begins to pitch, the confines of Gheorghe's
hiding spot now rising and falling with the currents of the sea. He
grows seasick and weak. And his *head*—its pounding has fallen in
line with the movements of the boat, mounting and subsiding
with each swell. Still, he's had far worse moments—once, in a Baia
Sprie copper mine, a charge placed by a drunken man collapsed a
section of tunnel. There was an explosion muffled by the walls of
the mine, and then Gheorghe and six others were trapped, without water or food, slowly growing woozy in the dwindling air. The
strange thing was that no one panicked, Gheorghe learning that
day that panic only happens as a by-product of options, and the
possibility of survival. They had all sat down wordlessly, accepting that the worst form of death was to be theirs. One of the men
cried, yet he cried so weakly Gheorghe got the impression his
tears were for show only—as if to prove to himself that the loss
of his life was something worth crying *for.*

Eventually, Gheorghe had turned off his miner's lamp, and
was surprised when the other men followed suit. *This is bad enough,*
Gheorghe had thought, *without having to watch each other die.* Slowly,
his thoughts had grown thick, and confused. He began to wonder

if perhaps he was already dying, his only regrets being that he had not had children, for he really did like them, and that he'd spent his whole life in a ruined place like Romania.

He had just begun drifting off when they'd all heard a gurgling noise, growing louder. A few minutes later, an auger tip broke through the blockage, and they could hear the whirring of fans. At first they took turns crouching around the hole, sucking up lungfuls of forced air. A second hole broke through, and a third, the resulting beam of lights forming a triangle against the far wall of their cave. The men began to turn their lamps back on, and hammer their fists against the wall, crying and screaming and suffering the onset of panic, for it suddenly felt intolerable, being trapped and hungry and ravaged by thirst. After a time, a hose appeared at the lip of one of the holes, and when drinking water started flowing they took turns putting their mouths to the nozzle. Far off, they could hear men yelling.

One and a half days they were in that hole, one and a half days of waiting and watching and panicking every time there was a break in the drilling. When they finally saw shovel tips poke through the seal of rubble, ore and earth, Gheorghe did a funny thing. Without thinking, he began to feel parts of his body. He touched his arms, his legs, his bristly face. He checked to make sure he was real.

Now that, he thinks, *had been a tough spot.*

Lying in his chasm, he feels sunshine fall hot on his face, and he stupidly opens his eyes. He shuts them immediately, a globe burning red and veiny on the inside of his eyelids. Slowly, the warmth moves off his face. He opens his eyes, and this time he sees only a sliver of the sun, hairband shaped and blazing. It moves out of the channel of sky altogether, and he realizes he's made it through the morning.

One more afternoon, he thinks, *and one more night spent looking up at stars, and the worst of it will be over.*

~

The next morning, he waits until the sky has been a clear, depthless blue for more than an hour, then stumbles into the pathway spanning the deck of the *Maersk Dubai*—his back and legs barely work, his head pounds, he feels as though he's suffering from a flu. He looks in both directions. For no particular reason, he walks to the port side and rests his hands on the gunwale. He gazes out over the gently swelling seas. He has never seen such limitlessness, and for some reason the sight of all that space makes him feel slightly better—he'd always suspected the world was this large, its possibilities this vast. He looks along the gunwale, all the way to the rear of the boat, and starts walking, marvelling at how much easier it is to manoeuvre the deck of a container ship in daylight. Looking around, he hopes to see Daniel, thinking he's probably in the process of giving himself up as well.

He spots one of the sailors near the rear of the deck, heading toward the bow. Instinctively, Gheorghe presses his back against the wall of containers and watches. As the man approaches, his features come into focus; large for an Asian, he has a broad chest and shoulders, coal black hair, and a round, light-brown face. Gheorghe continues to study the man as he nears: the measured way he places his feet, his upright posture, the stalwart positioning of his arms.

Gheorghe steps away from the wall of containers. The sailor, meanwhile, keeps his head down, and it becomes clear to Gheorghe that he's lost in thought. When no more than ten metres separate the two men, the sailor looks up and stops.

Gheorghe continues toward him, smiling broadly, for he knows that the next step is to demonstrate he's not armed, or angry, or in any way a threat. He lifts his hands, and shows his palms.

The man has rooted himself to the hard concrete deck. While Gheorghe had expected the man to be surprised, or annoyed, or perhaps slightly afraid, he never guessed he would look so stricken—his eyes widen, his lips part, his shoulders hunch. A second later, he looks down, as though Gheorghe is a light his eyes cannot tolerate.

"*Hola!*" Gheorghe calls out, inflecting his voice with cheerfulness. "*Hola, amigo!*" and still the man can barely flit his gaze upward. Instead he is lifting his hands, and waving them in front of him as though Gheorghe were an insect he's trying to shoo.

"No," the man says weakly.

"*Hola, amigo!*" Gheorghe calls out again, his voice now tinged with worry. When the man still doesn't answer, he gives up. Neither man moves—Gheorghe feels if he were to take a step forward, the sailor would take a step backward. To break the impasse, Gheorge calls out one of the few words he's learned in Spanish.

"*Venga,*" he says, "*venga,*" and when the sailor's eyes meet his, Gheorghe makes a sweeping motion, indicating the man should come. When he stays put, Gheorghe explains in Romanian, "Come, friend, come. I'll show you where I was hiding." The sailor lowers his head, sadness infecting both his movements and his expression. "*Venga,*" Gheorghe tries again. "*Venga, venga, venga . . .*" His voice drifts off. The sailor says something in his own language, maybe Chinese or Japanese or Filipino or Korean. In those confused seconds, Gheorghe becomes convinced that if he could only show this man the place where he has squeezed himself for the last thirty-six hours, the sailor would appreciate that Gheorghe is human, and living, and deserving of mercy.

The sailor switches to Spanish, that infernal language Daniel had picked up so easily.

"*No me importa*," the sailor says, "*no es mi problema.*" He speaks softly, and refuses to look Gheorghe in the eye. "*No es mi problema*," he says again, and this time Gheorghe understands that the man will not help him.

Two others are approaching now. When they are ten or so metres away, the sailor hears them and turns. The two men stop and manufacture the same shocked expression as the sailor. Not a word passes among them. After a minute, the two men turn and walk toward the white structure rising from the back of the boat.

The sailor's chest heaves. "No," he says, "no, no, no," and then, once more, "*no es mi problema, no puedo ayudar, no es mi problema, lo siento, lo siento . . .*"

He turns, and walks away. Gheorghe is alone now. The wind is lifting the few hairs on his head, and his shirt is luffing in the breeze. He cannot understand what is happening—he had expected to be yelled at, or locked in a state room, or given a free lunch, or put to work immediately. The last thing he'd expected was to be ignored. For a while he entertains the possibility that they want him to simply go back to his hiding spot, and not bother them, and then slip off the boat when it next reaches port. He would do it too, were it not for the hunger pangs coiling through his belly, and the sensation of thirst, just starting to sear his lips and throat and tongue. *What I would give*, he thinks, *for some beer, or some wine, or some ţuică.*

He decides to follow the sailor. He feels silly, trailing after the man like a lost puppy, and this embarrassment makes his body feel weak, his leg muscles barely able to absorb the bucking of the ship. He stops when he reaches the area of deck surrounding the accommodation; attached to the outer wall are fire extinguishers, hoses, a water fountain, and axes. Looking around, he notices that sailors are peering at him through windows in the first and second levels, the expression on each face as grave as the one worn by the sailor who'd found him. After a few minutes, even those faces slip away, and he is left alone with his confusion.

To prove to himself that he isn't dreaming, he turns and looks out over the choppy sea. *Yes,* he thinks, *it's definitely there; it goes on forever; I'm not imagining this.* He hears a door open, and when he turns he sees a procession of men step onto the deck—he can tell that they're officers, for they're wearing dark blue jackets instead of coveralls. They approach him in a tight huddle led by one of the men, who is perhaps Chinese and about fifty years old, with a strong square jaw and lines around his eyes. He says something in a foreign language, and there is nothing Gheorghe can do but smile, and shrug his shoulders, and say in his own language that he doesn't understand. The officer asks another question, and when Gheorghe can only shrug a second time, the officer comes closer. Again, the questions come, though Gheorghe thinks that maybe they are no longer questions, for the officer's tone is angry, and this signals to the others that they may crowd around Gheorghe and start haranguing him as well. Each word is spat in a language that Gheorghe will never know, a language of fits and jabs and sudden intonations, and it is the use of this indecipherable language that, more than anything, makes Gheorghe angry.

He drops his forced smile, he narrows his eyes, he tightens his chest muscles. He suddenly feels better, his temper causing him to forget how badly he's outmanned, and how far away he is from home, and how imprisoned he is by the endlessness of the sea. He starts an invective of his own, directed straight into the tightened face of the officer, the two men now barely a half arm's length away from one another. Gheorghe even begins to enjoy himself, for he has switched to Hungarian curses, picked up in the mines of Maramureș, Hungarian being the world's best language for swearing. He tells the chief officer to go stick a horse's cock up his ass, and he tells him to go use his mother's cunt for a soup bowl, and while the chief officer doesn't understand the exact meaning of Gheorghe's words he can nevertheless understand their intent. It is at this precise moment that Gheorghe seals his own fate, for in the middle of his tirade of insults he remembers that any fight—no matter what the odds—can be won through the twin elements of surprise and intimidation. He strikes the officer, throwing a sudden uppercut, never dreaming that the officer would so easily block the punch with a forearm and then throw a sudden, solid blow of his own, hitting Gheorghe hard in the face with the side of his hand. For the next few moments, Gheorghe can see only rockets against a curtain of black velvet. He smiles to himself—after all his bad luck, he has to go and pick a fight with somebody who knows karate. That is so, so *like* him. He puts his hands up to show that he's surrendered, and when the chief officer relaxes slightly Gheorghe throws a left-handed punch that lands hard and lacerating on the right side of the chief officer's forehead.

In that instant, they are all upon him, unleashed by the blood coming from the chief officer's head. Gheorghe absorbs punch after punch, and as his punishment mounts he departs from himself and rises somewhere above the deck. Really, he is proud of the man below him, and the way he's refusing to give up. Above, the departed Gheorghe feels contented. This surprises him, for he had always thought that dying would be such a sad experience, in which you reviewed all of your failures, and all of your wrongdoing, and all of the things you never got a chance to do. Instead, a wave of peacefulness passes over him. He pictures things from his boyhood that he hadn't thought about in years: strawberry festivals, Gypsies with dancing bears, kisses given by sweethearts. Yes, he was young once, he was. He looks down. The man is still refusing to give up. Filled with magnanimity, Gheorghe even admires the Chinese, for they are clearly hard men themselves, though he wonders why these distinctions had once mattered so much to him. There is no pain, no noise, only a wistful longing. Below, the huddle of men moves toward the perimeter of the deck. The stowaway is backed against the gunwale, and still he fights on, taking blow after blow. Watching this, Gheorghe feels a sense of relief, for he had always figured that he'd really died down in that mine shaft, and that the time given him had been a gift requiring too much responsibility. Then again, he *had* left Romania, hadn't he? He *had* tried for a better life, hadn't he? He couldn't fault himself *too* much, could he?

Below him, the man turns, his body bending over the gunwale, not so much fighting now as holding on for dear life. Blows rain upon his back. Above, Gheorghe feels sorry for this man below him, for in his refusal to go down he's showing a degree of fury that must have been difficult to live with at times— just look at him down there, badly beaten and bent over a gunwale and still, *still,* trying to elbow someone in the throat. *Really,* Gheorghe thinks, *it's like watching a child try to do a puzzle that's too advanced,* there being something in the human capacity for struggle that can be heartbreaking to observe. The man slips and loses his balance, and because he's so tall and the weight of the group is against him he upends, by accident, and falls into the water. The others look on, astonished, for despite beating him they hadn't realized they were going to kill him.

Watching from above, Gheorghe Mihoc wishes he could yell down at the man in the water and tell him everything is fine, and warm, and comfortable, where he is going. Below, the fallen stowaway seems to hear Gheorghe's thoughts. Either that, or he is exhausted from his beating, and from the temperature of the ocean, and from the demands his life never once stopped making. When his head goes under he starts kicking, his mouth breaking the surface and gulping air before he slips back under again. This goes on and on. It is difficult to watch. He is close now. The man comes to the surface, takes a last gulp of air, only to find that his lungs are filled with saltwater, and no longer function as lungs. He slips under yet again, the ocean's surface now disturbed only by waves, and white caps, and the bubbling wake off the big ship's stern.

THIRTEEN

He stands just inside the second-level exit, his fingers resting on the door handle, his heart pounding, and as he listens to the yelling he thinks, *No, no, it can't be happening again.* With a deep breath, Rodolfo pushes the door and peers out, careful to keep his body inside the accommodation so that none of the officers will see him; beneath, the other seamen have scattered. Or at least he thinks they have—in reality they've found their own surreptitious ways to watch the slaying of Gheorghe Mihoc, and are in the process of glimpsing his end through porthole windows, and cracks in door frames, and gaps in the stacks of containers.

The man is bellowing now, like a large wounded animal, and it is the awfulness of this sound, more than the spilling of blood, that makes Rodolfo pull his head back inside the accommodation. With a trembling hand, he shuts the door, the voices from outside turning to something muffled and distant. Back in his room, he falls to his knees and starts saying Psalm 91. When he gets to the end, he repeats the eleventh verse—*for he has charged his angels to guard you wherever you go*—until it stops being words, and becomes something that is all cadence, and texture, and grace. Tears come, the first since he saw the first two stowaways disappear in the big ship's wake. He weeps with his hands still folded on the bed in front of him, his body rocking slightly, back and forth. When he is done he sits on his bed and takes his logbook from his bedside table. In it, he describes not only what he has just seen, but what he knows has just happened to the third stowaway.

"They are killing him," he writes, "they are killing him as I write this." He pauses, and stares at the words, asking himself if there is any way they could not be true.

He adds: "I did nothing."

He closes the book, and is about to put it back in the drawer of his bedside table when something stops him; he looks around the room, suddenly seeing it not as a place where he sleeps, but as a place so small, and so neat, that he cannot find a hiding spot for a slim notebook. He discards the obvious possibilities—inside his pillowcase, beneath his mattress—before slipping it between the end of the bed and the frame. With a prayer, he hopes this will suffice, and he goes back to work, keeping his head down until lunchtime. Though he cannot imagine himself eating, he nonetheless proceeds to the mess, moving more like a robot than a sailor. Hardly a word is spoken. From another table, he hears one of his ABs—Marlou, he thinks—joke that the officers really got their exercise that morning. This is greeted with forced, nervous laughter, and a continuance of quiet. One by one, the men stand, and empty whole meals into the trash. Each then exits onto the deck, where they are met with a sight that stops them and leaves them unsure of what to do—the captain is hosing the part of the deck where the struggle had occurred. The sailors stand there, hands in their pockets, feeling that the passage of time was something sent to hound them, the captain too preoccupied to look over and command them back to their posts.

~

That night, the seven men meet in the oversized room of the oiler, Juanito Ilagan. There is little to be said, for they are frightened, and exhausted, and slowly succumbing to the sadness that is overtaking the boat with each passing day. The meeting lasts no more than ten minutes, just time enough for the men to say a prayer, and for Ariel Broas to reiterate that if there's ever any sort of problem they must somehow get word to him in the engine room, where he will use the radio to call the mainland. The other men nod, and disperse, Rodolfo and Manuel returning to Rodolfo's cabin. They undress, and crawl into their bunks, and stare at the ceiling.

After a few minutes, Manuel asks, "Bose, do you mind if I have a cigarette?"

"No, Manuel."

"Do you want . . ."

"No, Manuel, you go ahead."

Rodolfo listens to the ritual of a cigarette being lit, and the first pull of smoke being inhaled.

"Manuel," he says after a bit. "When did we first meet?"

The AB exhales.

"Maybe . . . fifteen years ago?"

"More like twenty, I'd say. At the shipping agency in Manila, no?"

"Yes, Bose."

"I remember hearing you say something, and knowing you were from Ilocos." Rodolfo smiles at the thought of them both being so young. "Tell me, Manuel. When did your family make the move to Manila?"

"I was seven or eight."

"Yes, like me."

"I couldn't believe all the cars, and the height of the buildings, and the noise."

"Oh yes, I remember the noise."

"And the neon signs."

"Yes . . ."

Manuel pauses to smoke and then says, "I remember the first time I realized that those girls, the ones out walking the tourist zone in high heels, were for sale. I couldn't believe that could happen."

"Manila is a big city. I don't always miss it. My country, yes. My family, yes. But Manila? I don't know. Sometimes it's like . . . a difficult child."

"Bose?"

"Yes, Manuel?"

"Have you ever paid for one of those girls?"

The question hangs heavy and dark.

"No, brother, no."

"I did, once."

Rodolfo says nothing, and wishes he wasn't being subjected to this.

"It took me hours to get up the courage, and then I couldn't even go through with it. She was older than I was, and had bruises on her legs. I hated myself for a long time afterwards."

"Did you still have to pay?"

"Yes. In fact, I paid her extra."

"We all do stupid things when we're young."

"Yes, I suppose you're right."

"We all do things we feel bad about."

"We do?"

"Yes."

"What about you, Bose?"

An answer pops immediately into Rodolfo's head—*I did nothing, Manuel*—and he is thinking about how he could possibly explain this, when Manuel resumes speaking. "Look at us," he says. "You, a bosun, running the deck of a big ship. And me still an AB. You've done well, Bose. I always knew that you would. I wish I had what you have. Tell me something. When all this is over, will you go to sea again?"

Rodolfo pauses, and feels slightly out of breath.

"I don't know, brother."

"Not me, Bose. I'm out. No more. I'll never work on a big ship again."

"But what will you do?"

"I don't know. Not this. Not this any more. I hate this. I hated it even before this tour. I miss my family. I'd get off at the next port, but how am I supposed to get home? No, that's it. I don't care if I have to shine shoes on Roxas Boulevard—anything would be better than this. I've just got to finish this tour. That's all I know. That's all I can do."

An uncomfortable few seconds pass. Manuel keeps shaking his head from side to side, as if trying to convince himself of something. Then he rolls over and pulls the covers over his shoulders. A long night ensues. If Rodolfo sleeps at all, it doesn't happen until the early hours, when he is finally overtaken by a light, tortured slumber. He awakes with a start. As quickly as possible he washes, and shaves, and dresses before heading to the bosun store. There, he finds the chief officer staring out over the deck of the big ship at the waters beyond. A bandage stretches diagonally over the right side of his forehead.

"Bosun," he says.

"Chief."

And then something foreign rises within Rodolfo, something that makes him forget about consequences. "How did you get that cut?" he asks.

The chief officer glares at him briefly. Then he turns toward the bow and mumbles, "It's nothing, some karate injury, Bosun. You are okay for work today?"

"Yes," he says, and without waiting for the chief officer to dismiss him he walks off, and finds his ABs grouped near the port-side gunwale. He tells them they'll start painting the areas they stripped over the first half of the voyage. The men keep their eyes down as they begin unloading brooms, brushes, paint cans, and drop sheets.

Rodolfo sets off to do his tour of the deck. Though he's supposed to be looking for slackened lassos, and container shifts, and leaking hydraulics, he cannot attend to his work. He keeps drawing in lungfuls of sea air so deeply he can feel it cool the inside of his lungs. His whole body feels shaky, as though he hasn't eaten for days. He reaches the upper ship catwalk and begins to cross over, though midway he stops, and looks out over the bow, and catches himself thinking that whatever force has taken possession of the *Maersk Dubai* has now taken possession of it completely. *I cannot believe,* he thinks, *I just walked away from the chief officer. I cannot believe I could do that.* He shudders, suddenly feeling alone and guilty, as though he was the one who'd sinned. He cannot stand another moment; the boat, and the ocean, and the sky become figments. He steps off the catwalk onto the port-side deck, the whole time thinking, *This is a dream; I have fallen into a bad, bad dream,* the bosun so lost in disbelief that when a bedraggled and hungry Daniel

Pacepa steps out of a compartment beneath the catwalk, Rodolfo is not even surprised, for these are the sorts of things that happen on a boat that is not real, that has never been real, that is a mirage in a dark blue infinity.

Rodolfo closes his eyes and tries to send it all away, only to find that he cannot—the vision has the tenacity of a real person. It keeps saying, *Por favor, amigo, por favor por favor,* while Rodolfo keeps his eyes trained on the deck of the ship, all the while thinking, *This is not happening, this cannot be happening,* and still the thing is talking, its voice weak in the churning breezes: *Hola, amigo, tengo hambre, amigo, por favor, amigo,* until Rodolfo decides it doesn't matter if he's fallen into a bad dream, or if the ocean doesn't exist, or if the boat is cursed. His shoulders lift to his ears, and the muscles in his forearms cramp. He feels exactly as he did yesterday, when the third stowaway presented himself.

I just want to go home. I just want to see my children again.

"No," he whispers, trying hard to convince himself. "*No es mi problema.*"

His eyes flit upward, and in that moment he sees it: the stowaway is taking a Bible out of the pocket of his pants, and is rubbing the front cover with his thumb. Immediately, Rodolfo motions at him, telling him in a loud whisper to move back, to please, *please* move back. The stowaway gapes at him, confused. Rodolfo's voice grows more insistent, his hands up and pushing at the bank of air between the two men.

"Please," he says. "*Por favor . . .*"

It doesn't work. The young man—he can be no more than nineteen, with mussed dark hair and a tall, angular frame—shrugs his shoulders and lifts his fingertips, as if to indicate he doesn't understand. He takes a step toward Rodolfo. "No," Rodolfo says, and again he pushes at air while whispering, "No, no, no," and when this stops the stowaway from moving forward, Rodolfo adds, in his own language, "If the Chinese see you they'll kill you!"

He makes a slashing gesture across his throat, repeating the words "Chinese" and "officers" over and over. The stowaway sees this, and his lips part. He neither moves forward nor does he return to the compartment where he's been hiding.

"*Vaya, vaya,*" Rodolfo keeps saying, "Go back, go back," and when the stowaway still doesn't move—his hands are in the air, fingertips up, palms exposed—Rodolfo says again, "If the Chinese they see you, they'll kill you, *van a matar,* so go back, please, *por favor, amigo, vaya, vaya.*"

The stowaway remains rooted to that spot on the deck. Rodolfo resumes the slashing motion across his throat while saying, "*El capitan, el capitan.*" Finally, a look of comprehension ebbs across the young man's face. Rodolfo quickens the sawing motion of his forefinger against his throat, for it seems as though the young man's understanding is so hazy, and so weak, it might vanish at any moment.

"Your friend," he says, "is dead. *Es muerto, su amigo . . .*"

The stowaway's shoulders drop. His lower lip trembles. "*Lo siento,*" Rodolfo says, and to explain further he forms a circle with his thumb and forefinger, and he holds it over his eyes. "Filipinos good," he explains, "*Son buenos, los Filipinos.*" The stowaway looks weakened, as though barely able to stand, and this encourages the bosun. Rodolfo tugs at the corners of his eyes and says, "Chinese bad. *Son malos, son muy malos . . .*"

He pauses and looks down. He realizes he's breathing hard. "*Su amigo,*" he explains once more, "*es muerto, su amigo, lo siento.* I'm sorry."

They both hear heavy, slapping footsteps. Rodolfo spins around—thank God it's Manuel, and not one of the other able-bodies, coming down the port side. When Manuel spots the stowaway, he stops and hangs his head like a guilty child; Rodolfo watches him swear under his breath, and rub his eyes as though they were suddenly painful. He comes forward, stopping about two metres from the bosun. Rodolfo doesn't even nod at Manuel. Instead, he moves toward the stowaway, and touches the young man's elbow, and gestures toward the compartment in which he'd been hiding.

"Wait here," he says. "*Espéra,* please, wait for me, *por favor.*"

The enclosure is less than two metres high, and barely a metre across. The stowaway bends himself around the bar spanning the entance, and crouches into its shadows.

"Wait for me," Rodolfo says again, "*Espéra.*"

He straightens and looks at Manuel.

"Go to work," he says in Tagalog. "Say nothing, act normally, say nothing . . ."

"Yes, yes, of course, Bose, whatever you say."

Rodolfo retreats to his cabin, where he calms himself for a few minutes before returning to the deck. He spends the morning helping his ABs swab and paint the port side. After an hour, he takes a can of primer and a brush, and he moves off by himself, away from the ABs he doesn't trust. The sun burns hot on the back of his neck, and his paintbrush feels heavy. He tries not to think of the stowaway, crouching close by in the gloom of a storage nook, and fails—the man's face is in every brush stroke, and in every stretch of metal, and in the stark blue sheet of the sky. At times he has to stop, and close his eyes, and rest his forehead on the back of his arm.

When the morning shift ends, he instructs his ABs to clean and store their brushes. Rodolfo returns to the seamen level, where he washes, and changes his clothes, and combs his hair. His feet move over dimly lit hallways. They strike against grated metal steps. He reaches the mess, and takes a tray of barbecue and rice and steamed bok choy. He heads toward a table occupied by the oiler, the fitter, and the third engineer, Broas.

He sits. He hears the scrape of chair legs against metal floor, and he hears greetings—"Bose, Bosun"—though they seem to come from far away. The steam from his food rises into his face, moistening his pores. He takes a bite of meat, only to find it tastes of sawdust. He is alone, in a bubble, quarantined by what he knows. Far off, there is the murmur of conversation, and there is the sound of four men, struggling to swallow, each one with his eyes glumly turned toward his food. Rodolfo finally puts his fork down, for he can no longer eat, not with what he has to say, choking its way up from the base of his throat. *There is hope,* he wants to tell them, *he had a Bible* . . . but no, no, that wouldn't make sense, at least not yet, at least not until they know.

In the plainest of voices, he says, "We have company . . ."

The three men look at him.

"We have company," the bosun says again, looking only at his food.

The other three men glance at one another, refusing to guess what this might mean. Rodolfo keeps his head lowered. He finally pricks the silence by saying, in a voice now hushed, "I'm sorry. There's another. I'm sorry."

~

That night, the only man who doesn't come is Manuel. The others wait for a minute or two, wondering what has happened to him, before beginning.

"So," the electrician eventually says, "what's this all about?"

"Yes," says the second cook, "what's happening?"

Broas looks at them both. Though he still wears sunglasses, he now moves, if somewhat hesitantly, without a white cane. "This morning," he says, "Rodolfo found another."

"Another?" says the second cook. "Another *what?*"

No one answers.

"My God," the electrician says. "Another stowaway? On board? Is this right?"

The others nod.

"He left him in an enclosure under a catwalk," Broas explains.

"This can't be! The boat, it's . . ."

"Yes," says Juanito. "It's been cursed. I can feel it." And with this statement everyone starts whispering at once.

"What do we do?" someone says.

"I don't know. I just know I've had it."

"Yes, I've had it too."

"They've gone too far, those damn officers."

"It's like they think they're gods."

"We have to stop them."

"Yes, yes, of course, but how?"

"We save this stowaway. He is a religious man."

"Yes, yes, we have to."

"The question is how."

"There must be a way."

"And if the officers find out?"

"They can't."

"No, no, if they did . . ."

"They'd kill us, they would."

"They're godless . . ."

"And cruel . . ."

"And I think even a little crazy."

"So what do we do?"

There is another pause.

"The bosun," Juanito finally says. "The bosun knows the boat better than any of us. He could hide him somewhere down below, maybe in one of the container levels."

"Yes," Broas says, "That's a good idea. He can bring him food. The cook can help."

Rodolfo's eyes scan the room.

"I don't know . . ." Rodolfo says, though even as he does he understands that they are right, that as the bosun he's the only one whose presence, anywhere on board, won't be questioned.

"But don't tell us exactly where you put him," Juanito adds. "Only you should know. If one of us is found out, we won't be able to tell if we don't know. If they try to do something, it won't matter. Only you can know. Our job will be to protect you."

The fitter, second cook and electrician all nod, and mutter, "Yes, it's the only thing we can do." Rodolfo looks imploringly at Broas; he too nods. Then they all turn silent, if only to allow the gravity of what they've decided to sink in.

"Maybe," Broas says, "we can get him off the boat somehow . . ."

No one speaks, for it is understood they cannot yet construct this part of the plan, and that what they are heading toward is unknowable.

"This will be difficult," Broas adds. Again, no one speaks, aside from a murmured agreement. After another minute, Broas stands; he has begun working again, and has to report for his watch in the engine room. When he has left, Rodolfo rises from his seat on the oiler's spare bed, as does the second cook. The two leave together, and descend one flight of stairs to the crew mess level. The second cook unlocks the door. As Rodolfo keeps guard, he gathers slices of bread and apples, and fills a plastic container with drinking water. He puts them all in a plastic bag, and hands them to Rodolfo.

"Good luck," he says, and they part at the door of the mess. Rodolfo descends another flight of stairs and exits at the rear of the accommodation, only to find that a damp, obscuring fog has come up. *Good,* he thinks, and from this point he's careful to stick to shadow, using his knowledge of the big ship's deck to guide him through stretches of black.

FOURTEEN

He doesn't know whether the person holding the flashlight is the sailor who found him earlier, or one of the officers who'd gotten rid of Gheorghe, and he doesn't care. His head is bursting, his body is racked with chills, his throat feels constricted and raw. He draws his legs up to his chest and rests the side of his face on his kneecaps.

"*Amigo,*" he hears.

He lifts his head and looks into the glare.

"*Amigo,*" he hears again, the voice a loud hiss. "Come, *venga.*"

For a time Daniel remains tucked in his enclosure, his arms wrapped around his legs. Slowly, he manoeuvres himself around the bar spanning the cubbyhole, a tight, cramping pain issuing through his back and legs. He looks up and sees the sailor he first met on deck, a forefinger across his lips.

The two men move along the length of the big ship, their way lit only by running lights and the moon's glimmer. They quickly pass the accommodation, and reach a passageway at the very back of the ship, in an area called the afterpart. Again, the bosun holds a forefinger to his lips; when Daniel nods he opens the metal door, the accompanying squeak an eruption in the quiet of the night.

Both men freeze. A light from inside the entranceway fans

over the deck. They wait, listening for anything other than the thrum of the engine and their own nervous breathing. Together, they slip into the passage, and move down a flight of steps, the sailor stopping in front of a heavy blue door. He opens it and the two men are greeted by the airy roar of the engine. They stand for a second on a grated metal parapet before moving down narrow steps, Daniel careful to keep both hands on the thin yellow railings. He is halfway down when he spots a man standing at the far end of the engine block, looking at him through sunglasses. Daniel freezes, thinking they have been caught, and is surprised when the man does nothing but nod in their direction.

On the floor of the engine room, Daniel follows the sailor along a short stretch past the front of the main engine and into a room containing the steering apparatus. This room is small, the only noise the squeaking of steering rams, and the spill of sound coming from the engine room. Daniel watches as the sailor pulls a set of keys from his pocket and crosses the floor of the steering room, where he stops at a locked door on the bow side. Here he tries one key after another, Daniel understanding that they'll be heading to a place rarely visited. When the sailor finally finds a key that fits, he turns to Daniel and says, yet again, "*Venga* . . ." and the two men step into a stairwell lit only by yellow emergency lights.

The sailor says to Daniel, "All right, we are safe, *seguro* . . ."

Daniel nods. Yet as he follows the sailor down flights of stairs, bypassing all of the container holds, he wants nothing more than to turn back. As they burrow deeper and deeper the air becomes hot, and stale, and thin, and if there's any place he doesn't want to be it is here, in the tomblike depths of the ship. His thoughts turn irrational—the sailor wears a large knife, and Daniel asks himself if he could be leading him somewhere to be killed. They pass through yet another doorway, into one of the two tunnels that run along the very bottom of the hull. It's like stepping into a hot, damp sponge, the air so thick it feels like something they have to push against. Daniel's pulse is reverberating through his forehead, and he can feel his legs turn weak—the tunnel is barely a metre wide, and lit only with the faint glow of emergency lights.

The sailor turns and says, "Please, no worry, *ne preocupa,* all is safe, all is *seguro* . . ."

Daniel nods. Droplets of sweat have appeared on the sailor's forehead, and on his upper lip, and on his thick, hairless forearms. "*Seguro, seguro* . . ." he keeps saying before turning and walking down the airless tunnel. Daniel follows. His stomach is churning, and he fears he might be ill. The sailor stops in front of an empty buoyancy tank. He opens it while motioning for Daniel to step inside. When he does, the bosun steps into the large, dank space behind him, and hands him the plastic bag.

Daniel takes it and looks inside. Though the prospect of eating sickens him—he's too afraid of being left alone, here, with whatever thoughts his mind might generate—he grabs the water jug and gulps, some of the cool liquid dribbling down the side of his mouth. When he's finished, he looks at Rodolfo. He is sweating, badly, and his face feels hot.

"You're from Romania?" Rodolfo asks. "*Es de Rumania?*"

Daniel nods.

"It's a terrible place? *Un lugar terrible?*"

"*Sí,*" he croaks, "it's terrible," though what he really wants to tell the sailor is that it wasn't always that way, that the capital was once the Paris of the East and that at least two people once found love there. Without understanding why, he reaches into his shirt pocket, and pulls out his photograph of Elena. He passes it to the bosun.

"*Su mujer?*" the sailor asks. "Your wife?"

Daniel shakes his head and says, "No, no, no. *Novia.*"

"Aaaah, your sweetheart . . ."

Daniel watches as the sailor looks at Elena, who is smiling in the glow of the flashlight.

"*Bella,*" the sailor says. "*Muy, muy bella.*"

He hands the crinkled photo back. Daniel takes it, and as he looks at Elena he thinks that the sailor is right, that all the light of the world must be contained within the roundness of her cheeks, and in the length of her eyelashes, and in the swirl of chestnut hair around her face. Looking at her, he chokes back both his fear and his near-desperate longing for *ţuică*.

He carefully slides the photograph back into his shirt pocket.

"One week," Rodolfo says, "you'll be here one week, *una semana, mas o menos.*"

Daniel nods.

"Do not go out," Rodolfo says. "Never leave this compartment." To indicate his meaning, he waves his arms in front of him, the flashlight beam dancing over the walls of the tank. "*No salga, nunca salga, comprende, amigo?* It's very important, *es muy importante.*"

Again, Daniel nods.

Rodolfo crosses a finger over his lips and says, "Shhhhhhhhhhh. All the time," he adds, "*todo el tiempo,* no noise."

Again, Daniel nods, though as he does another chill, this one worse than the others, ripples through him. With it comes a sharpening of the fear that he will lose his mind, down here, in this hot airless tank.

He squeezes his eyes shut, and reaches into the oversized pocket of his cargo pants, and runs a thumb over the cover of the Bible. His eyes burn. He has never felt so sick. He looks at

Rodolfo, who is pointing at Daniel's pocket and saying, "What do you have? *Qué tiene?*"

Daniel pulls out the Bible, and with shaky hands passes it to the sailor. Rodolfo accepts it, saying, "*Ah, tu Biblia,*" and he begins flipping through the pages, a smile coming to his face when he lands on his favourite page. He then hands the Bible back to Daniel, who sees the book opened to Psalm 91, a passage he barely remembers from Sunday morning sermons.

"Do you want to pray?" Rodolfo says. "*Quiere rezar?*"

Daniel nods, and watches as Rodolfo lowers himself to his knees. Daniel kneels painfully beside him, every joint in his body calling for alcohol. Rodolfo then motions toward the open page, gesturing that Daniel should read along. And though he tries, his mind is swimming and his Spanish is still poor and he only catches the gist of the words, the real comfort coming from the lilt of the sailor's voice as he quotes, from memory, in his own language, the following passage:

> *You should not be afraid of the terror by night; nor of the arrow that flies by day;*
>
> *Nor of the pestilence that walks in darkness; nor of the destruction that comes at noonday.*
>
> *A thousand shall fall at your side, and ten thousand at your right hand; but it shall not happen to you.*
>
> *For only with your eyes will you behold and see the reward of the wicked.*
>
> *Because you have made the Lord your habitation, no evil will befall you, and neither will any plague come upon your dwelling.*
>
> *For He has charged His Angels to guard you wherever you go.*

When he's finished Rodolfo stands. As he does, he understands that, for better or worse, all the moments of his life have
conspired to bring him to here, in this corroded tank, in the sweltering depths of the *Maersk Dubai*. "Do you believe in God?" he
asks Daniel. "*En Dios?*"

Daniel blinks, and confuses himself by saying, "*Sí.*"

Rodolfo pulls a penlight out of his pocket and hands it to the
boy. The stowaway takes it and turns it on, a small light dashing
over bare, splotchy walls. He notices a curling of old hoses in the
corner.

"This will be difficult for you," Rodolfo says in his own language. "You are frightened, and your *novia* is not here. I'm sorry.
Lo siento. I can't do anything about it."

The stowaway looks at him, clearly wishing he could understand more.

"I will come every night and give you food." Rodolfo gestures
toward his opened mouth. "I will bring you *comida,* I promise, *te
prometo,* I will bring you *agua y comida.* You'll be safe, *seguro, te prometo,*
I promise."

The stowaway nods.

"*Buena suerte,*" Rodolfo adds, to which the stowaway says only,
"*Gracias.*"

Rodolfo enters the tunnel. Instead of turning left, and retrac-
ing his steps back through the steering and engine rooms, he turns
right and exits via a stairway at the bow, emerging in the shelter of
the forecastle. He shuts off his flashlight so as to not be spotted
by anyone who might be in the wheelroom. The night is still hazy,
the moon lost behind a blanket of mist. As he looks out over a
flat, jet-black sea, he notes that the only movement of air is being
caused by the boat itself.

He takes a deep breath, and finds himself taking stock of all the things that he really and truly knows.

I am a bosun, he thinks. *I am a bosun, and I am from a poor country, and every minute I miss my wife and children.*

He thinks hard, and adds something else. *No one,* he thinks, *knows this boat like I do. No one knows her tunnels, her decks, her storage compartments. No one knows the way she lists in high seas, the way she groans when striking the peak of a whitecap, the way she complains like an old woman when docked too forcefully.*

He then questions whether these are good things, and whether these are the sorts of things that should represent a life half over. He doesn't know. He is, however, certain of one thing, and he makes this the final addition to his list.

This, he thinks, *is a thing that is happening to me.*

FIFTEEN

They come to the oiler not as dreams, exactly, but as the residue of dreams, recalled in the seconds after waking. They come to him as afterimages, as waxy pavement reflections, as the lights over Roxas Boulevard, looking bleary and sullen and warm. They come to him as the beckonings of nightclub shills, as the pleas of Chiclet kids, as the incessant honking of jeepneys, and with these visions come the acrid scent of diesel, and the hint of a sea breeze over traffic, and the honied smoke of street vendors.

One moment he is outside, looking down, and a second later he is in the club, swooping over people who are laughing and smoking cigarettes and drinking whisky, and a second after that he's on stage, looking out, smoking a cigarette and waiting for the first notes of "My Way" to come from the karaoke machine. He's eighteen, and he's making money, and who knows? Maybe he'll turn into a film star or a politician one day. Best of all, there are women, looking at him, sharing their thoughts with the subtlest lowering of an eyelid, or with the slightly suggestive way they hold their cigarettes. He is eighteen, and he's the king of a big city in the tropics, and he will never, ever, be a day older.

Juanito's eyes snap open, his heart speeding. He rises, washes, tries to eat breakfast, and descends to the engine room. *Don't think,* he keeps saying to himself. *Don't think about the stowaway, don't think about what he must be going through, don't think about what will happen if the officers find him. Don't think, don't think, don't think.*

Midway through his shift, the chief engineer comes and stands next to him. Juanito stops working and faces the man.

"Here," the officer says, and he hands him a cigarette. Juanito nods his thanks and lights it, the chief engineer heading back to the control room. As Juanito inhales, he wonders why the chief engineer would choose this morning to offer him a cigarette. Yes, it could be a chance occurrence—it has happened before, though not very often, and when it does it's generally because his boss is happy about some news from home. Or it could be that he's letting the oiler know he has his eye on him, and that any more small kindnesses would now come with a cost attached. This is a possibility, though it is equally true there had been something sheepish in the way the chief engineer had handed over the cigarette, as though embarrassed by all that has happened.

Oiler, please. Don't think . . .

At supper he finds himself in the serving line, chatting with the second cook, struggling to act as though a tension has not returned to the *Maersk Dubai.* (It's no use: eyes are watching him; he can feel them on his back, heating his skin, boring their way into his thoughts.) In the middle of their conversation, the second cook wordlessly deposits an extra piece of chicken on Juanito's tray. The oiler sits and begins eating, though as he does he keeps an eye on Rodolfo, the fitter and the electrician as *they* move through the serving line—one is given an extra potato, another a slightly higher mounding of greens, another an apple he won't eat.

They all join him, and as they eat they struggle to maintain a conversation about Filipino basketball, and what the Pepsi Mega has been up to lately. Two tables over, the four ABs who have separated themselves from the other Filipinos—Juanito barely even knows their names—sit together, and if one of them happens to look over, the oiler finds himself wondering if the glance was innocent, or whether it was designed to gather information. By the time Juanito leaves, the extra chicken leg has been wrapped in a paper napkin, and the napkin has been slipped into a pocket.

That night, he paces as he waits for them to come. Around nine o'clock he hears footsteps along the corridor, prompting him to throw open the door of his cabin and look out expectantly. Yet instead of seeing the faces of Ariel Broas and the others, he sees the second officer, inexplicably walking along one of the seamen levels. Their glances meet, and the second officer grins slightly. Juanito feels his face flush and grow hot. He nods, and then moves across the corridor to the washroom, where he leans over one of the enamel sinks.

Stupid, he thinks. *How could you have been so stupid?*

Shutting his eyes, he replays the second officer's grin in his mind, each time colouring it a different way: first a completely innocent greeting, then a taunt, then an icy way of saying, *We know, Oiler, we do.* When he realizes he can no longer picture the grin—by this point he's not even sure there *was* one—he looks at himself in the mirror, and silently indicts himself for being a poor man from a poor Asian country.

He crosses back to his cabin, and resumes his wait; he is lost now, in his own, perturbed thoughts. When he hears the cabin door handle turn, it feels as though he's being vacuumed through a tunnel, the details of his room—two beds, dresser, porthole—

blurring with movement. The fitter and second cook come in. Ariel Broas is next, followed by the electrician and then, after another minute, Rodolfo and Manuel. Everyone but Juanito takes a seat.

"Oiler," the second cook says, "what is it?"

"The second officer was just here."

"He was here?" the electrician asks.

"No, outside, in the hallway. I thought his footsteps were yours. I opened the door . . ."

There is an extended silence, each man thinking the same thing: *It is so hard, this. It is so, so hard.*

"We need a code," Broas says.

"Yes," they all echo.

"A special knock, so we know if an officer comes."

There is more hushed agreement, and then Broas says, "Two knocks, one knock, two knocks. Is that all right?"

"Fine, fine," they all mumble, and before Rodolfo collects the food each has taken from the seamen's mess, Juanito suggests they give a code name for the stowaway, and that they use it, always, in case someone happens to overhear their conversation. Again, this suggestion is met with agreement and another long pause. Rodolfo suggests they call him the *ibon,* the Tagalog word for "bird."

"Fine," says Broas, who then rises and says good-night. Though his eyes are still sensitive to light, he can now move under his own direction, and when enough time has passed for him to reach the engine room, Rodolfo stands as well. He leaves with a paper bag containing that night's food, his steps growing fainter and fainter along the corridor.

~

That night, Juanito has a restless sleep, for he is again haunted by the spectres of his old life, when he was a pop star in the night-clubs of Roxas Boulevard, and the world was his for the asking. At breakfast, he takes his tray and sits opposite the bosun. Seconds pass before the two men look at each other, the bosun giving a barely perceptible nod.

Good, Juanito thinks, *he fed him,* and for the first time in days he tastes his food—the second cook has chopped smoky red chilis into the eggs, and the flavour reminds him of his favourite food stall back home. After breakfast, he moves down to the engine room and begins work on one of the water coolers, which has not been registering at a normal pressure—the suspicion is that there are cracked lines in the system, and that water is leaking through the crankcase. He has started disassembling the cooler when an alarm rings through the intercom. A second later, he hears the captain's voice, calling all men on deck.

Shit, Juanito thinks, and he moves toward the stairs, cursing the way fire drills always seem to happen when they are their busiest. He steps on deck. The wind has kicked up, banishing the fog of the past few days, the big ship rolling up and over each trough in a slow figure-eight motion. The sun is as white as ash, and he wishes he'd remembered to bring his sunglasses.

Juanito reports to his station and waits for the captain to indicate where the make-believe fire is raging—there, he gestures, on the starboard side, beside the gunwale, as if a blaze could really appear on a stretch of cold, barren steel. It's the oiler's job to help unroll one of the eighteen-metre hoses attached to the forward facing of the accommodation. A minute after doing so, he and one of the able-bodies don fire suits and direct a jet of water at the imaginary flame; the spray hits the wind that is channelling over the side of the boat, and blows it back over the deck. As he works, it occurs to him that something is different that day, the captain letting the drill unfold at the sluggish pace chosen by the sailors. This, he thinks, is odd, for speed is the number-one requirement when containing a blaze, and usually the two officers spend the whole drill hollering at them to hurry.

He looks around. Sunlight is refracting off water vapour in the air, causing the deck to spark with colour. He then notices that neither the chief nor the second officer is on deck, where the fire is supposedly raging out of control. This, too, is strange, for during a fire drill the rules are unvarying: all hands on deck, with the possible exception of men assigned to fight fires below. The drill goes on, and as it does it gains a surreal quality, as though the same moments are playing themselves out, over and over, like the repetition of a dream. Finally, the water is shut off. The seamen return hoses and pack up their asbestos suits. Under the direction of the bosun, they winch the lifeboats back into place. By the time the fire drill has ended, the oiler's morning shift is over. He feels tired from standing in the hot sun, and from commanding the heavy spray. The dye from the fire hose has turned his hands a tawny red, so he decides to go to his cabin to wash, and to change his clothes, before lunch. He passes through doors, marches up a flight of stairs, and steps into the seamen's level.

Like all Filipino sailors, he keeps the outside of his room as clean as he does the inside—there is no graffiti scribbled on the door frame, and there are no *Playboy* centrefolds tacked to the door. His shoes are placed neatly to the side, on a grey rubber mat that he cleans periodically as well. He pulls a ring of keys from his pocket and moves to unlock the door, only to find that it swings open, practically by itself. He enters, and stops. His lips part. The

clues left behind are so obvious it is clear they want him to know
they've been there: drawers open, closet door left ajar, a pillow on
the floor. Never has his room been this way.

Juanito slumps on his bunk and stares at a spot on the wall
across from him. *I'm just an oiler. I shouldn't have to do this. I'm not
being paid for this.* He turns, swings his feet onto his bunk, and stares
up at the ceiling. A heavy pain comes to the front of his head. He
folds his hands over his chest, and closes his eyes, and struggles
to fight the feeling that the officers have not only been inside his
room, but inside of *him*.

That night, the other sailors come to his cabin again, Juanito
admitting them only after he hears the code, tapped so lightly as
to barely be audible. They file in: Ariel Broas, his face looking pale
and sensitive, along with the second cook, the bosun, the fitter,
and the electrician. Manuel comes a few minutes later, looking jittery and afraid; as he sits, he fumbles to light a cigarette, his hands
shaking so badly he can barely strike the match. The others say
nothing, and in so doing indicate that their cabins have been vio-
lated as well. When eleven o'clock comes, Broas leaves for his
watchman's post in the engine room. Rodolfo rises five minutes
afterwards to take that day's provisions to the *ibon*. As he does, the
other men keep their heads lowered, for they all feel certain that
tonight will be the night when they will hear the bosun call for
help, and they'll be forced to fight.

Rodolfo moves along the hallway. One hand is gripping the
bag with the stowaway's food, the other his bosun's knife, and as
he moves he thinks, *Thank God they didn't find the logbook.* The sign-
posts rush past him: poop deck, afterpart, Broas waving him
through the engine room. Then, the steering room, the cargo
shaft, and the tunnel, with its perpetually hot and stifling air. As

he moves through the gloom, it occurs to him that the officers do not know everything—if they did, he would not have been allowed to visit the *ibon* unbothered. His thoughts whir. Yes, they must know that another stowaway is on board, or they wouldn't have searched the cabins. Yet what they don't know is where he's being kept, and they don't know that the bosun is the one feeding the stowaway. As Rodolfo moves along the tunnel, his route lit by a procession of emergency lights, a single oppressive thought keeps running through his head.

It's only a matter of time.

When he reaches the enclosure he crouches and shines his flashlight at the stowaway, who is curled into a fetal position, facing the rear wall of the compartment. The boy's face turns slowly, his eyes squinting into the light. He stands painfully and limps toward the bosun.

Rodolfo holds out the sack. The stowaway takes it, Rodolfo watching as he gulps from the water bottle. The young man's hands are shaky, and when some of the contents spill down his shirt front he stops and looks up, as though suddenly aware of his surroundings. His hair is standing up in greasy spikes, and his clothes are stained from lying on the oily floor. When he has finished drinking, he plunges a dirty hand into the paper sack and pulls out a pork rib; soon, his mouth is rimmed with barbecue sauce. When the bone is stripped of flesh, he drops it and starts pulling out handfuls of cold noodles and stuffing them into his mouth.

"*Gracias,*" he says, breathing hard.

A thousand plans run through Rodolfo's head—he should warn him, or move him, or tell him to hide behind the wrecked hoses mounded in the corner of the tank. Yet in his heart of hearts, he can think of nothing that will help.

The *ibon* is chewing more slowly. Now that the first fiery pangs of his hunger are sated, Rodolfo can tell there is little to savour in the tangy rubberiness of the noodles. Daniel stops chewing, and looks at the bosun. His eyes are round and dark and exhausted.

"*Está bien?*" Rodolfo asks.

"*Sí, sí,*" says the stowaway.

"I cannot stay long tonight, *lo siento, no puedo quedar.*"

"*Sí.*"

"Things are very busy, *muy ocupado*. But everything's okay. Everything's fine."

"*Gracias, gracias.*"

"Yes, *todo está bien,* you don't need to worry."

"*Bueno, muy bueno, gracias.*"

"Okay, *adios,* I see you tomorrow, *nos vemos mañana,*" and with that Rodolfo turns and quickly retraces his steps along the tunnel and up through the engine room, feeling puzzled when he reaches his cabin without having had to defend himself. He steps inside, undresses, lies down, and stays awake all night, for it feels as though the ghosts of the officers are still in his cabin, going through his things, chilling the air. When he can stand it no longer, he rises from his bunk and reads from his Bible; much later, he watches the sun rise bursting and red from his porthole window. His eyes burn; he can barely think straight; he gets dressed. No amount of cold water, splashed on his face, or hot coffee, consumed over a plate of untouched eggs, helps. Time leapfrogs—one second he is in the mess, a second later he finds himself on deck, with no recollection of what passed between the two moments.

The sun is seeping through drifts of wispy cloud, and a slight cool breeze is blowing crosswise over the deck. Throughout his shift, he closely watches Angel, Carmelito, Marlou and Joe. How little he knows them, how little he understands of their lives—perhaps, he thinks, this is the reason he cannot trust them now. As they work, he does his best to search their faces for signs of betrayal. From behind the lenses of dark wire-frame glasses, he studies every glance and every nod, until he begins to pick up something beyond the discomfort felt by all of the sailors on board—something with shades of cunning, and subterfuge, and guilt. If anyone is passing information on to the officers, it has to be them. It is the only explanation.

That night, when seven exhausted men gather in the cabin of Juanito Ilagan, Rodolfo tells them, "It could be the other ABs. We all work so closely together—who knows what they might have picked up? Who knows what they might have overheard?"

The others mumble and continue looking at the floor. A second passes, Manuel fragmenting the silence by saying, "Yes, yes, you must be right, Bose."

"All right," Broas says. "Then we have to address this. No more ignoring the other four at the mess. We have to mingle with them—it's too obvious. And no more talking about the *ibon* on deck, or in the WCs, or in the corridors. We have to be more careful. Does everybody understand?"

They do not answer or so much as look up. Juanito knows why, for he feels the same abandonment of hope clawing at him as well. He looks at the third engineer, so as to wordlessly suggest that they do something to improve the morale of their little group. Broas returns the glance—because they are good friends, and because they work together in the engine room, and because they come from the same province, a decision passes silently between them.

"There was a letter," Juanito announces.

Rodolfo looks up. "A letter?"

"Ariel and I wrote a letter. To that Filipino priest in Houston. I mailed it in Algeciras. We told him everything."

"Yes," Broas adds. "We must make it to Houston. We have to last another week, week and a half—it all depends on the weather. If we make it to Houston, something might happen there. The Coast Guard or the Port Authority will meet us there, we can only hope."

There is the slightest lifting of voices in the room.

"Yes, yes," they stammer, "we have to make it to Houston."

SIXTEEN

As he writhes on the oily floor, Daniel wonders whether he will die from the chills running through his body, and from the pain issuing through every joint. His head pounds, his back and neck ache, he keeps slipping in and out of consciousness, often awakening with the belief he's been buried alive in an oven. His fingertips burn, his skin itches, his pulse speeds and then stops altogether, only to continue as a pounding, irregular lurch. He sees things, too—eels, furred at the head and tail, slithering over his legs. Spiders the size of small dogs, with grins and antennae, crawling over the walls. Or: he comes awake from a feverish dream and finds that his cell is a field of lime green sunflowers, with Daniel in the middle, frantically looking in every direction and seeing only more lime green flowers, and though he wants to scream for *ţuică* he can do nothing but hold his head and squeeze his eyes and pray that he isn't going permanently mad.

Then, as though a switch has been thrown, his visions downgrade to gauzy spectres. The chills dissipate, the pain in his muscles and joints subsides, and over the next half day his thoughts reorder. The only residue is a draining sadness, and the feeling that he is now empty inside—gone is the grace bequeathed to him by family, and the larceny bred into him by Romania. With this emptiness comes the feeling that, at any moment, he might succumb to tears.

He turns on his flashlight and inspects the floor, the ceiling, the flaking walls. At the corner of the cell is the pile of torn cloth hoses, wound into the shape of a barrel. He spots a hairline fissure, running along the top of the enclosure, and to pass the time he imagines he's an explorer, and that the crack is a river coursing through the leafy depths of the Amazon. Or India. Yes, India—he's on a trek through the jungle, seeing tigers and ruins and beautiful women with ruby red dots on their foreheads.

He spends hours searching the tank for the best place to sit. Though he eventually concludes that the perfect spot doesn't exist, he finds a shallow, bowl-shaped impression near one of the corners that is big enough to cup one haunch comfortably. He also finds a stretch of space near the centre of the compartment where the floor evens and he can lie flat. Here, he has his first real sleep since boarding the *Maersk Dubai*—with his mind so tired from hallucinating, his dreams are light, and barely remembered when he awakes. He sniffles and stands, and despite the sailor's warning, he ducks into the tunnel and slips into the tank beside his, where he urinates against the back wall. Exhausted, he re-enters his enclosure, lies down on his flat space, and falls asleep again. This time, he awakes feeling filthy, and wishing only that his sadness would evaporate in the same way his chills and delirium had.

He examines the hoses in the corner. There are three of them, two green and one black. He works slowly and meticulously, mentally cataloguing every spot where the cloth has grown thin. Working by the weak beam of his penlight, he unravels the hoses as best as he can and then coils them into a tight stack, the black hose between the two green hoses. He sits in the corner, and looks at his efforts. After a time he turns off his penlight. In the darkness, he finds himself thinking of home, and of Elena, so he turns his penlight back on, and trains it on the coiling of hoses—he's in India again, a python rising from the basket, Daniel controlling the movements of the animal with notes played on a frigolet. When the beam cast by his penlight begins to dim, he turns it off, and is plunged into darkness. To occupy his thoughts, he listens to music, played on a *ṭambal* in his head—after a while, it gets so he can listen to entire folk songs, from start to finish, playing in his mind. He rests his face against his kneecaps—despite his best intentions, it was inevitable that the music would make him think of home. He hears his mother speaking to him, and he sees the way that Elena's chestnut hair turns upward as it meets her shoulders. Alone in his cell, he can hear how the wind sounds when it blows over the mountains, rustling the pines as though they were wood-block chimes.

He hears footsteps and skitters to the corner of his enclosure, where he hides behind the coiling of hoses: every time, he worries it might be an officer, coming to kill him. A light falls over the tank, settling at Daniel's feet.

"*Hola,*" the sailor says.

He enters and, as always, hands Daniel a bag and plastic water jug. Daniel takes them and nods his thanks before drinking deeply. When he finishes, he begins working on his dinner: barbecued ribs in sauce, boiled potato halves, green beans. The sailor moves to the far side of the enclosure, and leans against one of the dry, flaking walls. It is the fourth night he has visited, and each time he speaks less and less, something Daniel attributes to the awkwardness imposed by the difference in language. As he eats, he glances at the sailor, who looks drawn and tired. He is also tapping his right foot, and the fingers on his left hand are drumming against the tank wall.

"Are you all right?" Daniel asks in Romanian. He then switches to Spanish, and says, "*Está bien?*"

"Sí," the sailor says, "of course, *por supuesto.*"

Daniel bites into a boiled potato and swallows more water.

"*Los capitanos,*" Daniel catches himself saying, "*ellos saben?* They know?"

The sailor stops fidgeting, and his mouth purses. A lattice of wrinkles appears at the corner of the man's eyes, and in the space separating his eyebrows. Just as quickly, the sailor seems to catch himself, and forces himself to smile.

"No, brother," he answers, "don't worry, *no preocupa.*"

Daniel studies the man. Something is happening, he knows it. Somehow, he can no longer describe the sailor's face as a soft, round, kind one.

"*Gracias,*" he says.

"*De nada.*"

Again, Daniel asks, "Everything is all right, *todo esta bien?*"

"Oh yes," the sailor says, "*sí, sí, sí.*"

They stand. Daniel's head roars with thoughts.

"Your flashlight," the sailor says, "*es buena?*"

When Daniel doesn't understand, the sailor motions at Daniel's breast pocket, where he keeps the penlight. He says it again, "*Es buena, su luz?*" and because he's distracted by the change that has come over the sailor, Daniel again misunderstands the question and says, "Sí, *sí, es buena, gracias.*" The sailor says something long and complicated, in a jumble of English and Spanish.

Daniel nods dumbly, and the sailor repeats himself, this time gesturing with his fingers. Finally, Daniel understands that the man is talking about batteries, about *pilas,* and how if Daniel needs new ones he will try to bring them.

"*Gracias,*" Daniel says.

Again, they look at each other. Daniel feels chilled, and weary. He's about to ask the sailor for more information, and is formulating a sentence when the man says *adiós* and ducks into the corridor.

Daniel pokes his head out and watches him walk quickly away—when he reaches the rear of the boat, a white light is cast through the opened door. Then, with a clank, the tunnel returns to a mustard gloom. Daniel steps into the tunnel himself and begins walking along its length. As he reaches each buoyancy tank, he stops and shines the faltering beam of his penlight inside. Most are empty, though some are filled with junk: rusting chains and ripped hoses and, in the case of one tank about two-thirds of the way along, an old coffee urn, the cord wrapped loosely around its rusting body. Daniel reaches the end of the corridor and places his hand on the door latch. He imagines turning it. He imagines breathing cool air and blinking away white light. Mostly he has to fight the urge to leave his sanctuary and find out what was causing the sailor's tense, grey expression.

Instead, he turns and walks the entire length of the tunnel; by the time he reaches the other end, he is damp with perspiration. Breathing hard, he puts a hand on the door latch. He hesitates, his face resting against his arm, and he thinks of Gheorghe. After a minute, he moves back along the tunnel. This time, as he steps inside his hiding place, he starts to think that the officers have probably figured out he is hiding there, and that they are just waiting for the right time to throw him overboard.

He surprises himself by falling to his knees, and placing the palms of his hands together, and letting his head fill with prayer. Then he lies down, rubbing the Bible in his pocket. After a time, he feels the onset of sleep. *Probably,* he thinks, *I will die here.* And though he's had this thought many times since he was first hidden in the bottom of the *Maersk Dubai,* this time it spawns nothing beyond a return of that terrible hollow sensation. His flashlight starts to flicker. He switches it off, the darkness now swirling with the faces of the children he will never have, each one pale skinned and dark haired and happy. He wonders if it's possible to say goodbye to those who have never existed, and who never will exist.

He rolls onto his side, pulling the Bible from his pants' pocket and using it as a pillow. As he lies in the darkness, he listens again to Romanian folk songs in his head, and this causes him to think of the other things he will miss: thunderstorms, the antics of his younger cousins, wooden churches—he could go on and on. And he does—hiking in the Carpathians, the smell of frying pork rind, the onset of spring—for he feels it is important to not let the bitterness felt by Romanians colour *all* of the life he has had. He knows his list is far from complete—the smell of coffee, bathing in hot water, mornings in autumn—and so he promises himself he won't sleep, that he'll only close his eyes to stop their smarting. Immediately, his thoughts grow slow and disordered. Sleep covers him like a comforter, and at first he dozes peacefully. Gradually, his body begins to shift on the floor of the cargo hold, the precursors of images entering his mind—dull-coloured shapes, ponds of light, segmented lines. The other senses awaken, and Daniel is visited with boyhood scents, with the touch of a favourite coat, with the call of his mother's voice.

He sees an area of dirt, no more than a metre square, off the side of his parents' house, where he used to play with wood bugs and centipedes, constructing shelters for them out of twigs and leaves and bits of cloth. He is called inside. He is six years old, he's had his supper, and with twilight coming his mother wants him to start getting ready for bed. The cottage is dimly lit, for Ceauşescu has just passed a law saying that only a forty-watt light bulb may be burnt in the evenings. He's even hired a squadron of thugs who drive around all night, drinking imported vodka and looking for those stupid enough to disregard the law.

In this weak light, his father scribbles away at an old pine desk that his own father had once scribbled on—"The only difference, Dani, is that *he* could spend all his time writing poetry. Can you imagine that? He spent all of his time writing poetry, or tales for his children, or stories that took place in the woods. I have not had this luxury. *You* have not had this luxury. But someday, Dani. Someday all that will change. By God, I promise you that."

He is a slight man, bespectacled, with a dark moustache and long, sinewy arms; he wears suspenders, belts serving little purpose on his spindly hips. During the day, he works in a *hanul* one village over, cooking and doing the books.

"What are you writing, Papa?"

"Nothing important," he answers, which is what he says when he really means, *Not now, Dani, I'm trying to concentrate.* His brow furrows, and his lips purse. "Please, Dani," he says, "off to bed." Daniel stands at his side, resting against the arm of the chair, for a few minutes more. Finally, his mother fetches him, and leads him to his room. There, she tucks him in, and tells him not to worry, that when his father gets in one of his moods that's just the way he is. She kisses him on the tip of his nose, on each cheek, and on his forehead—always, she gives these kisses in the same order, for she knows her boy will protest any deviation. She leaves his room. He lies in his bed, unable to sleep, for it is a warm, still night and he doesn't wish to let it go.

He hears his mother walk down the hallway and enter his father's study. For a few seconds there is quiet. Then their voices rise, Daniel listening to an argument he does not understand, despite having heard it more and more often of late.

"Please," his mother says, "enough of this nonsense. Enough of these letters. You're going to get us in trouble."

His father says something Daniel doesn't catch.

"But how do you expect to get away with it?" his mother asks. "How, when Ceauşescu is demanding handwriting samples from every man, woman and child? How, when all typewriters have to be registered with the nearest police station? How, when even the phones are bugged? How, Ilya, how?"

And then, his father is laughing, and saying, "Oh please, Ana, I've had enough of this. We live in a little backward town in the middle of nowhere! Do you really think they care about what happens here? To Ceauşescu we're a bunch of starving farmers. To him, we don't exist!"

From his bed, Daniel holds his breath, so as to hear every word, and every dissatisfied breath. *Yes,* he thinks, *you tell her, Papa.* When the argument resumes, his father states once more that they're just peasants—peasants in the remote, once-Hungarian region of Maramureş—and when was the last time she saw Securitate in those parts? When *was* that, Ana?

"Please stop writing those letters."

Again, his father chuckles. "But how else to get published in this infernal country? How else? He's already put every publisher

out of business. So how else? Please explain this to me? I know—
maybe you would have me working for the Ministry of
Information, writing bestsellers called *How Ceauşescu Is the Best
Despot Around?* Perhaps that's the answer?"

"Ilya! Please! Be quiet!"

"Well then, Ana, you tell me what I should do!"

A door angrily shuts. Daniel lies awake, disconcerted by the
ensuing silence, feeling slightly guilty at the way he always roots
for his father. He starts to feel drowsy and warm, and then he
drifts off, and time eases forward, and it's hard to say whether it's
the same night or another night altogether—the only thing he
knows is that he sits straight up in bed, his head alive with the
sound of sirens, and the barking of dogs, and the swirling of red
lights. He throws off his quilt and rushes to the window and looks
out, and there, right there, in front of his house, they have come,
black vans and snarling German shepherds and men in green uniforms with dark blue epaulets. His neighbours are there too,
standing still, like good Romanians, though they all start heading
back into their homes the moment that Daniel's father comes
rushing out, his pants hastily pulled on, his hair standing on end.
He barely has time to yell, "What do you want?" over the barking
of dogs when they are on him, knocking him down, striking him
again and again with the butts of their Soviet-made rifles, and
throughout Daniel cannot take his eyes off the flat, determined
faces of the Securitate as they pick up the letter writer and throw
him motionless into the black van, his mother screaming and
weeping and rushing into the street and it is at this moment that
Daniel awakes in the hot darkness of his cell.

As always, after one of his dreams, he is gasping and perspir-
ing and feeling as though he's been struck, hard, in the stomach.

Only this time, squirming in the furnace-hot belly of a big ship, he cannot turn the nightmare off. Though he is no longer sleeping, the pictures still come to him, projected on the wall of the storage hold, Daniel thinking he must still be dreaming so he forgets about the danger and he yells at himself—*Wake up, damn idiot, wake up!*—which of course doesn't work, for he's already awake; he is fully and completely conscious, and is being forced to watch it all.

They came back.

Two days later they came back, sirens whirring, *for they always used sirens,* though this time it is early evening, the sun hanging low, and they are shouting and their dogs are barking and they're firing rifles into the air, for this has nothing to do with a lone letter writer and has everything to do with neutralizing entire villages, one by one, as they drunkenly roam through the hillsides. They stop in front of the house. An entire village peers from behind pulled-back curtains, and gapes from slightly opened doors, and listens from nearby lanes. They wait, and they wait. The dogs, from somewhere inside the black van, calm. There is silence, a silence that goes on and on, more frightening than the sirens and the barking and the shooting of rifles into the air, until finally it is punctured by the squeak of van doors, opening from the inside.

Ilya Pacepa is dumped onto the lane, an example for all those who had ever thought of taking up a pen. In the last two days, things have been done to him—when he drops from the back of a black van he does not drop as a body should. There's no tension in the joints, nor is there the rigidity normally provided by the muscles. His limbs flop as he lands in an impossible heap of limbs, twisted in every direction. A Russian circus contortionist could not begin to do what he is doing, at that moment, in the unpaved street in front of his own home.

The black van pulls slowly away. Dust rises lazily from where the tires had made contact with the lane. A wooden door opens, and his mother moves down the walk leading to the front gate. Her head is held up, her shoulders are back, she looks almost proud. There is no need to rush. It is so quiet the other villagers can hear her feet, crunching particles of sand and pebble, and they can hear her grunt as she lowers herself beside him. She is not crying. She gathers her husband's upper body into her arms, and she begins stroking his hair.

"Oh, Ilya, you silly boy—you have lost your glasses! Now we have to make the trip to Satu Mare for a new pair . . ."

She continues sitting there, tenderly admonishing him: "You weren't thinking, were you? If you had lost your glasses in May, we could have gone in time for the strawberry festival, but now . . ."

A few more seconds pass. The corners of her mouth turn down, her lips begin to quiver, her eyes fill. From the doorstoop, where Daniel is watching, he thinks, *Why is Papa sleeping? Why is he sleeping there?* There is the wind rustling the trees, there is the calling of birds, there is an ox lowing, somewhere far off. Otherwise, there is silence. His mother is rocking now, back and forth. She grips her husband tighter, and puts her cheek to his, distorting both their faces. After a time she straightens and, while staring at her husband's face, begins to hum a folk song that many of the villagers know—a tune written long ago, when wolves still roamed the hills, and the harvests were so bountiful they continued past nightfall, the shirts of the men lit silver.

Seeing this—seeing *all* of this—Daniel begins to weep in his tank, so long and so hard it feels as though his pain will be with him always, as though his pain is the thing that he is. Eventually he rises, and steps into the tunnel. As always, the air is piping hot, though for some reason he doesn't mind: somehow, it is all right to feel his own body, working away, struggling to cool itself.

He moves toward the bow of the big ship and reaches the door at the end of the tunnel. He opens it and finds a metal staircase reaching three storeys toward a small landing and another door, which presumably opens directly to the deck at the bow of the ship. He begins climbing, his body coated with perspiration. As he reaches the top, he experiences the fluttery beginnings of panic, for it occurs to him the door might be locked, and he cannot bear the idea of being in the tunnel for one second longer.

Turning the latch, he steps out. He moves to one side and leans on the gunwale. His face dampens with mist, and far beneath him, the ocean churns. He tries to imagine what it will feel like—his lungs filling with water, his brain fighting for oxygen, his extremities numbing so quickly he cannot thrash his limbs for more than a few seconds. He struggles to find the strength. *At least,* he thinks, *if I do get it over with, here and now, it'll have been me who made the decision to no longer exist.*

He stares at the shifting black water. In the swells he sees the faces of people he will miss, and in the wind breaking over the forecastle he hears their voices. Of course, one of them is his father's. Though he was a small man, his voice had a deep, resonant quality, like a saxophone played well—Daniel had forgotten how it could calm him, how it could make him feel that good things were happening.

Papa?

Yes, Dani? Yes, my boy?

Would you do it, Papa? Would you?

And then he is standing beside him, a ghost, though he's not Ilya Pacepa the letter writer. No—he's the man who kicked a ball with Daniel when he was so, so little. He's the man who helped him with his reading, who cooked him cornmeal porridge and eggs on weekend mornings, who showed him how to pull trout from a mountain stream.

Daniel turns to the presence beside him; he touches him, and in turn feels warmer. He misses him so, so much.

Would you do it, Papa? he asks again.

The smaller man answers with a note of surprise in his voice. *Oh no, Dani. Never.*

SEVENTEEN

In the middle of the night, the boat crosses paths with a mild storm that has wound its way up from the tropics. The waves come from the port side, each swell causing the vessel to totter like a child learning to walk. Hot rain lashes the deck, and a blanket of vapour forms over the topside. Rodolfo lies motionless, staring at the ceiling, while his cabin pitches and rolls. He finds himself picturing the way that a big ship, in even the roughest of oceans, leaves a V-shaped swath of aerated water in its wake—a triangle that looks lighter, and creamier, than the water surrounding it. He also pictures the space through which the boat is travelling—he sees it as something being conquered, slowly but surely, by the big ship's bow. This is the way he tries to calm himself at night—he imagines space being digested by the boat, gradually bringing them closer and closer to the city of Houston, Texas.

He smiles to himself. He has never looked so forward to docking in that homeliest of cities. *Another week,* he thinks. *You can do this, Bosun.* Outside the ship, the horizon is being warmed by the arrival of dawn. The weather settles, the rain giving way to thin, white air. Throughout the big ship, the wristwatch alarms of those who rise early are going off. Around this time, Rodolfo finally drifts into a state approximating sleep. While he doesn't dream, his thoughts do manage to place him elsewhere for a short time, and in this dislocation he experiences the briefest of rests.

When he comes to, Manuel's bunk is vacant and neatly made, the blankets drawn in tight, straight lines. Rodolfo dresses and locks his cabin door and crosses the hallway to the WC, where he splashes cold water over his face. He catches his reflection in the mirror, and is transfixed by the grey flecking his temples. His face looks pouchy, and pale.

Yes, Bosun, he thinks, *you are tired today.*

He lowers his head. Again, he tries to splash away his fatigue. Water trickles down his neck and into his shirt. He shakes his hands over the sink, and then dries himself with paper towelling. He moves quickly along the corridor toward the stairs. He goes down one level and enters the seamen's mess, which he finds deserted. He pours some coffee into a paper cup, and takes it with him, a bit of it spilling as he steps over the lip of the accommodation exit. He swears, switches the cup to his left hand, and puts the reddened webbing of his right hand to his mouth.

Out on deck there is a coolness in the air, and the clouds overhead look chunky and damp. His able-bodies, as usual, are milling near the bosun store, awaiting instruction. Rodolfo heads toward them.

"Good morning," he says, and when only one or two grumble in return, he knows that something is happening. He looks toward Manuel, who keeps his eyes focused on the deck of the boat. After a few seconds, Marlou gestures at something with a nod and says, "Did you see it, Bose?"

Rodolfo looks at the wall of the accommodation, where a single sheet of paper has been taped.

"That?" he asks.

The others nod, and one of them says, "What's going on, Bose? What is it?"

"What do you mean?"

"Look . . ."

As Rodolfo nears the sheet of paper, and sees that it's a routing schedule, his heart begins to pound—the only reason for posting it would be to announce a revision. His eyes scan the places they have been—Suez, Malta, Spain—and he reads the list of places they are scheduled to dock—Halifax, Newark, Miami, and then Houston. His body is shaking badly now, and he plunges his hands into his pockets so that his crew won't see them tremor. *That's it,* he thinks, *it's over, we've lost.* No matter how many times he reads the list he cannot alter the information it conveys:

SZC SUEZ CANAL . . . . *ETA May 09, ETD May 09*
JMW MARSAXLOKK . . . . . *ETA May 12, ETD May 13*
ALR ALGECIRAS . . . . *ETA May 15, ETD May 16*
HAL HALIFAX . . . . *ETA May 25, ETD May 25*
NWK NEWARK . . . . *ETA May 26, ETD May 27*
MIA MIAMI . . . . *ETA May 29, ETD May 29*
HOU HOUSTON . . . . *OMIT.*

~

The news reaches the oiler in the engine room. His arms are blackened with grease, and his features are smudged with grime. He hears something and turns. The fitter is coming toward him—his face is taut, and he is carrying a wrench the size of a crowbar. "They've changed the routing," he says. "The boat's not going to Houston."

A long moment passes between them. The heat in the room, a product of boilers and trapped air, grows uncomfortable.

"What about the containers?"

The fitter shrugs his shoulders. "What do we do?"

"I don't know, Fitter."

"This means . . ."

"Yes, I know."

"This means it's one of us. It's not the other four ABs. It's one of us who's been talking."

"Yes."

"The other four didn't know about Houston . . ."

Juanito nods his head gravely.

"If I find out who," the fitter says, "I'll kill him."

"I'll help you," Juanito says, though even as these words come from his mouth a much different thought is entering his head.

It could be you, Fitter.

~

At break, Juanito sits with the fitter, the electrician, and Manuel. Nobody speaks, except to comment on the weather or to ask for a creamer to be passed, their collective silence indicating that from now on, they will not be meeting in the cabin of the oiler.

The electrician stands so suddenly his chair legs scrape against the mess room floor, the other three men looking away. *Perhaps,* Juanito thinks, *he's angry with himself? With something he's done in a moment of weakness?* A minute later, Manuel shakily stands, his face wan, his eyes haunted *and perhaps this is the expression of a man tormented by feelings of guilt?* The fitter stands as well, his movements looking slower and more careful than usual, and at this Juanito cannot help thinking that maybe the shakiness of his movements are a facade meant to hide what he really carries inside him.

Juanito returns to the engine room, and goes back to work. The time passes so slowly that he shakes his watch and holds it to his ear to check that it still works. With fifteen minutes left in his shift, he collects his tools and scrubs his arms with degreaser. He leaves right at shift end, passing the second engineer, who nods and says simply, "Oiler."

Juanito returns the nod and struggles not to hurry. His plan is to leave the engine room, make it unseen to the lower officer level and find Broas before he leaves his cabin. He moves through corridors plastered with ship plans, and safety posters, and red-handled axes encased in glass. Every sign on board—from WATCH YOUR STEP to REMEMBER FIRE SAFETY!—is in English, and for some reason Juanito chooses this minute to notice this absurdity. He actually smiles—he can't help it, he's going crazy—though he sobers when he hears the sound of shoes against metal. He looks up and sees Broas slowly navigating the steps. As he makes his way down the stairs, he watches his feet through eyes that still look slightly puffy in the glare of corridor lights.

"Ariel."

Broas looks down at Juanito, blinking until his eyes focus. Juanito climbs a few more steps, so that he's within an arm's length of the Filipino officer. Before saying anything, he looks along the corridor, ensuring the metal doors at either landing are closed. He then takes Broas's elbow and leads him back to his cabin. They enter and sit.

"Ariel," Juanito says. "There's news."

Broas looks at him; his head tilts to one side. "Yes?"

"They've posted a new routing sheet. The boat's not going to Houston. We cross from Miami . . . we go no farther than Miami."

Broas swallows. "So they know."

"Yes."

"Someone told the officers about the priest in Houston."

"Yes."

"That's means they know that you and I . . ."

Juanito nods, and looks down. A clammy fear passes through them. They will be next. Nothing will stop this from happening.

"There must be something . . ." Broas says. Juanito looks up, and takes a deep breath, and pulls his thoughts back to the present. He hunts for options, for possibilities, and finds none.

"Oiler?"

Juanito blinks, and says nothing.

"Oiler," Broas says again, "what do they know, exactly?"

"They know—" Juanito stops, and thinks about this. *What is it they exactly know?* "They know about the *ibon*. They know we've hidden him. They know we were trying to get help in Houston."

Broas coughs, and rubs his sore eyes. "Yes," he says. "They know all of that."

"But they don't know where the *ibon* is hidden. If they did they would have gotten him by now. They know he's hidden somewhere, but they don't know where. It's still only Rodolfo who knows."

"Yes."

"So we know the squealer isn't Rodolfo."

"Yes, of course, of course."

"So we have the second cook, the fitter, the electrician, or Manuel."

"Yes."

"Four men."

"Which one?"

"I don't know."

Broas thinks. "Juanito," he says. "Do the officers know the stowaway is somewhere below deck?"

"Probably not—they would have searched . . ."

"And yet, *we* all know that Rodolfo hid him somewhere below deck. So why hasn't the squealer told them that? Why don't the officers at least know *that*? That's what I can't figure out. That's what I don't understand."

Juanito pictures how it must be happening—the stoolie passing on certain bits of information, yet playing dumb with others.

"He's frightened," Juanito says in a low voice. "He's doing it because he's scared."

"Yes, I think so."

"He doesn't really want to do it. He's telling them just enough to save his own skin. He's scared out of his wits."

"Yes, I believe so."

"He hates himself for doing it . . ."

A few seconds pass.

"Who do you think, Oiler?"

Juanito shakes his head. He doesn't know, doesn't want to know.

"Who would act that way?" Broas presses.

Juanito looks up. His throat clenches, so that when he says the man's name it comes as a whisper.

~

Rodolfo's face is in his hands. His head is ringing with the memory of a thousand card games, a thousand conversations about their northern province back home, a thousand beers they've had, late at night, watching action videos in the seamen's rec lounge.

His stomach hurts, his eyes sting, he wants nothing more than to sleep. *No, Bosun,* he keeps telling himself, *you don't know that. You don't know that yet.* Still, he can't help recalling what Manuel had said the last time they'd spoken alone, about how he would do anything to survive his last voyage as a seaman. Recalling this, Rodolfo could kick himself for taking so long to understand what he had meant, or for understanding why Manuel could not look him in the eye earlier that day.

But no, Bosun, you are tired—maybe your brain is adding it up all wrong. And so he rises and crosses the cabin. He steps out and moves through corridors and stairwells. The mess and rec hall are empty and silent; Rodolfo asks himself when it was that he last heard the gunfire of a Jet Li film, or the cooing pop songs of a Bollywood actress, or the sound of men hollering at a sports event. He retraces his steps, thinking his AB might have gone to his own cabin for some reason.

When he reaches Manuel's cabin, he stops and hears voices speaking in hushed tones. He presses his ear against Manuel's door, and can hear only that a conversation is taking place in poor English. The conversation rises slightly in pitch. There are two speakers. The first, of course, is Manuel, though the other is more difficult to make out, for he's standing farther into the room, perhaps near the porthole. *For the sake of God,* he thinks, *please let it be another AB.* . . . Rodolfo strains to hear, feeling only a sad resignation when he identifies the voice as belonging to the second officer.

The bosun shuts his eyes, and holds his breath, and leans against the corridor wall.

I could kill you, he thinks. *This is something I could do now.* Inside the cabin, voices rise. The Chinese officer says something, and is met with silence. He says it again, in a louder voice, and this time

Rodolfo can make it out: "But I see! I see you meet in oiler room! AB, you not know what they going to *do* to you?"

"No, no," Manuel sputters, "please, my head, it hurt me. . . ."

"I know, AB, I know!" and then the second officer lowers his voice, his words no longer loud enough to carry across the cabin and through the heavy door.

"Please," Manuel answers, "is difficult, is difficult to say . . ."

The officer says something.

"But they not tell . . ."

Again.

"I know, but I . . ." And the officer begins speaking once again, his words a muted, hostile patter. From the corridor, Rodolfo catches only the odd word—"sea" and "*Maersk Dubai*" and, yes, "stowaway." The officer goes on and on. Finally, after a full minute, he stops speaking. A silence descends upon the room. It lasts so long that Rodolfo wonders whether the conversation is over, and whether he should move away to avoid being caught. Finally, he hears Manuel's voice, still coming from somewhere near the door.

"Okay," he says. "Please, okay, please . . ."

From outside the stateroom, Rodolfo holds his breath, thinking, *Don't, just don't.*

"The bosun," Manuel says. "The bosun he feed him, at night, after the meetings, he feed the *ibon.*"

Rodolfo feels his face drain of colour, and his heart deaden. His fingers crook at his sides. Inside the cabin, the officer says something Rodolfo can't hear, Manuel answering, again, "Follow him tonight," and it's the way he's divulged their secret not once but twice that causes the bosun to seethe, and to harden, and to act.

～

A light tapping comes at the door—two knocks, one knock, two knocks. Juanito and Broas startle, their heads snapping in the direction of the cabin door. They don't know whether they should answer, for they don't know if the secrecy of the code is another thing that has been lost to them. The tapping comes again, this time followed by the voice of the bosun—he's whispering loudly, as if trying to be heard only by those inside the cabin. Neither Juanito nor Broas moves. They look at each other.

"Oiler," Rodolfo whispers again. "Please . . ."

Again, they don't move, the bosun having to say, "Please, I know something," before Juanito opens the door just wide enough to peek at Rodolfo and make sure he's alone. He opens the door a little wider, allowing the bosun to enter. Rodolfo stays on his feet, running fingers through his hair. Juanito and Broas wait as the bosun calms himself. Finally he sits, and clears this throat, and starts to shake.

"It's Manuel," he says.

"Yes," Broas says, "we think so."

"No, no, no," he says, "I know it's Manuel. I heard him. He was talking to the second officer in his cabin. Tonight they'll wait for me—tonight they're going to follow me."

The three men look at one another. One is thickly built, one has a moustache, one looks much younger than his years. Otherwise, they all bear the same fatigued expressions.

"He's not with the containers," Rodolfo says. "He's in the tunnels. I put him in one of the buoyancy tanks."

~

They move quickly. Ariel Broas heads to the engine room, and if anyone asks why he's there in the middle of the day he'll say he's fallen behind in his computations, that with his damn eyesight coming back he can finally do some catching up. Rodolfo and Juanito go to the mess, their footfalls echoing along corridors. Once there, Juanito keeps watch while Rodolfo combs the galley kitchen for a large, empty orange juice container. He finds one that is big enough for several days, and begins filling it with drinking water. When he finishes, he moves around and sets down the jug at the beginning of the serving line. Then he curses, for only fruit and bread have been left out.

He is about to put the first apple into a paper sack when he hears Juanito rush into the room and stand beside him.

"Bosun . . ." he whispers.

Rodolfo glances up, and sees that the Chinese head cook is entering the kitchen from the far side, nodding at both the ship's oiler and the bosun.

Juanito reaches out, and begins to pour coffee from the urn that sits, running, all day, at the end of the serving line. The fluid is thick and jet black, and it spills over the brim before Juanito releases the black triangular spigot. Rodolfo helps himself to a cup of coffee as well, and follows Juanito to one of the tables. There, the two sit and nervously sip the bitter, burnt coffee while pretending to have a conversation. At the other end of the room, in the kitchen servicing both messes, the cook hacks at large cuts of meat coated with tenderizer. Every few seconds, the two sailors nervously meet each other's gaze—if the cook were to enter the mess and see the jug of water sitting on the floor, the game would be over.

There is another Chinese voice. Juanito leans slightly to his left, so as to see around Rodolfo.

"The second officer," he whispers, and for the next few

minutes they listen to them speak, in Mandarin, across the room. The conversation fades in volume before disappearing altogether.

"Wait," says Juanito. He gets up and moves toward the door of the mess. He peers up and down the hallway. Without looking at the bosun, he signals for him to hurry.

Rodolfo starts filling a plastic bag with as many apples and slices of bread as he can carry. He picks up the water jug and stands in the door to the mess. He looks along the short hallway leading to the accommodation exit. Juanito is there already, standing in the open doorway, looking from left to right. Again, he motions for Rodolfo to come.

This is madness, Rodolfo thinks, *this cannot be done in the middle of the day,* but still he hustles along the brightly lit hallway, conscious only of the sound of water sloshing in the heavy jug. He joins Juanito at the doorway. They are together for a second only. Moving quickly, Juanito crosses the deck to the stairwell leading down to the engine room. From here, he looks back and indicates the coast is clear; Rodolfo then crosses the deck himself, thankful he can be seen neither by the officers on the bridge nor by the able-bodies working at the far end of the ship. He reaches the passageway and looks down; Juanito is already on the landing beneath him, ensuring they are alone. Again, Rodolfo follows, quickly descending the two flights of steps. Adrenalin is coursing so swiftly through him that the water jug feels weightless, his feet unconnected to his body. He stops on the landing outside the engine room. The oiler is peering out through the opened door—three metres to the right, along a grated parapet, is the door to the steering room. From where Juanito looks out, he cannot see the glass-paned control room, which sits above the main engine block and overlooks the space they have to now cross. He can, however, see Ariel Broas, pretending to write on a clipboard.

Broas looks over. His face looks tight, and the muscles beneath his jawline flex. With a slight, almost imperceptible movement of his jaw, he shakes his head, *no*. Juanito ducks back into the stairwell, and puts a hand on Rodolfo's chest. He keeps the door open just enough that he can look at Broas.

They wait. Each man is trembling and, without realizing it, holding his breath. Rodolfo lowers the water jug and, with his free hand, touches his bosun's knife. *Today*, he thinks, *I use this. Today I will, I don't care.* Finally, Broas glances up at the control room and sees some change. He looks at the oiler and gestures in the direction of the steering room. Juanito sees this, stands out of Rodolfo's way, and says, only, "Go."

~

He is alone now, moving along the engine-room parapet. He does not look up, nor does he look at his destination. Instead, he keeps his head down, focusing on the movements of his feet. He opens the door to the steering room and steps inside. Here, he puts down the water jug, and leans against a wall, panting; he is safe, for the moment, assuming that no one has seen him. The muscles in his forearm hurt, and he cannot stop his legs from quivering. Beside him, the steering rams jostle and creak. He moves across the room and unlocks the door at the far side. He stops to catch his breath, and to think, *Keep going, Bosun*, and the next second he finds himself moving down steps, the atmosphere growing hotter, and denser, and moist, his feet lit with the yellow glow of emergency lights. His thoughts roar in the humid silence. He reaches the bottom of the boat, steps into the tunnel and moves along the port side, his steps accompanied by the groan of metal on a large mass of water.

He reaches the compartment housing the stowaway. The *ibon* hears him, and begins whispering, "*Hola? hola?*" into the darkness. Rodolfo withdraws his flashlight and shines it into the enclosure, the stowaway's knees caught in the beam's weak perimeter.

Daniel is sitting against one wall, hugging his legs, looking up. His lips tremble, and his face looks drained of colour. Rodolfo places the provisions against the space of wall beside him, surprised that the stowaway doesn't leap for the water. He lowers himself to one knee, and looks into the stowaway's face.

Something has happened.

"You are all right?" he asks. "*Está bien?*"

The stowaway nods. The grime on his face looks streaky, as though he's been weeping. Rodolfo realizes, with a start, he doesn't even know the *ibon*'s name.

"*Como se llama?*"

Daniel looks at him blankly.

"Your name? *Su nombre?* Brother, what do they call you?"

The stowaway's voice sounds scratchy.

"Daniel."

"Yes?" Rodolfo says. "Daniel? *Soy Rodolfo, Rodolfo Miguel.*"

Daniel blinks at him curiously, for he truly doesn't understand why this man is trying to save him. He doesn't understand, for these types of things do not happen, not in the world he knows. He watches as the man uncaps the water jug and holds it to Daniel's lips. Then he tips it, helping Daniel drink, the water flowing cool and metallic over parched lips. His stomach constricts painfully, and starts to gurgle. Hearing this, Rodolfo lowers the jug.

"*Me llamo* Daniel Pacepa," he says again. Then, in Romanian, he adds, "My father was Ilya Pacepa, and he was a dissident, and he was murdered by the Securitate when I was six years of age. I know this because I saw it happen. I know this because I was there."

Rodolfo peers at him, curious about what the man might be saying.

"My name is Daniel, and I am from a place where they used to kill you for writing a few letters. Did you know this? Can you imagine there was such a place?"

Rodolfo pulls an apple from the paper sack and extends it to Daniel. The stowaway doesn't seem to see it, and continues mumbling away. *Yes,* Rodolfo thinks, *all this time, trapped in a pitch-black compartment, something bad is happening to him.* The bosun says, in his own language, the only thing that comes to his mind. "You know we are brothers, you and I. We are both from places ruined by a stupid man and his greedy wife. We are both men who have been forced to go to sea. We are brothers, *hermanos, somos iguales.* We are the same."

Daniel looks up, and stares into the face of the sailor. It fascinates him that the man's features have given way to something different, to something harder. He tries to find the Spanish words to express this thought, and cannot. He wants only to curl up and sleep, dreamlessly, for the rest of the trip.

"Daniel," Rodolfo says, "there's enough water for a week here. Maybe more. And there's food for at least a couple of days. I may not be able to visit you as often, but you'll be all right, this I promise, so don't worry if you don't see me, because everything is fine. The boat—it's delayed, but otherwise everything is fine."

Daniel looks up; he knows only that he wants to survive now. Meanwhile, the sailor has continued speaking in his own language.

"You," Rodolfo keeps saying, over and over, "will be safe. I will keep you safe. I don't care what I have to do, but I'll protect you. I will."

He pauses and lowers his eyes, as though ashamed of himself.

"God forgive me," he says, "but I will."

~

That night, Juanito goes to bed with a long, glinting kitchen knife lent to him by the second cook; as he tosses and turns, it lies beside him, nestled in sheets, tip pointing downward. He does not sleep, nor does he sleep the night after that—anytime now, the final confrontation with the officers will come. As his exhaustion deepens, his ears start to ring, an incessant high-pitched whine that bothers him whenever he's in a quiet place. One afternoon, while lying sleeplessly in his cabin, he listens to the noise in his ears, and as he does its seems to take on texture, and characteristic, and meaning. He focuses harder, until he realizes that hidden within the noise is a second frequency that he hadn't previously noticed, and that between the two frequencies he can hear the cries of the first two stowaways, just before their raft was sucked under by the big ship's wake. Other times, he thinks he can hear the *ibon* calling from below, and it haunts him that there is a man down there, and that they dare not go to him.

So he stops thinking. It causes him too much pain. He stops imagining the way the fight with the officers will come, for it takes too much energy, and causes him too much fear. If he concentrates at all, it is on matters of the most basic survival: the way an oil gun works, how you unscrew the top of a toothpaste tube, how you keep the door to your cabin locked at all times. His fingertips turn slightly numb; he has to shake them in order to regain sensation. Common smells, like coffee and fried bacon, start to make him feel ill. One morning, he picks up a wrench, and peers at it, as though it is the most fascinating thing he has ever seen.

I don't know what this is called. I know what it does, but I don't know its name.

He does not speak with the other sailors, and with the exception of Ariel Broas they do not speak to him. He has not slept for more than two days now. His dreams, unable to express themselves during the night, struggle to invade his waking hours—in the middle of supper, his thoughts turn illogical, the food on his plate suddenly grey and foreign. His body, at all times, feels as though it is slogging through ointment. At odd moments, he finds himself fighting tears, his fear being that he has somehow ceased to be a sailor, and has instead become one of the coffee spillers and cigarette stealers that roam the nooks and crannies of a big ship. It is a fear promoted by his own reflection, caught in the bathroom mirror on the third morning without sleep: his cheeks have started to sag, and his skin is as white as a sheet. Rodolfo, Broas, the fitter and the electrician all look the same way, for they have stopped sleeping as well.

We look like phantoms, Juanito thinks. *We're turning into ghosts.*

The boat pulls into anchorage sixteen kilometres off the shore of Halifax. From where they have dropped anchor, other boats can be seen in the distance, like a row of bath toys waiting to be played with. They are stopped for two days. During that time, Juanito overhauls fuel injector valves and replaces the turbocharge

filters; this is difficult, given that he's clumsy with sleep depriva-
tion and a sense of hopelessness. One afternoon, he hears that
the pilot has come; within an hour, the engine room has received
the order to switch fuel and rev the propulsion engine. The boat
docks, Rodolfo and his able-bodies now busying themselves by
disconnecting lashings, and opening hatch covers, and helping to
take on food and oil stores via the afterpart crane. Juanito, wearing sunglasses and a cap pulled low, goes on deck. While watching
the dock workers on shore, he thinks, *How can they not notice? How
can they not tell we are different?* He stays out until the pain in his head
turns piercing. Then he goes back inside the boat and heads to his
cabin. He lies down, and stares at the ceiling, and monitors the
ringing in his ears. He has no idea how much time goes by
between the docking of the ship and the knocking that comes at
his cabin door.

He sits straight up and listens intently. There, it is coming
again—two knocks, one knock, two knocks. He throws open the
door, not caring, not any more, and sees the second cook standing in the corridor, his eyes as red as an ocean sky at dawn. He
is wearing a white T-shirt, sneakers, and an apron stained with
food. His cooking knife is in his hand—he hasn't been without
it for days—and it drips some sort of moisture onto the grey,
metal floor.

Juanito continues to stand there, peering at the second cook.
When the cook's words finally come, they are without inflection
of any kind, his tone like that of a man heavily drugged.

"There are police," he says. "On board."

The two men stand looking at each other, the oiler too
fatigued to understand this new information.

"Oiler," the cook finally says. "You have to come."

Juanito nods, and crosses the hall, and washes his face. By the time he exits the WC, the second cook has wandered off, leaving Juanito alone in the corridor outside his cabin. For one second, he is struck by a glimmer of hope—*Perhaps,* he begins to think, *Father Albano sent word* . . . But no, it's no use; lack of sleep renders the thought fleeting and disjointed, the idea vanishing before it fully forms. He stands blinking, wishing he could get it back, for it had seemed so much better than the thought he is having now: that this is another trick, that the whole thing is drawing to an end, that these will be his final, violent moments.

He trudges along the corridor, finds the stairs, and descends to the officers' mess. He steps inside and there, right there, are the Filipinos, and the officers, and a half-dozen men wearing sky blue jackets and dark pants. *My God, it's the Port Authority,* and then one of the men in uniform, a huge man with a moustache and glasses, starts saying that they've received word that something has happened on board, and would anyone care to comment? Out of the corner of his eye, Juanito watches as the other Filipinos fidget, and look down, and say nothing. Meanwhile, the officers treat the whole thing as a joke, the captain saying, "Oh, no, it is just some mistake, perhaps other boat but not this one . . ." This goes on and on, the officers acting as if the whole thing were an amusing error, the Filipinos saying nothing, their weight shifting from foot to foot.

The men in the Port Authority uniforms finally notice this, and they separate the two groups, the officers still laughing and saying, "Oh no, this is all mistake. This is not necessary. Don't worry, they'll tell you," as they are led to another part of the ship. The Filipinos are then taken to the corridor, where they wait outside one of the officers' cabins. Another man comes, and he announces that his name is John Parsons, and that he is from the International Transport Workers' Federation, and that he and the Port Authority men will be asking some questions, and is there a Juanito Ilagan here?

Juanito's heart skips a beat. The other Filipinos are careful not to give him away by turning to look at him. Meanwhile, the ITF man is consulting a crew list, as though worried he might have mispronounced the name, and then he is saying, again, "Juanito Ilagan? Is he here?"

Juanito steps hesitantly forward. He is led into a cabin with the ITF man and two of the Port Authority police, one of whom is the big man who had spoken earlier. Juanito shakes hands with the ITF man, and the big cop, and another man whose name he does not catch.

"Juanito," says Parsons. "A Randolph Albano, a priest at the mission in Houston, received a letter."

Juanito looks at him blankly. *I don't know you. How can I trust you if I don't know you?*

"Do you know anything about this?"

Juanito shakes his head, and in English says, "No, I don't know anything."

This causes the three men to look uneasily at one another.

"Juanito," the ITF man says, "are you sure?"

Juanito nods, and watches as the ITF man reaches into an inner pocket of his coat, and pulls out the very letter that Juanito mailed in Algeciras, when he'd told the chief officer he'd needed to go ashore to wire money back home. It is the sight of the letter, gingerly held aloft in a stranger's hand, that cuts through the haze of Juanito's exhaustion and causes him to realize that maybe, maybe, their plan had somehow worked.

Still, Juanito hesitates, so as to let this new possibility wrap itself around him. It feels warm, and good, like a facecloth dampened with hot water.

"Yes," he finally says. "It was me."

~

Rodolfo is the sixth Filipino to be called into the room. He enters, and introductions are made.

"Mr. Miguel," the ITF man says. "You are the bosun?"

Rodolfo nods.

"And apparently it was your crew who built a raft for the stowaways?"

Rodolfo squints and puts a hand to his forehead. He, too, hasn't slept in days—their questions are like bright lights, shone directly into his eyes. His head pounds, his eyes burn. *I'm too tired,* he thinks, *I'm too tired to start.*

He nods.

"And you were the one who found the stowaways?"

"Yes."

"And you were the one . . ." And this time the question fades into the mire produced by exhaustion.

He cannot answer any more questions, he cannot. So instead, he stands and says, "Come."

The ITF man and the two Port Authority police look at each other questioningly.

"Please," Rodolfo says again, "come."

Again, the three men look at one another, until finally the biggest of the men says, "All right, Mr. Miguel," and a second later they are following Rodolfo into the corridor. The four then descend a flight of stairs, and go to the bosun's cabin. He unlocks the door, and beckons the men inside. They follow, Rodolfo noticing that they are now the ones who look nervous, for they are glancing at every corner of Rodolfo's room, as though expecting it to be booby-trapped.

"Here," Rodolfo says. He reaches between the end of his mattress and the bedframe, and pulls out his logbook. He then hands it to the ITF man, who begins riffling through the pages, and reading random sections.

After a minute or so of this, the two Port Authority police begin to look impatient, the smaller one saying, "Look, Mr. Miguel . . ." Before he has time to finish Rodolfo reclaims the small, spiral-bound book, and opens it to a page near the back.

He then returns it to the ITF man, and says, wearily, "Please . . ."

The man reads for a few moments, struggling to decipher Rodolfo's handwriting. His eyes stop. His lips part, and he looks up at the two police officers.

"What is it?" the big one asks. The ITF man holds up a hand, indicating he needs a moment to think. His eyes return to the passage, and he reads for a few seconds more before looking up at Rodolfo and saying, "Is this true? There's another?"

For Rodolfo, the question is so inane as to be a string of meaningless sounds. Instead of answering he moves his head, slowly, up and down, his eyes trained on the faces of the three men.

"Yes," he says. "He's below."

~

For the first time, he takes the standard route to the tunnels, in full view of the bridge. With three men following him, he marches down the accommodation stairs and exits onto the deck, where the officers have been gathered. Though they are still chatting and laughing, enough time has passed to add gravity to the situation, and their jocularity is starting to look forced. When they see Rodolfo and the three men, they stop talking altogether.

Rodolfo leads the ITF man and the two Port Authority officers along the port side, until they reach a manhole halfway along the length of the big ship. Rodolfo unlashes the cover, and crawls in, descending a ladder that leads to the depths of the boat. At the bottom of the ladder, he jumps off and looks up at the circle of daylight: the three men are struggling, and it is all Rodolfo can do to stop himself from yelling at them to hurry. Slowly, they come down, unsure of their steps in the darkness, apprehension and the heat of the tunnels causing beads of perspiration to arise on foreheads and upper lips. They stand in the tunnel, looking at one another, catching their breath.

Rodolfo motions with his flashlight for them to follow. They fall in behind him, glancing from side to side, nervously appraising their surroundings. It's a short walk to the stowaway's enclosure. Rodolfo shines his flashlight down, near the front of the tank, so as to not startle Daniel. Meanwhile, the ITF agent and the two police officers look on, aghast, their eyes wide with disbelief.

"Daniel," the bosun calls.

They all listen; there is no answer.

"Daniel," he calls again. "It's me, Rodolfo," and again he hears no answer, though he thinks he can hear rustling coming from the back of the tank.

"Daniel," he calls for the third time, and as he does he lets the beam carry over the buoyancy tank—there, right there, is a man, slowly rising to his feet. His face is grimy, his clothes filthy; he looks starved. His arms rise to block out the beam cast by Rodolfo's flashlight, and when he shows a hesitancy to come forward Rodolfo says, "Please, *no preocupa,* the boat is at shore, we've arrived, *hemos llegado . . .*"

The stowaway inches forward, his hands held out, and as he comes forward so does his stench. When he spots the three strange men, he hesitates and shields his dirty face again.

"No," Rodolfo says, "*no preocupa.* They are police. They will help you, *van a ayudar.* Everything is okay, *todo está bien,* believe me, it's okay."

Hearing these words, Daniel lowers his hands, and looks at the men. For the first time, it registers that his ordeal might be over. He begins to weep, and move toward the bosun. For a minute, they all stand in a circle in the depths of the boat, the stowaway sobbing fitfully into his hands, Rodolfo finally reaching out and touching the stowaway's shoulder. It is this touch that helps Daniel pull himself together, and act once again like a man.

～

They regain the deck of the boat. This time, when they pass the Taiwanese, and the officers see the surviving stowaway, their faces harden. The captain and second officer glare. Daniel is taken to the accommodation, where he is given food, and a hot shower, and a change of clothing. The officers are then told to take the ship back out to anchorage and await instruction; later, they do so, never dreaming that in three days they will be taken, grim-faced and handcuffed, to jail.

All of the Filipinos, meanwhile, are escorted off the boat. When Rodolfo touches shore, he is approached by a chaplain from the Mission to Seafarers in Halifax, who has been waiting for hours on the concrete jetty. Immediately, things become clearer to

Rodolfo: this must be the man Albano contacted, and this must be the man who alerted the authorities. Rodolfo stares at the chaplain's soft features. He is so numbed with fatigue it doesn't occur to him to thank him, or so much as say hello.

"Do you understand where you are?" the man asks.

Rodolfo nods.

"Do you know why you're here?"

Again Rodolfo nods. Seconds go by.

"Then trust me, my son. The police will take care of you. Everything is going to be all right."

Rodolfo is placed in a police car and taken to the Port Authority building. There he is led inside, along with every other Filipino who'd been on board the *Maersk Dubai*. Rodolfo is the first to be called. He is ushered into a small room, where the two police officers he'd taken to the tunnels are sitting at a small table. They offer him coffee, Coke, pizza, cigarettes, anything he might need. He accepts the offer of coffee and then slowly takes a seat, preferring to keep his eyes down.

"Mr. Miguel," one of them says, "we want you to tell us everything you know."

Everything? That's easy. I have fear and hatred in my heart. That is everything. That's the whole story. I have fear, and hatred.

A few seconds pass. There is a knock, and a tall uniformed officer comes in with the coffee; the two men both nod toward Rodolfo. The cup is placed in front of him. He takes a sip, and the fact that it is so much better than the coffee afforded Filipino sailors on board a big ship makes him angrier still. He lifts his eyes, and looks at a space between the heads of the two men.

"If I begin to talk," he says in English, "you must hear everything. You must not stop me till I am finish."

"Yes, yes," the two men say. "Of course, we've got all the time you need. Take your time, Mr. Miguel."

Rodolfo takes another sip. The beverage warms his lips, his mouth, his throat. How he loves the flavour of coffee, how he adores its aroma. How he craves the way it wakens him, after a long night spent on a tossing ship. His mind focuses, and he puts the cup down.

"The boat," he starts, "was a day from Algeciras."

EIGHTEEN

He waits, his nervousness prompting him to note every detail. The hall is long, and lined with bulletin boards, and lit by fluorescent light fixtures. The bench on which he's sitting is a hard, dark wood, and the floor is an old speckled linoleum. Across from him there's a locked glass case containing a fire hose. At the end of the hall, to his left, is a window facing onto a clear, white afternoon. To his right sits a translator, some Romanian guy they dug up in town; as they wait, the man crosses his arms over his chest, and bounces his foot against the floor. They do not chat, and Daniel finds himself wishing that the translator weren't so taciturn.

Farther along, there is a Coke machine, glowing fire-engine red, and beyond that is some kind of station where a woman in a police uniform operates a telephone. The place is buzzing with activity: doors open and close, people rush by, a badly distorted voice keeps coming over a crackling intercom, its speakers mounted at intervals along the hallway. He doesn't know whether this police station is always like this, or whether the arrival of the boat has caused this frenzy. When he asks the translator, the man shrugs, and lifts his eyebrows, and without turning his head says, "I don't know, maybe, who knows?"

After a time, a woman in a dark blue skirt and blouse and cap gives him Coca-Cola and a slice of pepperoni-and-green-pepper pizza. When he finishes, the woman comes and asks, politely, if he would like another serving. Or at least he thinks she does—he turns to the translator, who is sitting beside him, arms crossed over his chest. The translator, who has started to daydream again, suddenly realizes that two people are waiting for his services.

"You want more?" he asks Daniel.

To which Daniel, who has not eaten properly in days, looks at the women and says: "*Da,* please, yes."

~

As more time passes, he begins to realize that this is a strange type of police station, this Port Authority office, for there are no German shepherds, and there are no prisoners being dragged by the shoulders, and there are no doors muffling screams. It does, however, look like a place where everyone is too busy to attend to him—the police officers who brought him in keep walking up and down the hallways, going from room to room, hollering for more coffee. He catches a glimpse of the sailor Rodolfo, down the hallway, surrounded by men in suits, being led into a room. The afternoon wears on, and Daniel grows bored. He's offered more pizza and Coca-Cola, and is told that if he needs anything else he should just let them know. He has also been given magazines, and he thumbs through them, looking at pictures of smiling young woman wearing skimpy clothing and handsome men with large muscles. One is Brad Pitt, and he supposes that the others are stars he hasn't heard of.

Finally, a man wearing a light blue jacket and dark pants approaches and sits on the bench beside Daniel and his translator.

He explains that they're still taking the crew members' statements, and that they'll have to interview him tomorrow. In the meantime, he explains, Daniel will be billeted in the Holiday Inn. The man then passes an envelope toward Daniel. At first, Daniel is afraid to take it, for he's sure it must be some sort of deportation notice or arrest warrant. The man waggles it slightly, and then smiles, as if to indicate that nothing is the matter. Finally, Daniel accepts it. When he opens it, his eyes widen with surprise. The man then says something, the translator explaining, "For small expenses. If you have any."

Shortly after that, he's escorted from the offices of the Port Authority. The day is warm and sunny, and the moment Daniel steps outside he breathes deeply, filling his lungs with clean air. A large, dark car pulls up. He gets in, as do the translator and the man who gave him the envelope. The translator sits in the back with Daniel, while the Port Authority man sits in front with the driver.

As they drive through downtown streets, Daniel looks through the slightly tinted windows, admiring the height of the buildings. When they pull up in front of the Holiday Inn, Daniel is taken into the lobby, where he cannot stop craning his neck and looking around. For a while, they do some paperwork, the details passing between the Port Authority officer and the smiling young woman at the front desk. Meanwhile, the translator stands with his arms crossed, saying nothing.

The men take Daniel toward a bank of elevators; he is nervous, for in Romania the elevators generally don't work well enough to be trusted, meaning that most people ignore them and take the stairs. After a minute, the doors open, and he gets in with the two men, his heart pounding. They ride in silence, the floors counting off in red numbers at the top of a panel to his right. When the elevator stops, he hears chimes, and the doors open. They walk into a long carpeted hallway. At the door of the room where he will apparently stay, he notices that instead of a key they use a plastic card embossed with small bumps, like something a blind person would read.

They step inside, and Daniel looks around: he can't believe he will stay here, in this room, with its huge bed and TV and clean fluffy towels and even what looks like a hair dryer, free for him to use should he wish. Outside the room, through a thickly paned window, he can see lights, and traffic, and an illuminated bridge.

The man from the Port Authority says something, the translator turning to Daniel and explaining, "A car will come for you at eight o'clock tomorrow morning. Is that all right?"

Daniel nods, though he does so distractedly, for he's too busy poking around the hotel room, thinking that it's probably nothing compared to the ones they have in New York City.

"Daniel," the translator says, his voice a little impatient. "Did you hear me?"

"Yes," Daniel says. "I'll be ready."

~

He flips through stations on the television. After a bit he turns the set off and admires the view through his hotel window, thinking only that he has done it, that he has somehow survived. He feels as though he should really phone Elena to tell her all is well. There is, however, one problem: he can't read the list of instructions he finds next to the phone, and so he gives up, thinking, *They'll probably send me home anyway*. This thought depresses him, though he cheers considerably when he notices what looks like a small black refrigerator built into a wall unit opposite his bed. There's a tiny key protruding from a lock in the front of the door. When he turns it, the black door pops open, and he cannot believe his eyes, for it's filled with little bottles of liquor and beer, all cold and ready to be consumed.

He takes out the first little bottle of Smirnoff. For one or two seconds he hesitates, thinking of the horrible withdrawal he'd gone through in the bottom of the boat. But then he remembers the memories that had visited him there, and he recalls how hungry and thirsty he'd been toward the end, and he remembers how he had cried in front of complete strangers. He remembers all of these experiences, and he understands that he will forever have to acknowledge them as horrible, and real, and his own.

No one, he thinks, *deserves a drink more than me.*

He upends the miniature bottle and consumes its contents in a single, wheezing gulp. He sits on his bed and lets the warmth of the vodka find its way to his stomach, where it signals a snug, hopeful comfort in his brain. Smiling, he helps himself to the next little bottle—something called "Canadian Club"—and when he drinks it he is reminded of the tall, iced drinks that were so popular among the old men of Algeciras. To cure the heat in his throat he opens one of the cans of beer, and drinks it while munching on a bag of peanuts he finds in the fridge as well. By the time he's consumed the four little bottles and the four cans of beer, he finds himself wishing that the liquor had packed the same wallop as țuică, and that the beer had the same kick as the homemade brew back home. He lies back, and links his hands behind his head, and stares up at the ceiling. While it's true there is no such thing as happiness, it could also be true that there is more of *this* feeling to be had out there, in a world having nothing to do with Romania.

He falls asleep in the clothes given to him on the boat, his legs bent over the edge of the bed, his feet touching the carpeted floor. After an hour or two he starts to come awake, and for the first few seconds he thinks he's on the container ship, sprawled on the floor of his compartment, going out of his mind with hunger and fear. Slowly, he becomes conscious of the soft mattress supporting his back, and of the motionlessness of the room, and of the soft streetlight outside his window. He stands and groggily remembers the envelope given to him by the police officer. He retrieves it from the top of the television set, and looks inside.

Jesus, he thinks. *Fifty dollars. I left Bucharest with only a few* lei. *With fifty dollars, who knows how far I could go? Who knows what I could do?*

His hotel room—which had seemed so heavenly just a few hours earlier—suddenly feels lonely, and quiet, and small. He looks inside the little refrigerator, only to remember that he cleared it out prior to sleeping. He has to get out, if only to stretch his legs and breathe some fresh air. Stupidly, he'd forgotten to ask if he was free to do this—he doesn't know if his hotel room is guarded, or whether he can leave the hotel without triggering alarms. He dresses, and pokes his head into the carpeted hallway. It is still, and quiet, and when he gets on the elevator he's half surprised that nobody tries to stop him. He gets out at the lobby, and walks calmly toward the brass-handled front doors. As he walks, he's careful not to look at anyone, not even at the smiling girl at the front desk. Yet when he begins to move toward the front door, a man in a blue Holiday Inn jacket heads toward the door as well. Daniel stiffens, and in the back of his mind he can hear the snarling of dogs, and the whirling of sirens.

Instead the man smiles, and opens the door. He also says something that Daniel doesn't understand: "Have a good evening, sir."

~

Daniel stands outside the hotel, looking around. The night is humid and still, though not in any way hot. Every minute or so a breeze kicks up, carrying with it the faint odour of salt. Daniel begins walking, the streets quiet enough that he can hear the echo of his footsteps on pavement. This confuses him, for anything he has ever read or seen on TV indicated that in North America the streets stay alive until the early hours of the morning, the bars and restaurants serving people with all kinds of money until dawn. Instead, the whole city looks locked up; only the odd store on a corner, and the odd restaurant serving something called *falafel,* is open.

Soon, he has left the part of the city with tall concrete buildings, and has entered a place where people seem to live. Here, the streets are lined with small wooden houses that, under moonlight, look to be painted hues of green and blue and yellow. There are automobiles, and trees, and mailboxes the colour of apples. Clearly, this is a neighbourhood where there are lots of children, and where crime is not a problem—there, over there, is a stroller, left out on a verandah, and over there is a tricycle, completely unattended. He passes tidy green parks, and a ball diamond, and a steepled church, and more streets lined with wooden houses. Oddly, he feels safe, as though nothing could happen to him. *Perhaps*, he thinks, *this is the promise of North America*—a place where a man can do what he wants, without anybody ordered to bother him.

He is walking faster now, his arms swinging like a soldier's. He has started to think that if he goes back to the hotel, they might put him on a boat or a plane to Romania, and what would he do then? Soon, he is practically speed-walking, and oh how good it feels, all that oxygen flowing through his body, reddening his blood, energizing his muscles, stretching tendons left cramped and tired after a week in a buoyancy tank. He takes deep, lumber-jack breaths. He won't go back to the hotel, not unless they catch him. He'll go on to New York, the city so nice they named it twice, or maybe he'll continue on to Mexico, or Brazil, or the southernmost tip of Chile. *Yes, Tierra del Fuego, that sounds good, they speak Spanish there, I bet I'd like it, I bet the girls are pretty there.*

And then, just like that, his hopefulness evaporates, his elation turning to a dull, hurtful foreboding. Daniel stops and rests his hands on his knees, letting the moments of his life course through his body like thick, cold blood. He returns to his hotel, and spends all of the next day giving short, terse answers to the Port Authority interviewers, which are then made shorter, and terser, by the sullen translator. At dusk, they take him back to the hotel, where he is given a chit for room service. He eats a roast beef sandwich and french fries in front of the television set, though is disappointed to find that they have restocked his little refrigerator with juice and snacks only. This impels Daniel Pacepa to take another long walk through the city, his Bible and photograph of Elena tucked firmly in his pocket, and it is on this night—a night that has turned cloudy and thick, muting the colours of the small wooden houses—that he does not turn back.

The Stowaway started as my attempt to document, with as much fidelity as possible, the ordeal suffered by the crew members of the *Maersk Dubai* during the months of March, April and May of 1996. Everything described via the perspective of the Filipino sailors was the result of exhaustive interviews with Rodolfo Miguel, Juanito Ilagan, and Ariel Broas, who at no time asked to be paid for their stories. Without their patience, grace, and heroism, this book would not, in any way, have been possible.

My thanks also go to Father Randolph Albano, who supplied me with the letter written to him by Juanito Ilagan. (At the request of Rodolfo, Juanito, and Ariel, I changed the name, and identifying characteristics, of the crew member called Manuel Pacificador, as it was their wish that *The Stowaway* not bring embarrassment to the man's family.)

In May of 2001, I travelled to Algeciras, Spain, and researched the way that young Romanian men were reaching North America in the early- to mid-nineties. As a result of this trip, I found myself becoming more and more fascinated by Romania's tragic recent history, and by the social realities facing the citizens of that country. By the summer, I had decided that the story of the *Maersk Dubai* would not resonate in the way I wished it to without the inclusion of the surviving stowaway's tale. As this was unavailable to me, the life of Daniel Pacepa is a fiction, albeit one intended to represent the pressures experienced by many Romanian immigrants from that period. (The details of Daniel's tale are only true when they intersect with Rodolfo's—he *did* hide under a catwalk, he *was* found with a Bible and a photograph of a girlfriend, and he and Rodolfo *did* have the conversations presented in the book. Necessarily, the characterizations of the other three stowaways were also a product of my imagination.)

My thanks go to the staff of El Faro for showing me a facet of Algeciras missed by tourists. I also thank the following Romanian Canadians for sharing their tales with me: Daniel and Bianca Levu, Elena Dumitru, Radu Iatan, Jean Masare, Nicu Branzea, Elena Enia, and Stephen Danas. Many of their recollections of life in Romania, or their trips to the New World, appear at some point during Daniel's story.

Though I consulted too many resource materials to list, the book *Red Horizon* by Ion Mihai Pacepa most helped me appreciate the increasingly paranoid and psychopathic way that Nicolae and Elena Ceaușescu governed Romania between 1965 and 1989. Thank you, Jean, for recommending it. I also thank Scott L. Malcomson, who wrote a lengthy *New Yorker* article about the case, which I consulted frequently.

I am also deeply indebted to Captain Barry Scott of Halifax, Nova Scotia, who for a year and a half acted as an unpaid technical consultant. For answering all of my questions regarding the functioning of a big ship without once sounding exasperated or bored, and for helping me get on board a big ship in Halifax, I say thank you, thank you, thank you. I also thank Captains

Walter Davis and Spiros Andolopolous for giving me tours of boats under their command, and for sharing with me their experiences with stowaways. Captain Angus MacDonald also helped with certain technical details, and RCMP constable Tom Townsend graciously furnished me with details regarding the capture of the *Maersk Dubai*. My thanks also go to: Roland Riedmann, who showed me a construction site of a house very similiar to the one built by Daniel et al. in the south of France; and to the Reverend Canon Milton J. Barry, who offered advice regarding some of the book's theological points. As well, I would like to make clear that although the *Maersk Dubai* was built by Maersk-Sealand, the company had nothing whatsoever to do with the operation or maintenance of the boat during the period described in *The Stowaway*, and in fact were helpful and open during the research of this book.

Finally, I have to thank my editor, Anne Collins, for her unerring guidance; my agents, Jackie Kaiser and Nicole Winstanley, for their tireless cheerleading services; my wife, Susan Greer, for making things fun; and my daughters, Sally and Ella, for everything else.

~

Following the capture of the *Maersk Dubai*, the government of Romania attempted to extradite the officers so that they could stand trial for the murders of Petre Săngeorzan, Radu Danciu and Gheorghe Mihoc. Rodolfo Miguel, Juanito Ilagan and Ariel Broas agreed to stay in Nova Scotia to testify at the ensuing extradition hearing, a decision that came at great personal cost: to survive during their unexpectedly lengthy stay in Canada, they took jobs in a fish-packing plant, and shared a basement apartment. As the hearing wore on, their families in Manila began to receive anonymous death threats, prompting the men to apply to the Canadian government to relocate their families.

At the culmination of the extradition hearing, a Canadian judge named J. Michael MacDonald ruled that the stowaways Săngeorzan, Mihoc and Danciu did perish on board the *Maersk Dubai*, and that there was sufficient evidence to suggest that they had met their ends as a result of actions taken by the officers. (The surviving stowaway, whose real name is Nicolae Pasca, had by this point disappeared; he is currently living illegally in a large American city with his wife and three small children, and would not co-operate with the writing of this book.) MacDonald also concluded, however, that any extradition of the officers was beyond his jurisdiction, as the drownings occurred in international waters. All of the officers were deported. In Taiwan, the captain, chief officer, and second officer were charged with a crime that roughly translated as the "negligent offence of homicide," in the cases of Săngeorzan and Danciu. While charges against the chief and second officers were later dropped, the captain became the subject of a marathon trial that did not finish until May 30, 2003. Throughout, it was the captain's defence that Săngeorzan and Danciu were dropped close enough to the Moroccan coast that they had survived. (Evidence from a Romanian inquiry, indicating that friends and family of the two men had never seen nor heard from them again, was discounted.) Without recovered bodies, the judge ruled that he could not be absolutely sure that the murders had occurred, and he ruled in favour of the defendant.

Rodolfo Miguel, Juanito Ilagan, and Ariel Broas continue to live in Halifax, Miguel and Ilagan with their families. In 2002, after six years of working at minimum-wage jobs, Juanito Ilagan and Ariel Broas found employment with the Coast Guard. Rodolfo Miguel is currently employed at the Halifax Wal-Mart.

ROBERT HOUGH's first novel, *The Final Confession of Mabel Stark*, was nominated for the Commonwealth Writers Prize for Best First Book and the Trillium Book Award, was published in fifteen countries, and is in development for a motion picture. He lives in Toronto with his wife and two daughters.